LORA LEIGH'S NOVELS ARE:

"TITILLATING."
—*Publishers Weekly*

"SIZZLING HOT."
—*Fresh Fiction*

"INTENSE AND BLAZING HOT."
—*RRTErotic*

**"WONDERFULLY DELICIOUS ... TRULY
DECADENT."**
—*Romance Junkies*

ALSO BY LORA LEIGH

RUGGED TEXAS COWBOY

TWO BOOKS IN ONE

Cowboy and the Captive
&
Cowboy and the Thief

LORA LEIGH

St. Martin's Paperbacks

This is a work of fiction. All of the characters, organizations, and events portrayed in this novel are either products of the author's imagination or are used fictitiously.

Originally published separately as *Cowboy and the Captive* and *Cowboy and the Thief*.

RUGGED TEXAS COWBOY

Copyright © 2017 by Lora Leigh.

For information address St. Martin's Press, 175 Fifth Avenue, New York, NY 10010.

ISBN: 978-1-250-15087-5

Our books may be purchased in bulk for promotional, educational, or business use. Please contact your local bookseller or the Macmillan Corporate and Premium Sales Department at 1-800-221-7945, ext. 5442, or by e-mail at MacmillanSpecialMarkets@macmillan.com.

Printed in the United States of America

St. Martin's Paperbacks edition / December 2017

St. Martin's Paperbacks are published by St. Martin's Press, 175 Fifth Avenue, New York, NY 10010.

10 9 8 7 6 5 4 3 2 1

COWBOY
AND THE
CAPTIVE

PROLOGUE

The enemy's promises were made to be broken.
—FROM AESOP'S FABLE
"THE NURSE AND THE WOLF"

Luc Jardin knew Miss Maria Catarina Angeles was going to be trouble the minute she stepped into the small hangar where he and his friend and partner, Jack Riley, were waiting to see if they could pick up a last-minute job flying out of the small South American airport.

This job was looking too good to be true. He never did like the ones that were too much of a good thing, and this woman could be described no other way.

She was slender and graceful, her skin a bit pale, but otherwise appearing as soft as satin. Her green eyes were vacant, but he had recognized her right off the bat. A spoiled little rich girl with too much time and money on her hands. It wasn't exactly the demeanor Luc had glimpsed the few times he had been forced into the social circles she moved in, but it wasn't the first time he had been wrong about a beautiful woman. He was sure it wouldn't be the last.

He and Jack had always been suckers for redheads,

though, and Maria Catarina Angeles was a true redhead. And she had the one thing they needed desperately to keep their foundering air delivery service off the ground. Money. Lots of money and a name that should be trustworthy.

The American businessman Jonathon Angeles was considered one of the richest men in the nation, and Maria Catarina was heralded as an angel of mercy and light.

What could it hurt to help her out?

"I'll give you a hundred thousand dollars and a night you'll never forget," she purred sweetly as she stepped up to Luc, rubbing her lithe little body against his harder one.

The feel of her moving against him almost made him forget the little niggle of worry that tapped at his brain. The one that warned him there could be more to this than returning a simple little crate filled with supplies to the charity's home office. But damn if it wasn't hard to think about danger when slender fingers were loosening his belt and undoing his jeans. All he could think about was sex and the lack of it in the past few months.

"Consider this a down payment," she murmured.

When she finished Jack off, leaving him damp with sweat but satisfied—just as Luc had been before him— she rose to her feet, wiped her mouth delicately, then looked back to Luc.

"Do we have a deal then?"

A hundred thousand dollars to transport her and the crate of supplies back home from the South American jungle before the rebels could figure out she was there. It was a short flight. She had the crate sitting outside, and it wasn't as though they were overbooked. She could have gotten a much better deal if she had bargained for it.

"Where do you need to go?" Jack was all for it.

"A small private airfield just over the American border." She smiled sweetly. "My friends will be meeting me there to take the crate, and the neighboring town has the cutest little motel we can spend the night in."

Easy enough. So why were his guts sending out warning signals? Luc shook his head at his own suspicions. He was getting too cynical. Maria Angeles was known for her flights of mercy over international borders. The fact that she was flying supplies into America raised a question, but not enough of one to have him cutting his nose off for the answers. He wanted the money. He could survive without the fuck, but he needed that money to finance the cargo operation he had started the year before.

"Get ready to fly." Luc shrugged. "We'll load the crate."

The small South American airfield where they were cooling their heels wasn't the busiest in the country. They were unlikely to get a better deal. Hell, they hadn't had a better deal in the year they had been running the plane anyway.

The flight from the airfield to the small California border town was uneventful, but then most flights were. The fact that she directed them to a nearly deserted, dusty field to land in should have been his first warning.

"This doesn't feel good, Jack," he said softly into the headset he used to communicate with his buddy in the copilot's seat.

Maybe it was time to return to the ranch, Luc thought. The plane wasn't turning a profit and some of the jobs they were offered were less than legal. Some were downright life threatening. And this one was just plain making him nervous.

"There you go, letting the good things slide by you again, man." Jack laughed as he pushed a wave of long blond hair back from his face. "Go with the flow. What could happen?"

But Luc was worried enough that he checked the gun he carried at his hip before landing the plane. As Miss Angeles had predicted, there was a truck waiting at the end of the airfield, along with several of her friends.

"We're right on time," she announced happily from behind him as he and Jack rose from their seats and headed to the back of the plane.

Luc watched closely as she picked her purse up from the seat. He pushed the box down the small ramp Jack was lowering and watched as it slid to the ground. Several of the "friends" were moving closer. Luc liked to think he wasn't an overly suspicious guy, but the bulges under those coats were definitely messing with his nerves.

"Thank you for the ride, Mr. Jardin." Maria's voice was unusually high, her pupils dilated.

Luc stared at her closely then glanced to the cargo area, thinking about the crate.

His suspicions were getting worse and screaming that the crate held more than just supplies for the various charities the woman worked for. Drugs. He was sure of it.

Son of a bitch. He kept his expression impassive as he watched her move into the cargo area, her hips swaying with a sensuality that hadn't been present before. She was too relaxed now, smiling too sweetly as she kissed Jack on the jaw before moving down the ramp.

"My friends will take care of your fee." She giggled like a young girl as she turned back. "But I don't think they'll let me fuck you after all. My boyfriend gets pretty possessive." She watched them closely now as she stepped to the ground. "The money should be enough, though."

Luc glanced at Jack in concern. This job was about to go from sugar to shit real fast.

Shock lined the other man's face as he saw the men who came to a stop at the ramp. Several grabbed the crate and hauled it away as Luc quickly estimated their chances of survival. They weren't good considering three of them had their hands disappearing beneath their jackets.

"Get back!" he yelled to Jack as he hit the control button for the ramp and threw himself at the other man.

Maria's scream echoed around him as she jumped from the plane and turned to look back into the interior. Luc pushed Jack into the recessed frame and prayed for a miracle as the ramp began to rise slowly. Too damned slowly.

"Come on! Cockpit," he yelled at Jack as he caught sight of the automatic weapons her friends were aiming into the plane, glee reflecting on their faces as their fingers tightened on the triggers.

Gunfire ripped through the plane as he ducked and jerked Jack back, nearly falling as the other man stumbled against him, a stain of red blooming over Jack's chest. Luc threw him into the copilot's seat before taking his own and accelerating the plane back down the runway.

"Son of a bitch," Jack wheezed as he gripped his shoulder. "Dammit to hell, Luc, this shit hurts."

Bullets pinged against the hull of the plane while Luc sped down the runway, fury enveloping him as he realized Jack hadn't been the only one hit. His leg was bleeding profusely and the ranch was over an hour away. He prayed harder. But amid the prayers was a fury that surged hot and sweet through his brain. Angel of mercy, his ass.

That bitch would pay, he swore. And he would make certain she paid well.

ONE

Family obligations shouldn't involve life or death, Melina Catarina Angeles thought as she faced her parents across the brightly lit living room. The sun shone through the large arched windows to one side, reflecting back from the highly polished hardwood floors and lending an air of comfort and warmth to the expensively decorated room.

Antiques were her mother's passion, and the living room reflected her love for them. Being surrounded by everything her parents had worked for in their lifetime should have comforted Melina; instead, it left her cold as she stared back at them, fighting to hide her shock.

She was one of two daughters, the younger of a set of twins. The quiet, studious one. The one who had always stepped in to save her parents the humiliation of what her older twin had wrought. But she couldn't do it any longer.

They had rarely associated with her in two years. Not

since the last fiasco her sister, Maria, had managed to cause. With that one, she had nearly killed two innocent men, and through her selfishness had almost caused Melina's death months later. She had sworn then that she would never step in to play Maria's part ever again. Her parents had retaliated by cutting her out of their lives. Until now. Until Maria had once again gotten herself into a mess she couldn't get out of.

"This isn't my fight." Melina faced her estranged parents in her father's mansion and finally put her foot down. "Maria has gone too far this time, Papa. I refuse to cover for her."

She held back the pain that they would even ask it of her. Her twin sister was once again in a scrape that their money couldn't buy her out of without the proper presentation. They needed Melina for that presentation. And after the last time, there wasn't a chance in hell. She had spent a week in jail, during which time her father had been out of town and supposedly had not received her messages.

Thankfully, the police had already fingerprinted Maria, and Melina had been spared the horrifying knowledge that her fingerprints were on file as a criminal. A drug addict. A thief. Good God, her sister was deteriorating rapidly. And now this. Arrested for smuggling drugs into the country. Again. It was a certain prison term, and Melina was sick of paying for her sister's crimes. There was no way in hell she was going to take a chance on going to prison for her sister. Not after the last debacle.

Two men could have died the last time. When Lucas Jardin had arrived on her father's steps two years before, furious over his friend, her father had almost broken the man financially as well as personally. If Jardin hadn't been a highly respected rancher and businessman, her father would have succeeded. All because of the addiction that was growing closer to destroying not just her sister, but her family as well.

"Melina, Maria needs all our help right now. She can't fight this addiction alone," her father argued passionately. "It's little enough to do."

Melina turned from the pleading eyes of the man who had sired her to glance at her mother's miserable, tear-filled eyes. Margaret Angeles loved all her children, but her older twin daughter was destroying all their lives.

"No, Papa," she repeated gently. "It was enough that I spent a week in jail for her and you ignored the messages I left both here and on your answering service. I told you then, I won't ever make the same mistake."

She remembered the look in Luc Jardin's eyes when he entered the house and saw her standing with her parents. He had thought she was Maria, and Melina had been too shocked to deny it. After learning the reason for his fury, she had wanted to kill her sister. Jardin was a man unlike any Melina had known in her life. Not just tall and broad, but rough enough around the edges to make her long to smooth them. He was untamed, and she was woman enough to want to tame him.

He was man enough to despise her, though, when her parents introduced her as Maria. It was then she began to suspect the position she had allowed her parents to place her in. The week spent in jail had only cemented it. She had sworn then she would never lift a finger to get her twin out of trouble again.

Convincing her father to cease his crusade of vengeance against the pilot hadn't been easy. He had flatly refused until the day after Melina had been released from jail, walked into the lawyer's office, and threatened to publicly side with Jardin if it did not cease. She had moved out of the family house the next week. But she had never forgotten Lucas Jardin or her reaction to him.

"Melina, your sister could go to prison," her mother sobbed then, tears spilling from her eyes. "I cannot imagine one of my babies in prison."

Melina pushed her fingers through her shoulder-length red hair as she faced her weeping mother. She hated to see her mother cry.

"Momma, you said that when it was a jail sentence," she argued desperately. "Maria didn't spend any time in jail, but I did." And she hadn't forgotten it. She still had nightmares about it.

"It was a mistake, baby," her father exclaimed fiercely. "You were supposed to get probation. The lawyer assured us that was all. He even said everything was fine when we called."

"The point is, you left." She crossed her arms over her chest as the remembered horror and fear swept over her. "You weren't in the courtroom, you weren't there to make certain I was protected, and on top of it, you knew that lawyer would lie for her. They were sleeping together, for God's sake."

Jonathon Angeles flinched. "I was wrong. It won't happen again."

"I won't do it." Her heart clenched as her mother's weeping grew louder. "Papa, you have to make Maria accept the consequences. She's going to kill herself at this rate if you don't."

"I promise. We'll put her in a clinic," Jonathon swore.

"You promised that last time," she argued painfully. "Papa, please don't ask this of me. I can't do it. I won't do it. Please don't make me feel bad for it."

"There is such a thing as loyalty to the family, Melina," her father snapped. "Your sister will never convince the judge she had no idea what was happening. You know she can't."

"Because she would have to lie," Melina retorted. "You never see her lies, Papa. The rest of us do, but never you. Maria is killing herself and this family, and I refuse to let her destroy my life in the process."

Silence met her harsh words. Her father placed his arms around her mother's shaking shoulders and tried to comfort her weeping, and though Melina didn't shed a tear, inside her heart was breaking. It was a reenactment of the last crisis her sister had caused. Only then, Melina had given in. She had sworn she never would again.

She turned from her parents and paced over to the large window that looked out over the private lake of her parents' home. She had grown up here. Had learned to swim in the lake and had realized as she grew up that she would never measure up, in her parents' eyes, to Maria. Somehow her twin had drawn complete loyalty from them, whereas Melina had drawn only their distant affection.

"Melina, I cannot believe you would see your sister suffer in such a way," her father accused. "This would be no hardship for you."

"This is a federal offense with a mandatory prison term if convicted." She turned back to her parents as hurt and anger rolled over her. "With Maria's record she's certain to get time, no matter how great the argument. I will not go to prison for someone who stood aside as her criminal friends nearly slaughtered two men. It's bad enough she has no loyalty to her family, but she has no respect for life, either.

"I'm sorry, Papa, but spending time in prison would be considered a major hardship for me." She shook her head, fighting the memory of her week in jail. It had been horrible, locked into that tiny block room, at the mercy of the guards as well as the other prisoners.

She had been without protection. The bribes to the guards that would have ensured it hadn't been paid, and Melina hadn't been strong enough to defend herself.

"You will not go to prison." Her father surged to his feet, his portly body shaking with anger. "I have told you, I will not allow it."

He was furious. She hated it when her father was so angry with her. It made her want to please him, want to wipe the derision from his eyes as he looked at her. But she had learned to stand alone in the past two years and she wasn't going to fall back into the trench of despair that saving her sister always created.

"I'm sorry, Papa," she whispered again, her voice bleak. "I can't do this for you. You know as well as I do that all the pleading and good behavior in the world is not going to save Maria this time. You would do better to petition the courts or the prosecutor for a plea bargain. They would look more favorably on that than they would a sweet little protest of innocence. Surely even your lawyer has told you that."

"He has assured me this will work." His hand sliced through the air furiously as her mother's sobs filled the background. "I am asking you for nothing. Nothing. This matter is so slight it will take only a single afternoon."

Melina pushed her shaking hands into the pockets of her jeans and lowered her head to hide the misery in her eyes. How many times had they argued just like that?

That it would take so little for her to take her sister's punishments. All her life she had been standing in front of Maria, taking the blame and the punishment in her name. She wasn't willing to do so anymore. Maria had turned into a vapid, heartless conniver. All that mattered was the drugs. Nothing more. Not family or friends or even personal honor held any meaning to her.

"I can't do it, Papa," she whispered miserably, hunching her shoulders against the tension that filled the room.

She was too sensitive. She had known that all her life. Her parents' happiness and her family's success had always meant more to her than her own happiness. At least it had until she faced Lucas Jardin and the knowledge of how far Maria would go to save her own skin and escape punishment. She hadn't slept for months after her brother had finally managed to get her released; even now, two years later, the nightmares plagued her.

"I cannot believe you would say no." His voice clearly reflected his surprise. "I cannot believe you would allow your sister—your twin, for God's sake—to suffer so horribly."

"My sister isn't an innocent here." Melina's head rose as her own anger came to the fore. "She uses you to get her out of trouble and then goes on with business as usual when it's all over with. She's getting worse, Papa. You know it and I know it. I won't suffer her punishment for her."

"What punishment?" He threw his hands into the air a second before he clenched his thick silver-and-brown hair in frustration. "There will be none if you just do as the lawyer directs you."

"I won't take that chance again," she cried out painfully. "Papa, they beat me—more than once—and almost raped me. You know this. You know what I suffered in that jail, and still you ask this of me? How could you?"

Melina couldn't understand her parents' complete loyalty to her sister. It made no sense. They were trading the daughter who loved them unconditionally for the daughter who loved only their ability to get her out of trouble.

"Almost," he blustered, his face paling as it had the first time she had told him. "I will not let it happen again."

"No, Papa. *I* won't let it happen again," she said gently, trying desperately to hold back her own hurt and anger. "I had enough two years ago, you know this. I won't let her ruin my life."

Her mother was wailing now. Deep, pain-filled sobs interspersed with ragged prayers for her "baby." Her "sweet Maria." Melina wanted to crawl into a hole and cry herself. She gazed back at her father's disappointed face, the helplessness reflected in his deep-brown eyes.

"I cannot believe you would do this," he whispered.

"Go, Melina. Leave this house until your mother can deal with this betrayal you have dealt us. I will tell your sister of your refusal and pray it does not break her."

Melina blinked back at him in shock. "You're disowning me?" she whispered, her voice bleak. "Papa? You would disown me for this?"

His gaze was hard, remote. "I do not know you. You are not the child of my heart as I believed, Melina. Until you can aid your sister as you should, then you are of no consequence to me."

He turned from her and went to her mother, enclosing Margaret in his arms and letting her weep against his chest. Later, he would hold Maria the same way. Console her, pat her back, and whisper his love to her. He hadn't held Melina like that in years. Even when he'd arrived at the jail to learn she had been beaten and nearly raped, her face bruised and horribly swollen, he hadn't comforted her. It had been her brother, Joe, who had picked her up from the gurney, whispering senseless phrases of grief as he carried her from the jailhouse.

It had always been her brother who had eased her fears, her tears. But even he was gone now. He had left the family and the business before Melina had; his own disgust at his parents' foolishness where Maria was concerned had gone too deep for him to stay. She wasn't even certain where he was now.

Sighing deeply, holding back her tears, she did as her Papa ordered and turned and left the house. The butler was silent as he held the door open for her, his expression impassive. She knew there was little sympathy to be found there. All loyalties were given to Maria exclusively. Melina had never understood it, but she accepted it.

Night had fallen, casting hazy shadows over the Pennsylvania countryside and wrapping around Melina with trailing fingers of warmth. On nights like this, she thought of Jardin. Wondered if his friend had survived his wounds, if he had ever realized the young woman he had cursed so vehemently had been the wrong woman.

She shook her head mockingly. Her parents accepted praise for the work Melina used to do as Maria's successes. The charities had been in Maria's name, the work attributed to her until that day. They had all fallen apart when Melina left. Just as the rest of the family was falling apart.

She turned the key in the ignition of her car and pulled out of her parents' driveway. She fought back the tears and the regrets and thought about trying to contact her brother before too long. She knew a few of his old friends who might know where to find him. Joey had always seemed to care about her and seen past her likeness to Maria. He would understand the grief tightening in her chest even if she didn't.

She should have answered his messages those first few months after her release from the hospital, she thought regretfully. Facing him hadn't been easy, though. He knew what had happened to her, and every time she thought of the pity she would have seen in his face, or heard in his voice, she had cringed. It was time to put it behind her, time to make the final break with her parents and her sister. Joe knew how to do that and, hopefully, he would now teach her how. Because she'd be damned if she knew.

TWO

Luc narrowed his eyes against the darkness of the apartment and waited. He was a patient man. He had planned this night down to the last detail and he wasn't going to rush it. He had watched the parking lot carefully for her car to drive in. He didn't want her surprising him by coming in unannounced.

He knew she had been visiting her parents, likely pleading for help after the last scrape she had managed to get into. The woman was heading down a path of self-destruction and he was more than willing to help her along. After he got his pound of flesh.

She had made her parents relent in their war against him, but she had started the war to begin with. She had paid for Jack's medical bills and recovery then called and turned ol' Jack's heart with her tears and her apologies. But Jack was well known for his soft spot and his love for a pretty woman. Especially one who could suck cock like a dream and swallow without a grimace.

She had even called Luc.

Luc remembered the overwhelming rage and fury he had felt at the quiet dignity in her voice as she whispered her apology and offered to pay for the plane he had crashed upon landing that day. He had heard the thickness of tears in her voice, but she hadn't sniveled. She swore she hadn't known what would happen and had no idea what was in the crate. He didn't believe her. Hell, he knew better. But she spun a damned fine tale; he had to give her credit for that one.

He had waited two years for his chance for vengeance and, surprisingly, it had come from someone he'd least expected it to. It wasn't that he didn't have other things to do in that time; vengeance hadn't consumed him. But seeing her face plastered all over the papers over another drug charge brought it all back. He could do society a real favor. Clean her up and teach her the value of a hard day's work, all with the permission of her family.

He smiled slowly. He knew his main problem was boredom rather than revenge. It had been too long since he had allowed himself to ride the edge of danger. The ranching was easy. Hell, some days it was too damned easy. Jack took care of the business stuff when he wasn't running around the fool planet trying to sell the horses.

Luc took care of the actual ranch, oversaw the training and breeding of the prized Clydesdales, and worked at making the ranch even more successful than it had become in the past two years. But he hadn't forgotten the blatant disregard Maria Angeles had shown with her decision to allow her drug-running buddies to ambush them.

Boredom could do strange things to a man. Make

him do things like accept her brother's suggestion that maybe his sister needed a place where she would have no choice but to clean up her act. Make him plot and plan and carry out a kidnapping that was sanctioned by her brother. There was no fear of legal reprisals, and he had complete control of her. That was all that mattered to him.

Her bags were packed and stored in the trunk of the car; a private plane was waiting at the nearby airfield. Before Miss Maria Catarina Angeles knew what hit her she would be on the road to recovery. He chuckled in amusement, imagining the coming battle. He thrived on a good fight, and teaching the spoiled little brat how to be a drug-free member of society was going to be a battle.

He shook his head at the thought. He'd never understood the attraction to drugs. The loss of control, the addiction, and the mistakes that came from it. He was still just pissed enough to have very little mercy for the young woman he was about to kidnap. He wouldn't hurt her, but he'd be damned if he wouldn't paddle her ass good if she didn't toe the line. He was starting to think that might well have been her problem all along. Her daddy should have spanked her more often.

As he hid in the shadows moments later, he heard the key turn in the lock. Stepping farther into the darkness behind the bedroom door, he listened closely as the door opened and the sounds of entrance could be heard.

"Mason, Momma's home." Her voice struck Luc immediately. Husky, tear-filled, and miserable. At the same time he watched in surprise as the dark lump on her bed moved. A black shadow rose and stretched into the form of a fat cat that glanced at Luc disdainfully and jumped from the bed.

Hell, what was he supposed to do about the cat? He'd have to call Joe and have him collect his sister's little familiar. He didn't like cats much anyway, and black cats were even worse.

"There's my baby," he heard her croon softly moments later. "Are you hungry yet or are you still pouting at me for leaving? I'll take you to the park tomorrow instead. How's that?"

Luc frowned at her voice. She didn't sound drugged. She sounded immeasurably saddened. Almost broken. That wasn't the voice he remembered, but he admitted the events of that day were so fuzzy now that he couldn't be certain. He knew it was Maria, though. He had seen the car drive up and watched her step from the vehicle minutes before. He had the right woman. And it was just his luck she had a cat. A small smile tipped his lips. She didn't seem as hard as he remembered. She sounded softer, sadder. More a Catarina than a Maria. The Maria he remembered would have never bothered to look beyond herself long enough to worry about feeding a cat.

"Hungry little thing, aren't you?" she said from the other room. "Let's hope Momma can keep the goodies coming. If I don't get that job tomorrow, we might be raiding trash bins." She didn't sound like she was joking. "Sucks when your parents hate you, Mason."

He lifted his brows. She had a strange definition of *hatred*. They had likely managed to buy her out of a damned drug-smuggling charge. That didn't sound like hatred to him.

As he heard her moving around again, he slipped the chloroformed cloth from his jacket pocket. She would have to come into the bedroom eventually, and when she did, he would be waiting for her.

"Shower," he heard her mutter. "Damn if Papa can't make me feel like dirt after listening to his accusations. And I think he disowned me, Mason." She sounded lost. "Being out of the family isn't nearly as bad as being disowned."

Luc ignored the funny little feeling in his chest, the one that warned him he was about to feel sorry for the waifish-sounding hellcat. If she had paid attention to her father's pleas years ago, maybe she wouldn't be in this mess now.

He remembered his visit to the mansion. She had been surprised at first when her father had introduced her to him. As though he had needed the introduction. Then resignation had filled her gaze. She hadn't even known who the hell he was. His cock had hardened, though, despite his fury, despite his need to beat some sense into her. He had been stone-hard aroused in ways he had never been before, even the day she had sucked his dick down her throat.

Hell, she had looked so innocent that first day at the ranch, he would have sworn she wouldn't know what to do with a cock if he did push it between her lips, let alone how she would react to having his semen filling her mouth. But the thought of it had fueled more than one hot daydream.

"Enjoy dinner, Mason. I'm going to shower and see if I can't get hold of Joey. Maybe he can help us."

Luc smirked. Joe had already taken care of her.

He palmed the damp cloth and prepared himself to place it over her nose and mouth. He heard her quiet footfalls, heard the cat meow, then she was walking into the room, flipping on the light and passing by him.

Luc moved. He had a second to glimpse her wide, terrified eyes before they closed and she slumped against him. Catching her in his arms Luc moved to the bed, lowered her onto it, and gazed at the cat that jumped up after her. The beast stared at him with narrowed eyes.

"You're going to be a problem, aren't you, boy?" He sighed as the animal growled low in his throat. "I thought cats were supposed to be aloof, uncaring. You're a cat, not a dog."

He placed his hands on his hips and watched the confrontational animal.

"Hell, just what I need. An attack cat. I wonder if she has a carrier for you."

He found the carrier. He received a brutal scratch for catching the animal by the thick fur of his neck and stuffing him in. He'd have to remind Joe that he wasn't a cat lover next time he talked to him. In explicit terms.

"Well now, let's get you ready." He lifted Catarina in his arms, caught the carrier with one hand, and carried her quickly out of the apartment and to the nearby service elevator. It was a short trip to the car parked next to the elevator doors in the basement. Once there, he laid her in the backseat, quickly bound her hands, and set the cat's carrier on the floorboard.

Mission accomplished. Well, partially anyway, he thought with a grunt. He still had to control her once she woke up. Thanks to the chloroform, it should be several hours, though. By then he would have her safely at the ranch and everything in place to teach her the error of her ways.

As he started the car and headed for the airport, his gut warned him it couldn't possibly be this easy. He grimaced at the thought.

Pulling the cell phone from the carrier on his belt, he punched in Joe Angeles's number and waited for the other man to pick up.

"You have her, Jardin?" The other man sounded worried.

"I have her. We're headed to the airport. Is the plane ready?"

"Fueled and ready to go. Just pull into the hangar; the guard is waiting on you. Remember, it's a company airfield so you shouldn't have any problems. Did you get her cat?"

Luc frowned at the other man's tone. He almost sounded as though he was afraid to ask.

"Yeah, I got the black bastard," Luc told him. "I'm still bleeding for my efforts, too."

Joe chuckled, suddenly sounding more relaxed. "Mason is a bit protective of her, but he's easy enough to get along with. Keep me updated and make sure you don't fall for any of her tricks. She's really a good kid, Luc. I know you don't believe that right now, but you'll see."

Luc shook his head. Her brother's belief in her was to be commended. Stupid, but commendable.

"Good kids don't turn a blind eye to murder, Joe. But I promise I won't hurt her. You know me better than that."

Joe had come to the ranch two years before, after Luc's trip to the Angeles mansion.

For months, Luc had had no idea who he was as the younger man worked with the horses and they formed a wary friendship. Finally, Joe had come to him with the truth, that he needed to know how far his parents were willing to go to protect Maria, so he could protect them. Luc had understood it, but damn if he hadn't been pissed for a while.

"Yeah." Joe sighed. "I know you won't hurt her, Luc. That's the reason you have her. You're the only one I can trust with her. I'll talk to you soon."

"I'll call you when we lift off," Luc promised. "Later."

He disconnected the phone and turned away from the apartment building, heading for the airport. Joe hadn't seemed quite this fond of his sister during the long talks they had shared through the past two years.

The brotherly concern he was showing now didn't sit well with Luc. Not that he thought Joe was lying. It was just a bit odd considering the other man's reticence in discussing his family, or his sister. That boy hated lies, but something wasn't right. He shook his head and sighed wearily. Whatever it was, Luc thought, he had no doubt it would rise up and bite him in the ass soon. When it did, then he would deal with it.

Until then, he had vengeance to secure.

THREE

Joe hung up the phone and stared across his desk at the tall, slender figure of his father's butler. Johann held the same cool, aloof expression that Joe knew he always held. He had seen it crack once in the past thirty years. And only once. The week before when Johann had shown up late in the evening and informed Joe that his parents were going to attempt to convince Melina to once again stand in Maria's place.

"Mr. Joe, if she walks into the courtroom as Maria, she might as well stick to it. Miss Maria is going to be locked up, one way or the other; I've already found that out. Her parents know it, but they won't accept it. If Melina stands in for her, they'll lock her away, and she's just not hard enough to survive that."

Johann had shed tears at the thought of it. His faded-blue eyes had welled with the moisture and they spilled down his cheeks as fear overcame his reserve.

"Miss Melina doesn't deserve this," he had sniffed.

"She's a good girl, Mr. Joe. They'll hurt her worse next time she gets locked up."

Joe had been in shock. Not because of the tears, though those had contributed, but because of his parents' depth of ignorance. Maria slept with every lawyer they hired for her, and they would tell her parents whatever she wanted them to hear. And as usual, she wanted Melina to take the fall.

"What are the chances of her agreeing to it?" Joe had asked him.

Johann had shaken his head. "You know Miss Melina. She'll rage and cry but when her papa speaks sharply to her, he will gain her agreement. She dreams of their love, Mr. Joe. I'm terrified she'll agree to it."

Now, a week later, Joe was reasonably satisfied that Melina wouldn't be agreeing to anything their father wanted. Sending Luc after her thinking she was Maria didn't sit well with him, but he'd be damned if he would see her nearly broken, almost dead, as he had after taking her out of that jail two years before. Not that Maria had cared, even though it had been her fault her sister had endured it.

Rather than contacting their parents, she had gone on a weeklong high and merrily allowed Melina to face a punishment she didn't deserve.

"He has her," he finally told Johann, watching the other man slump in his chair in relief. "Now where's Maria?"

"Your papa has her confined to her rooms." He shook his head dismally. "You know how long that will last."

"How close are they to buying her out of it?" Joe finally asked, knowing his parents would spend any amount of money to do just that.

Johann sighed bleakly. "I heard them discussing information their investigators had that could embarrass the judge, as well as the prosecutor. They will blackmail her out of it just as they did the last time. They have paid off one of the arresting officers and are now attempting to do so with the other."

Joe sighed wearily as he pinched the bridge of his nose, assuring himself he would not strangle his parents next time he saw them. "What are they asking for?"

"Complete dismissal. They have disowned Miss Melina, though. Poor child left crying. It was all I could do, Mr. Joe, not to cry with her." Johann shook his head compassionately. "Poor little thing feels so alone. It's not fair we had to do this to protect her."

One problem down, one to go. Maria. Joe fingered the file he had before him. The private clinic in Switzerland would cost him an arm and a leg once he delivered Maria to it, but it would be worth it to have Melina protected after all this was over.

"If they manage to pull this off, Johann, you let me know," he said. "I'll take care of Maria after this. Just keep me updated."

Johann rose wearily to his feet. "That Mr. Jardin won't hurt her, will he, Mr. Joe?" he asked softly. "He was a hard man. I wouldn't want her hurt."

"Luc won't hurt her, Johann. I give you my word." Joe was positive there would be no true danger to Melina. He wouldn't have contacted Luc if he thought there were.

Luc was just the only man he could trust to do the job and not go to Melina's parents for more money to release her.

It was becoming harder to protect Melina than it was to keep up with their parents' attempts to protect Maria. They had always seen Melina as stronger, needing less love than Maria. Joe wasn't certain why his parents had made a stronger bond with Maria, unless it had been that incessant wailing she had done as a baby. Melina had always lain quietly, while Maria would scream for hours. Often it had been Joe who had picked up the newborn Melina, fed her, changed her, taken care of her as her parents concerned themselves with the other, more demanding, twin.

When Maria had begun getting into trouble, his parents had learned that Melina had a natural innocence and inborn depth of honesty that could get their troublemaking daughter out of her messes. It had been then that they had begun using the younger twin, almost unconsciously, as though it were Melina's job to keep her sister from facing the consequences of her actions. Now Maria had sunk to new levels, uncaring of the harm she created because she knew her parents would use Melina to get her out of it.

Joe had had enough the day he learned Melina was in jail in Maria's stead. Melina had tried calling her parents for days with no success. If it hadn't been for Johann's call to Joe's secretary, he would have never known the danger Melina was in.

"I must return to Mr. Angeles then." Johann rose slowly to his feet, his expression weary and grief-stricken. "Each day, Mr. Joe, I think more often of retirement, hearing them disown that child . . ." He shook his head painfully.

"If you decide to do so, let me know, Johann." Joe nodded respectfully. "I'll make certain there are no repercussions."

Johann drew in a hard, tired breath. "It is a shame, Mr. Joe. A shame. Once, your parents were good people. Good people. Now . . ." He tucked his hands in his pockets and moved for the door. "Now I just don't know."

And Joe agreed with him. Like Johann, he had no idea what had happened to his parents. More to the point, he had given up on them ever returning to the caring, decent people they had once been. If they had ever existed.

FOUR

She had been kidnapped. Melina fought to hold back her terror as she woke to realize her hands and feet were bound. She was lying on a surprisingly comfortable bed. Not that comfort meant anything. She was certain even serial killers could have comfortable beds. But she knew it wasn't a serial killer who had kidnapped her. Damn, the more she thought about it, the more she was beginning to fear that her chances could be better with a nutcase than they were with the man she had glimpsed in one blinding second the night before.

She fought to still the fear as she remembered the face of her kidnapper. For one heart-stopping moment she had stared up at him and realized that once again, despite all her efforts, she was going to pay for Maria's sins.

This was great. Like he would believe she wasn't Maria. How many people knew her parents had two daughters? She could count them all on ten fingers and have a few left over. Since she was a child, she had been content to be left alone with her dolls, her books, her various hobbies, rather than be the social butterfly her sister had started out as. And her parents had been willing to leave her behind. The fewer people who knew Maria had a twin, the easier it might be to get the older twin out of trouble later. That lesson had been learned early.

She opened her eyes, her senses groggy from being drugged, her mind sluggish.

She needed to think clearly, to clear the fog out of her head and figure out how to handle this one. There was no doubt Jardin was out for revenge. And she couldn't blame him. The surprising part was that he had let her live long enough to wake up.

"Awake, are you?" His voice sounded behind her.

His voice sent shivers up her spine. It was deep and rough, like the growl of a hungry predator. It sent a chill of dread through her and had her licking her dry lips in response to the nervousness suddenly flaring through her body.

The man most likely to kill you shouldn't sound so damned sexy seconds before doing so. Melina swallowed tightly. She should be more frightened and less aroused by that voice.

Her darkest fantasies had been filled with the image of him for two years. She had often woken in the middle of the night, her hips lifting, reaching for the dream vision ready to impale her. She was as sick as Maria, she thought in disgust. The way she lusted after him made no sense.

"I assume you are at least reasonably clearheaded,"

he drawled mockingly. "Pretending to sleep won't save your ass, little girl."

Melina winced at the pet name. She wasn't a little girl, dammit.

She breathed out in resignation. She had to use the bathroom and her mouth felt like cotton. She might as well give in and get it the hell over with. Jardin hadn't seemed like a man who would easily be sidetracked or sweet-talked. Not that she had ever been very good with the sweet talk anyway.

That didn't mean she had to like the unusual response to him. Why, of all the men in the world, did she have to be so attracted to this one? She was certain he would just as soon kill her as look at her. And knowing that, why was her pussy heating, her breasts tingling, her body so sensitized in response to his voice?

Drawing in a deep breath, she prepared herself to face him. The sooner she did so, the sooner she could possibly find some peace.

"Do you think you could untie me long enough to use the bathroom before you begin tormenting me?" she asked him coolly.

She wasn't about to roll over and make the pain in her shoulders worse by lying on her back, bound as she was. It was damned uncomfortable with her hands tied behind her. She also felt too vulnerable, too helpless. She was at his mercy, and being in such a position was much too arousing.

Arousing? It should be terrifying, not arousing.

Melina trembled as he moved. She felt cold steel slide between her bare ankles, slicing through the ropes, then between her wrists. Flexing her hands, she eased into a sitting position, placing her feet tentatively on the floor. Glancing through her lashes, she saw the lean, strong legs that moved into her line of vision.

She raised her eyes as her heart stopped in her chest. He was releasing his belt. Oh God. She gasped for breath as his fingers, callused and very male, began unbuttoning his jeans.

She wasn't going to whimper, she assured herself. She would not show her shock and arousal by actually letting that helpless little sound free. But as he pulled his thick, hard cock from the depth of his jeans she knew the sound squeaked from her throat as his broad hand stroked over the dark flesh suggestively.

"Come on, Catarina," he whispered darkly. "Open wide, baby, and let me have that tight throat again."

Her gaze flew to his. He was watching her with a deep vein of amusement and lust, his handsome face taut with arousal and demand. Melina wanted to laugh. She almost did. She wouldn't know what to do with it even if she did consider "opening wide" as he suggested.

"Uhh, I really need to go," she whispered faintly, trying desperately not to gaze at the hard cock only inches from her mouth. "Really bad."

His lips quirked mockingly, his dark-gray eyes darkening further. "Then pay the price," he suggested softly. "Come on, Catarina, it's not like it's the first time."

It wasn't? It was the first time for her, she thought with disbelief. Surely he didn't think she really would? Melina never had, but she was well aware of the fact that Maria would do it and had done it.

He moved his arm, his hand lifting, fingers threading

her hair, the touch sending tingles of sensation to her scalp as he held her still and moved closer. Her gaze dropped nervously, her vision filled with the dark, pulsing flesh of the head of his cock.

He really thought she was going to? Thought she could?

The broad, purpled head touched her lips, throbbed, then spilled a soft pearl of semen against her lower curve.

Before Melina could stop herself, she jerked back, a cry of outrage escaping her mouth as she rolled clumsily across the bed. Shaking with nerves, she fell over the side and scrambled to her feet before staring at him across the mattress.

"No," she snapped out, though her response was rather late, she thought as she watched him redoing his jeans with a quizzical frown. He appeared both amused and bemused by her reaction.

"That's all you had to say, Catarina." He shrugged. "I don't remember you being so hesitant last time."

Last time? She wasn't hesitant? She was going to kill Maria. Seriously. Honestly.

First chance she had, her parents were being cut down to one daughter in truth instead of just in wishes.

Would he believe she wasn't Maria? Melina clenched her teeth in fury, weighing her options carefully. He didn't seem determined to kill her at this point. He was lazily amused, perhaps a little sarcastic and mocking, but he didn't appear murderous.

"Look," she finally said, fighting to keep her voice steady as she heard the betraying quiver in the words. "You've made a terrible mistake here. Really. I'm sure you'll find it quite funny . . ."

He frowned. The look sent fear rioting through her system. Thick black brows and stormy gray eyes darkened, his lips flattened, the high cheekbones standing out prominently. The look was a warning and sent Melina's heart pounding in her chest.

"Really?" he drawled. "I never imagined for a moment that there wouldn't be a good explanation." He crossed his arms over his chest and watched her through narrowed eyes. "I think I should tell you right up front, Catarina, that there's no getting out of what I have planned for you. You may as well forget any excuses, lies, or tricks. This is hell, baby, and I'm your warden. So get used to it now."

Melina's eyes widened. "What do you mean, you're my warden?"

He smiled. The hard curve of his lips sent a pulse of warning through her nervous system.

"Exactly what I said, sugar. You're here to finish drying out and clean your act up. And I know just how to ensure that. You, sweet thing, are getting ready to learn how the other half lives. No drugs, no servants, no booze, no pampering. Now get showered. I'll be up to get you in half an hour. Be dressed and ready or face the consequences." He watched her intently, his eyes dark and steady, frightening. "And I promise, the consequences won't be pleasant."

FIVE

Melina gaped at her captor in shock as she blinked just to be certain she was awake and not having some horrible nightmare. He was actually threatening her. Had set himself up as judge, jury, and executioner and thought she would go along with it. She would laugh if he didn't look so damned serious about it.

"You're joking." She couldn't stem the horror that she knew reflected in her voice.

"Nope." He crossed his arms over his chest arrogantly, staring back at her with cold, mocking eyes. "No joke, sugarplum. You play, you pay. If the courts can't do anything with you, then I can sure as hell try. Consider it punishment for the little crimes you've escaped in the past years. All rolled into one." His smile wasn't comforting.

Melina drew a hard, deep breath. Patience was a virtue, she reminded herself. Only cool, calm heads solved extreme problems. She had faced the wrath of her parents, been disowned, and been turned down for the last three jobs she'd interviewed for. She could handle this. She hadn't killed anyone yet. She really didn't have to start with this ignorant cowboy.

"What in the hell makes you think I'm going to go along with this?" she asked him incredulously. "Do I have STUPID written across my forehead? WIMP? GO AHEAD AND STEP ON ME BECAUSE I'M TOO STUPID TO LIVE AND I ENJOY ABUSE?" She threw her hands up in frustration as she faced him in disbelief.

He looked at her closely. "Hmm. Not that one could see. But I'll reserve judgment. You never know what may show up after a good hot shower."

She was going to lose her mind. Right there, in a strange bedroom, facing the sexiest, most aggravating, most arrogant man she had ever laid her eyes on. She was going to commit murder. Namely, on him.

"Look, Mr. Jardin." She tried for a smile that held none of the fury she was beginning to feel build up within her. "I'm sure you think what you're doing is right. I'm certain you're even convinced you have the right person to punish. But you're not and you don't, and I'll be damned if I'll pay for any more of my sister Maria's sins. I'm not Maria. I'm her twin, Melina."

He smirked at her. Melina bit her tongue as her eyes narrowed on his smug expression, and her fists clenched at her side as she fought not to jump across the bed and claw his eyes out.

"Sweetheart, I'm sure you wish you had a sister who could get you out of this," he said complacently. "But since we both know you don't, you can stop with the innocent act because I'm not buying it."

Melina drew in a deep breath. If she could get her hands on Maria, she would strangle her now, she thought. As though the past twenty-two years and all the times she had willingly tried to save her sister weren't enough. Now Mr. Hardass, who thought he could reform the wrong damned woman, had kidnapped her. It was too much. Even for her.

"That's fine," she gritted out. "Because I'm not trying to sell a damned thing. I assumed you were a reasonably intelligent person . . ."

"Just like you assumed you could let your buddies kill me and Jack when we helped you deliver that crate of drugs?" he asked snidely. "Or how you assumed your parents could ruin the names of two good men when charges were brought against you? How about the assumption that your parents' money can get you out of anything?

"This is the end of the line, little girl. You might as well buckle down and save the lies for someone willing to believe them."

Melina could feel the fury brewing in her chest. Vivid and hot, it flared in front of her eyes like a matador's cape.

"Or save the truth for someone with enough brains to see what's right in front of his face," she snapped back heatedly. "Get real, Mr. Jardin. Do I look like a drug addict to you?" She waved her hands to her side, indicating her body.

She expected him to look; she just didn't like the flare of arousal that lit his gaze when he did so. Nor did she like the way her nipples beaded as his gaze paused on them, or the heat that flared in her pussy when his eyes then moved to her thighs.

She could feel her skin sensitizing, her vagina dampening, and she didn't like the sensations in the least. It was bad enough she had done nothing but fantasize about him for the past two years; she didn't need to become aroused after he kidnapped her as well.

"Look, I know you're angry over what Maria did to you and your friend. But this is a mistake . . ."

"The mistake is yours." His sharp voice caused her to flinch in surprise. "Don't think for a minute you can lie to me again. Now get your ass in the shower and get ready to face the day or you can get on your knees and see if you can't convince me another way."

On her knees? Convince him? She blinked in outraged surprise at the suggestion.

And she was ignoring the crazy flash of desire and hunger that seared her body at just the thought of accepting his cock into her mouth. The brief touch of it on her lips was enough of a temptation, thank you very much. She did not need to find herself lusting after this man any more than she already did. As a matter of fact, she needed to be as far away from him as possible.

"You're crazy. I'm going home. Now."

She turned on her heel, heading quickly for the bedroom door. She'd had enough of this. Accepting Maria's punishment because she decided it was okay was a far cry from accepting because this man decided she would. She didn't think so. It didn't matter how big or how good-looking he was. It didn't matter that he deserved his pound of flesh. She wasn't about to let him take it out of her hide.

Her hand had just wrapped around the doorknob, her fingers tightening on it, when a broad palm smacked the wood above her head and a hard male body pressed her tightly against the wall.

A hard, hot, muscular body. One that surrounded her, his heat pouring off his flesh in waves and wrapping around her. A male presence that smelled of long sultry nights and forbidden desires. Melina swallowed, feeling the aura of danger that suddenly emanated from him.

"You don't want to piss me off, little girl," he warned her softly. "Especially not right now. That bullet you let your friends put in my leg hasn't been forgotten. Neither has the fact that they would have preferred it being my heart. Now shut the hell up, get your ass in the shower, and get dressed. This is a ranch. Everyone does his or her part here, and you're here to pitch in. Whether you want to or not."

He moved then, one hand insinuating itself between the door and her body as he unwrapped her fingers from the knob and pushed her lightly toward the bathroom. She wasn't about to do a damned thing that he ordered her to do.

Melina turned, staring back at him furiously, shaking with the need to smack the knowing smirk off his face as she retreated.

"You're wrong," she informed him angrily, though she could tell he had no intention of believing her. "Won't you even check it out? I have a brother. Joe Angeles. At least contact him. He'll tell you who I am."

She didn't like the amusement that glinted in his eyes. "He wouldn't tell me anything new, little girl."

"I'm not a little girl." She felt like stamping her feet in fury. "And I'm not Maria. I have to go home. I have to take care of my cat. Who's going to take care of my cat?"

That sudden, horrifying thought slipped into her mind. She had forgotten all about Mason. Her baby. What would happen to him?

He would be all alone. He would be frightened without her. Lonely. He had been the only creature in the world who had stayed by her side all these years, and now she wasn't there to care for him?

"Don't worry about that mangy animal," Luc suddenly snarled. "He's in the barn with the other—"

"In the barn?" She practically screamed out in surprise and fury. "You put my cat in the barn? My baby is in the barn?"

She stared at him, unable to believe the words that came from him. Who would be cruel enough to put sweet little Mason in a barn? He couldn't do this. Her fingers curled, flexed, as she ached to attack him.

There went his arms over his chest again. "So?"

"So. You can't put Mason in the barn." She propped her hands on her hips, fighting mad now. She would not allow him to abuse her cat. "You go get him now."

He frowned at the harsh demand in her voice.

"If I were you, I would worry about my own problems, not that black mouse chaser," he snorted.

Outrage flew through her. She felt fury vibrating violently through her body.

"Mason does not chase mice," she informed him

coldly. "And Mason does not sleep in barns. He sleeps in my room, on my bed, next to me. I want my cat. Now."

He tilted his head, watching her with a sudden, inquisitive expression.

"How bad do you want that cat back, Catarina?" he asked her softly.

She wanted to slap his smug face. At least he was calling her by part of her given name. Even if it was one she shared with Maria. He was going to blackmail her. She could see it in his eyes, in his expression. The son of a bitch was going to use her baby against her. She wanted to tell him to go straight to hell.

Instead, she gritted her teeth, counted to ten, and said, "What do you want?"

Melina was aware there had to be something wrong with loving a black ball of fluff that rarely gave her the time of day. Unless she cried. Then he was all over her, comforting her, letting her hold him, even if it was with an air of supreme boredom. He had gotten her through the past two years when there had been no one else. She wasn't about to leave him in a dirty, dusty barn.

Luc stepped back to her, pulling her against his harder, taller body as she stared up at him in shock. She hated the awareness that flared in the pit of her stomach as his hard cock pressed into her. Hated the hunger she could feel welling within her.

Her lips parted as he stared down at her, his eyes flickering with heat as they settled on her lips. Melina trembled. She could feel her pussy heating, dampening, and cursed her response to him.

She braced her hands against his shoulders, resisting—not just Luc, but herself as well. He had the most kissable lips she had ever seen on a man. That full lower curve fascinated her, made her want to eat him up. But he had set the boundaries with this kidnapping. There wasn't a chance in hell she was going to lie down and let him walk all over her. She was tired of being anyone's doormat.

"I thought you were my kidnapper, not my rapist," she snapped when she managed to find her voice. "Let me go, Luc. I won't whore for my cat. But I'll be damned if I'll cooperate in any way without him."

His brows snapped into a frown as his arms tightened around her. Eyes narrowing, he gazed down at her thoughtfully for long seconds before slowly releasing her.

"Take your shower and get dressed. We'll discuss terms downstairs after you've managed to cool off and act decently. I might allow you the cat, if you can control yourself and follow the rules." With that said, he left the room, closing the door quietly behind him.

She was going to kill him, she assured herself. Then she was going to kill Maria.

SIX

An hour later, freshly showered and dressed in a pair of jeans and white cotton shirt, Melina entered the large kitchen at the far end of the house. The two-story ranch home was laid out fairly simply, so the kitchen wasn't hard to find. Of course, the banging of the cabinet doors might have helped a little.

Tucking a stray reddish-gold curl behind her ear, Melina checked the French braid she had arranged her hair into for neatness and stepped into the kitchen. She knew the second she walked into the room that she loved it. Too bad it belonged to the big, arrogant cowboy frowning into the depths of a cabinet.

The stove was to die for. It was a modern cook's dream with a gas grill in the center, four large burners on the side, and adequate ventilation above it. The floor was hardwood with an area rug beneath the six chairs and kitchen table that sat near a large picture window. The cabinets were cherry, though dusty and appearing dull in the light of the morning sun. But there were plenty of them. A large central island was located several feet from the sink, yet still near enough to the stove to make it handy.

It might have been a cook's dream but it was a housekeeper's nightmare.

Luc was turned just slightly away from her, giving her a clear view of his muscular back and the taut, well-rounded curves of his butt beneath his snug jeans. He had an ass to die for. The sight of it made her fingers itch with the need to touch. As though she would know what to do with it if she did touch, she told herself sarcastically. Still, she had always admired a nice male backside, and his had to be the best she had seen yet.

Drawing in a long, deep breath, she glanced away from the temptation.

"You need to fire your housekeeper," she told him expressionlessly as she stared around the room once again. "She's not doing her job."

The kitchen resembled the living room she had peeked into, as well as the dining room she had walked through. Dusty, unloved. As though the home wasn't really a home but merely a place to spend the night.

Luc turned to look at her, his brows lowered in a dark frown as she hunched her shoulders and tucked her hands into her jean pockets. She was still dying to claw his eyes out; she figured it better to restrain her hands enough that she would at least have a second to think before actually trying to do it. He was sure to make her madder before the hour was out.

She watched as he followed the move, a smirk tilting his lips as though he knew the reason behind it. Melina fought to keep her expression clear, the anger glowing in her chest from reflecting on her face. Damn him. She had never met a man more stubborn in her life.

Shoring her patience, she straightened her shoulders and met his look head-on. She had resigned herself to the fact that he wasn't going to listen to reason, which meant she was going to have to try to find her own way out. She had a feeling that escaping Luc wouldn't be easy. But before she could even consider escape, she had to have Mason.

"I've showered, I've dressed, and I've met you in the kitchen," she finally said with careful control. "Now where's my baby?"

Irritation flashed in his stormy gray eyes. It was obvious that there was something about her and her cat that he didn't like. Of course, it could just be Maria he hated, she thought with morbid amusement, which didn't bode well for her, considering he thought she was Maria.

"How anyone can call that fat-assed black ball of fur a baby is beyond me," he growled. "That animal should be put down for its temper alone."

Melina's eyes widened in sudden fear at the sincere dislike in his tone and the implied threat to the little animal. Her baby. He thought Mason should be killed.

And Mason did not have a temper. He was just a little spoiled, that was all. That was no excuse to be mean to him.

"You hurt Mason and I promise you, I'll make what Maria did to you look like a day at the park," she warned him, completely serious now.

He could punish her all he liked, and in a way she could even make some sort of twisted sense of it. But he wasn't going to hurt Mason. She'd had enough of Maria's thoughtless actions impacting her life in such painful ways. She blamed herself. She had allowed the trend to continue as they got older, but no more. She would not lose anything else due to her sister's selfishness and utter cruelty.

He crossed his arms over his chest. She was coming to heartily dislike that action.

He was still frowning at her, the low cast of his brows giving his expression a dangerous appearance. Melina fought back her fear as she met his gaze silently.

"You're in no position to be giving out threats here, sugarplum," he told her softly, his voice almost too gentle to suit her. It reminded her of the eye of a violent storm. She would have been more frightened if it weren't for the fact that she was hopelessly in love with that stupid cat. Even she didn't understand it.

"Listen, mister, I understand you think you have a problem with me. Really, I do," she assured him sincerely. "I can even, almost, understand the mistake you're making.

"But if you harm so much as a hair on Mason's body, then I promise, you're going to regret it. That's my cat. He adopted me when no one else wanted me and I'll be damned if I'll let you mistreat him."

"Baby, maybe more people would want you if you toed the line a little bit closer. You know. Give a little, get a little?" he suggested mockingly.

Melina flinched at the painfully cruel words. Give a little, get a little. She would have laughed at the thought if it weren't so ironic. She had given everything she had for so many years . . . for nothing. All she had to show for it was a black cat that deigned to curl in her lap and shed on her whenever she became weak enough to cry. But the warmth of his fat little body and his soft purrs had kept her sane through the aftermath of her nightmares.

"I'm sure you think your opinion of me should matter," she said reasonably, stilling the furious words that rose to her lips instead. "I'll even pretend it does for as long as I have to. But not as long as my cat is in that barn suffering."

If she could go to jail for Maria, then she could stand up to one temperamental cowboy for her baby. She could think of few things as horrible as that week she had spent in jail for her sister.

"At least he's alive," he grunted hatefully. "Have I mentioned I hate cats?"

Melina pushed back the fear rising inside her. Maria had nearly caused the death of this man as well as his friend. Killing a cat he believed was hers would be small compared with her crimes. But it was Mason. He didn't belong to Maria. Maria couldn't care less and she wouldn't spend a second grieving his loss. And she sure as hell wouldn't care about the pain Melina would suffer without him.

She bit her lip as she fought the fear that Luc would hurt him. She looked up at him silently, swallowing dread. She had a feeling her need for comfort from her fears might well be her downfall.

"Please," she whispered. "I just want my cat."

Melina saw the interest that suddenly flared in his eyes, the knowledge that the animal could be leverage against her that he might not have considered before.

"In exchange for?" he asked, confirming her worst fears. There wasn't a lot she would say no to in her effort to save Mason.

"I already asked what you want." She tried to still the frustration thickening her voice as she attempted to reason with a man who had already proven himself unreasonable. "I'm willing to cooperate as much as possible," she said nervously. "Fine, you want to punish me for what Maria did, but don't hurt my cat."

If his frown could have grown darker, it would have. She saw the anger that instantly flared in his gaze and knew she had just made a major tactical error.

"Admit to who you are, and we'll talk."

Admit to who she wasn't. A sense of resignation overcame her. The cost of one small comfort would be once again allowing herself to be mired in Maria's identity. She slid her hands from her jeans, linking them together, trying to still the tremors that wanted to rush through her body.

"I told you who I am," she said as desolation washed over her. "Don't make me lie to you. Please. Because I will, for this."

His arms uncrossed, his thumbs catching at the front of his jean waistband.

She shouldn't notice the tight, hard abs that the action displayed, or the lean, muscular hips and, below, the thick bulge of his cock. She shouldn't be wet, shouldn't be longing for things she knew she couldn't have.

His brow lifted mockingly. "You would lie for something so small?" he asked with sarcastic disbelief. "Don't make this any harder on yourself than it already is," he suggested easily. "Come on, tell me who you are and we'll go get the cat."

Melina drew in a tired breath.

"Catarina Angeles," she finally said, fighting to hold her temper back now. If she let her anger free, she would never see Mason again.

He shook his head slowly, destroying any hope she had that he would, by chance, let this go. "Nope. Come on, sugarplum, full name. Admit to who you are and we'll go get the cat. Otherwise, he takes his chances outside."

She met his gaze directly, holding back the screams that longed to pour from her throat. "Don't do this."

Could she survive without Mason? She shuddered at the thought of the nightmares that were sure to come without his comforting presence. How would she hold on to her sanity without something or someone to comfort her?

"Your name," he demanded again.

"Maria Catarina Angeles," she whispered despondently. It wasn't the first time she had done so, but at least this time it served her rather than someone else. "May I please have my cat now?"

He should have been satisfied. Luc stared at the expressionless face, the weary green eyes, and felt anything but satisfaction. He felt like a damned monster. She had spoken the words as her shoulders lowered marginally, as though the weight of the admission had placed an invisible burden on her that was too great to bear.

The admission, though given as he asked, was voiced with such a lack of emotion that it made him regret forcing the issue. And her eyes. If he had ever seen such weary resignation in a woman's eyes, he couldn't remember it. They darkened, turning so vulnerable, so filled with shadows and pain, that something about it twisted his heart.

She had spoken the words with an automation that seemed almost . . . rehearsed. He tilted his head, watching, as she stood silent and cool in front of him. Her fury of earlier that morning seemed extinguished and weariness had taken its place. He felt like a complete bastard and didn't even know why. Damn her. It wasn't his fault she wanted to play games.

He hated cats. What in the hell possessed him to consider letting that demon into his house? He probably shed, Luc thought in disgust. Just what he needed. But he'd be damned if he could stand that look in those dark velvet-green eyes. They were haunted, filled with an inner pain that he couldn't quite describe. A pain he had caused.

He snarled silently, lifting his lips in self-derision as he grunted in irritation.

"Come on, let's go get the bastard. But if he scratches me again I'll feed him to my dogs. He'd make a hell of a snack."

SEVEN

The barn was within sight of the house, but still nearly an acre separated it from the main building. Melina moved quickly behind Luc as his long legs ate up the distance.

She couldn't keep her eyes off his strongly curved ass, no matter how hard she tried, or the bunch and flex of his hard thighs beneath his jeans. He had the long-legged gait of a cowboy. That undefined, strolling strut that made a woman's mouth water and her fingers itch to clench into all that male strength moving so temptingly before her eyes.

His buttocks were lusciously curved for a man, and the low-riding jeans showed them off to perfection. His back was like granite beneath the T-shirt, each muscle defined by the cloth that had been tucked into his pants. The whole picture was irritatingly sexy. She didn't want to lust for him anymore. It was fine when he was just a distant figure she could drool over in private, but now?

She snorted silently. He had to be the most aggravating, ill-tempered man she had laid eyes on in her life. But good heavens, if he wasn't the most delicious-looking man she had ever seen.

Melina grimaced in self-disgust. The man had literally forced her into lying about who she was. He had blackmailed her with poor Mason's helpless life, and she was lusting over him. Her cunt was weeping, not just wet, but drooling in hunger. Like a man starved and presented a banquet, only to be told he couldn't partake. It wasn't fair.

It was the most unjust act of deprivation where sexuality was concerned that she could have envisioned.

Following close behind him, her head lowered, her gaze on the delicious curves of his male rear, she was completely unprepared for his abrupt stop.

"Omphf." She smacked into his back, stumbling, her face flaming as he turned to her and shot her a frown.

"Are you okay?" His hand shot out, gripping her arm as she jumped back again and nearly fell flat on her ass. "Dammit, you can't be on anything. I made sure there wasn't a pill in the house before I kidnapped you."

God, he would be perfect if he would just keep his damned mouth shut.

Jerking her arm back she flashed him a look, intending to convey the pure violence toward him that suddenly surged in her head. Too bad her body wasn't listening.

"Moron," she sniffed, moving around him to the open doors of the barn. "I assume this is where Mason is?"

As she spoke, a cat's plaintive wail filled the air, causing her eyes to widen at the lost, pitiful sound. She turned, shot Luc a look that promised retribution and moved quickly into the shadowed interior.

"Mason." She gasped in surprise at the bedraggled black ball of fur that cried out at her from a bed of straw.

He was pitiful. Dusty, his fur matted, his amazing blue eyes damp and miserable.

He wailed again, a feline sound of misery that broke her heart as she went to her knees in front of him and pulled him gently into her arms.

"Oh, Mason," she whispered against his once soft coat, ignoring the bite of his claws into her arms as he cried out plaintively once again. "My poor baby. It's okay. I'll take care of you now." She turned back to Luc, ignoring his dark frown. "You have abused my cat. There's no excuse for that, Luc. I didn't think you could truly be cruel until now."

His brows lifted in surprise, his hands going automatically to his hips as he stared back at her incredulously.

"Abuse? The little bastard was doing his best to take a bite out of me. All I did was shoot him a time or two with the water hose. Hell, he barely got wet."

Mason wailed again as Melina groaned silently. The water hose? Oh hell, Mason detested getting wet.

"He will hate you for life now." She sighed as she shook her head. This was not going to be a pleasant incarceration.

"This is supposed to bother me?" He arched a brow mockingly.

Melina smiled tightly. "Well, let's see, I paid your blackmail for him, which means he's now a resident in your home. Let's pray there's no leather furniture, shoes, or boots you're particularly attached to. If so, they're his the minute he gets his chance."

His eyes narrowed. "I'll kill him."

"Tsk-tsk, Luc." She shook her head with a knowing smile. "You gave your word, remember? I upheld my end, and I didn't tell you to abuse him, so . . ." She shrugged. "Unless your word means nothing, I guess you're just screwed."

"As long as it's by you," he murmured, his voice dropping, deepening to such a sensual pitch that chills chased over her flesh.

Melina swallowed nervously, her grip tightening on the bedraggled Mason as she fought back the panic welling in her chest. God, it was bad enough she ached for Luc; he did not have to make it worse.

"Only in your wildest dreams, cowboy," she snapped. "Now I need to feed Mason."

That brow arched again. That was never a good sign.

"Was feeding him part of the deal?" He surveyed the cat thoughtfully. "I don't remember that part, sweet pea."

"You've gotten all you're going to get from me, Jardin," she warned him quietly. "More than you know. If you want any cooperation from me at all, you'll let this go."

Her voice was quiet, her look direct. She could go so far, and only so far. She could see the way his mind was working and she would be damned if she would whore herself to feed her cat. She had, quite literally, had enough. Good-looking was all fine and well, sexy as hell was even better, but there came a point when what came out of a man's mouth just overwhelmed any appeal he might have. Luc Jardin was easing into that shadowed area really fast.

"Hmm." The rumbled sound skated over her spine with a sensation too close to anticipation to suit her. When combined with the drowsy sensuality in his gaze, it was potent. "Come on. I'll get you started in the house. Keep that mouse chaser away from my leather or your ass will hurt for it, not his. I'll outline your duties and we'll see how appreciative you can be of my generosity."

"If you had any generosity, I might appreciate it," she grunted as she turned back toward the house.

She could only imagine what her "duties" would entail. If he thought cleaning that nasty house was going to be much of a chore, he was dead wrong. The house was a dream, and it was a sin the shape it was in.

"Careful, sweet pea," he said as she passed, his voice diabolical in its sexuality. "I just might show you exactly how generous I can be."

And if she remembered correctly, he had plenty of reason to threaten generosity.

The memory of the head of his cock resting on her lips, the small pearl of seed catching on the lower curve, slammed into her. She could almost taste the heady male essence of him once again. And that wasn't a good thing. He didn't need more ammunition to use against her.

"As I said," she shrugged, feigning nonchalance with no small amount of effort, "only in your dreams, cowboy."

His dreams could get pretty vivid. Luc followed her closely, watching the smooth sway of her shapely hips as he listened to that damned cat cry. But he could handle the feline theatrics for the chance of watching that pert little ass bump and sway across his ranch yard. And he owed her. He was well aware of why she had walked into his back earlier.

He had felt the heat of her gaze on his ass as he walked in front of her. It had been a bit disconcerting, a sensation he wasn't used to. Never had he felt a woman watching him like that, knowing beyond a shadow of a doubt where her look was directed. And he was fairly confident she was pleased with what she was watching. But no more than he was.

He smirked as he noticed her efforts to control the ultra-feminine sway of her hips.

Could she feel his gaze as well? Hell, yes she could, he thought a second later, refusing to believe he was the only one in torment. That would not be acceptable.

He couldn't remember Catarina inspiring this hunger in him two years before. He had been amused. Hell, he had been willing to fuck the tempting little redhead, but he hadn't hungered for her. He hungered for her now. If he didn't trust Joe so damned much, he would half suspect she really wasn't the woman who had gone to her knees with experience he couldn't imagine her possessing now.

Luc shook his head as they neared the porch of the ranch house. The cat wailed again. Dammit, that fat black excuse for a mouse chaser was going to be in his house, shedding on his furniture, likely eating his food and tormenting the hell out of him.

And only God knew what his wolf hybrid, Lobo, was

going to think of the addition to the house. He only hoped his canine friend was as well trained as he had tried to teach him to be. Otherwise, that cat would be wolf chow and an unpleasant memory in a matter of hours.

EIGHT

It wasn't that the punishment was onerous; it was that the situation was pissing her off, Melina thought as she prepared to sneak out of the house. Cleaning house was child's play, and cooking was one of her favorite hobbies. Not that she had let Mr. Neanderthal know that. She had stayed mulishly silent, procrastinated, shot him ill looks as he watched her, and generally done her best to get out of whatever work he assigned her after the confrontation the day before. She could tell it was no more than he expected.

She loved the house. But it wasn't her house and she wasn't Maria, and she sure as hell didn't think much of his stubbornness and refusal to hear the truth. Furthermore, she wasn't going to calmly bow her head and accept his idea of punishment. She was finished with playing Maria the day she had nearly died in that jail cell.

"Come on, Mason," she whispered as she lifted the

fat cat and slid him carefully into the sling she had made of one of the pillowcases. She wasn't about to toss him down two stories. He would never forgive her, and it would be her luck if instead of landing on his feet he ended up on his oversized head.

The bedsheets were tied together and anchored to the heavy leg of the bed, giving her just enough room to slide down to about a four-foot drop below the end of the sheet. Mr. Know-It-All had locked the door to her bedroom but forgotten about the windows, she snickered.

Mason sighed his little breath of boredom as she slid the sling to her back and crawled over the window ledge. Gripping the sheet, she slid carefully down its length until she was forced to let go of the material and drop the final distance.

She landed easily and smiled in triumph. She had no idea where she was, but she would find out fast enough. There was a road that led to the house, and roads always ran into towns some damned place. It might take a while to walk out of there, but at least she was free. Free of Lucas Jardin's sexy drawl, the heat that emanated from his big body and his sexy smile. Free of the temptation those two years of sexual fantasies had caused.

Moving quickly, she sprinted across the flat harsh terrain, keeping the road in sight but staying a careful distance from it. If he happened to check on her and find her gone, he would most likely start searching the road first. Melina assured herself she wouldn't be a stupid escapee. She was going to succeed.

Well, he had wondered how long it would take her to make her first escape attempt. Luc chuckled in amuse-

ment as he caught sight of the sheets tied together and
leading out of the window to the ranch yard below. His
little captive had sprung her cage, and rather than the
fury he would have expected, he felt anticipation rising
instead.

She intrigued him. Damned if she didn't. He hadn't
expected to be touched, amused, or intrigued by her,
but he was. And damned if the thought of chasing her
wasn't giving him a hard-on like no other he had ever
had.

Shaking his head at the phenomenon, he moved back
to his bedroom, collected his rifle, and commanded
Lobo to follow him. The wolf hybrid would be a hell of
a surprise when he managed to track her down. Lobo
wouldn't eat her or the cat, but he would give her an idea
of what could be waiting on her when she roamed the
East Texas landscape alone.

The wolf followed at his heels as he moved through
the house and out to the backyard. Using the small penlight he carried, he checked the tracks under the sheet
and estimated she had a good thirty-minute head start
on him. Not nearly enough to do her any good.

Shaking his head as he smothered his laughter, Luc
cut a large strip of the sheet off and lowered it to Lobo
to get a good sniff.

"Find our girl, Lobo," he said softly as he smiled in
anticipation. "I'll be right behind you."

What was it about her? Luc shook his head as he set
off after the animal. There wasn't a chance in hell that
she wasn't Maria, but things weren't adding up. This
was a drug-addicted, spoiled little rich girl he was holding captive. But there were no needle tracks on her

arm; her skin was creamy and silky smooth, rather than sallow and pale as he remembered it two years before.

Her eyes were a vivid, dark green, her body lush and graceful with the most intriguing scent of heat and woman that he had ever smelled. It made him wonder constantly how sweet her pussy would be. And all those lovely red-gold curls that fell around her pixie-like face . . . It was enough to make a man's mouth water. Not to mention what it did to his dick.

It wasn't long before Lobo's yips alerted Luc to the fact that he had found the little escapee. Luc picked up his pace, jogging in the direction of the wolf's excited sounds as he carefully herded Maria toward him. He chuckled when he finally heard her voice, thick with fear and bravado as Lobo snapped at her heels.

"You think I don't know he sent you?" she snapped at Lobo as he playfully pounced toward the sack she carried in front of her. Likely that damned cat. "And no, you cannot have Mason." Yep, it was that damned cat.

Mason's wail of fear could be heard inside the cloth prison.

"Go away, you flea-bitten creature." He could hear the threat of tears in her voice as he watched her attempt to resume the direction she had been heading. Lobo wasn't to be denied, though. He nipped at her feet, causing a squeal of outrage to fill the desert night.

"You bite me and I promise you, your master will be bald next time I see him. Stupid cretin. Get away from me."

Lobo had the tail of her shirt in his mouth, dragging her back, ignoring her desperate swipes at his head as he pulled at her.

Luc stood back and watched. Damn, she was adorable. She called Lobo every nasty name in the book, but as each minute went by he could hear the shadow of laughter thickening in her voice as Lobo played with her.

Lobo growled as she pulled at her shirt, a deep, warning rumble that was nowhere as threatening as Luc would have expected it to be. The wolf normally took his duties a bit more seriously. He was supposed to frighten, not tease.

"I'm not going back there." She strained against the tugging animal. "Now let me go."

The shirt ripped, but Lobo wasn't about to be deterred. He grabbed at her pant leg instead and pulled back sharply, sending her to the ground, flat on that pretty ass. Luc expected her to be up, fighting, raging; instead, he watched as she merely sighed wearily.

"Dammit. I'm going to kill Maria," he heard her mutter. "I swear to God, first chance I get, I'm killing her."

There was a deep sigh of resignation before she laid her head on her upraised knees. She was breathing roughly as Lobo watched her with canine curiosity before turning back to Luc for guidance.

Luc watched her curiously. She had to be aware he was there, but her whispered words still bothered him more than he wanted to admit. He knew Maria was slick; she had to have been to sweet-talk her way out of so much trouble over the years. The reports he had seen on her various court appearances were astounding. She could sway a judge better than the most accomplished defense lawyer. She had walked away more than once with a slap on her wrist and a firm lecture rather than the jail time she should have received.

He couldn't blame the judges or the prosecutors too much, though, because right now, he wanted to believe every excuse out of her mouth. And the thought of that didn't set well with him at all.

Mason meowed plaintively from within what appeared to be a pillowcase converted into some type of sling.

"Be quiet, Mason," she mumbled. "If I let you go you'll become dog food. Is that what you really want?"

She was quiet now. As though she knew it wasn't going to do her any good to fight any longer. Conserving her strength, he thought in amusement. As aroused as he was right now, it might be the sensible course for her. He was so damned hard that if he did manage to get her into a bed, it would be a long time before she got out of it.

Shaking his head, Luc walked toward her, staring down at the mass of red-gold curls that had been tied back behind her neck, revealing the perfection of her pale profile. He hesitated to touch her. Rather, he stopped inches from her feet and stared down at her with what he hoped was a forbidding expression. It wouldn't do for her to see how easily he was softening toward her. Or how much he desired her. She was becoming a hunger. A need. In little more than a few days she had set his senses on fire, and despite the confusion, he found he had little resistance against it.

"Are you ready to go back yet?" he asked her sternly, pressing his lips together tightly to still the grin that would have edged them.

"Not really." Anger laced her tone as she kept her face buried in her knees.

She had to be exhausted. Despite her best attempts to appear as though she wasn't cleaning the house, several of the rooms damned near sparkled. He couldn't understand it. When he'd first set out the wealth of cleaning supplies he had bought her, she had lifted her lip in contempt. But with each room he dragged her to, the improvement had been almost immediate.

Luc bent his knees, lowering himself until he could stare into her eyes whenever she deigned to look up. She kept herself still, refusing to raise her head.

"You proclaimed your innocence almost convincingly the other day," he said softly. "Then you do exactly what I would have expected of Maria. Only a guilty child runs from her punishment, Catarina. Not an innocent woman."

"Oh God, the world has gone insane!" Her laughter was edged with disbelief as she shifted the cat to her side and sprawled out on her back, staring up at the black velvet, star-studded sky. "Did he even hear what he said?" she seemed to demand of the heavens. "A crazy man has kidnapped me. Have mercy, please," she prayed with exaggerated patience before staring back at him with glittering eyes. "What about innocent people who have no desire to clean your filthy messes?"

Luc watched her curiously, as did Lobo. The animal was a bit more forward about it, though. He scooted close to her, nudging her neck with his nose before yipping demandingly in her ear. Mason cried out plaintively within the crude sack that had fallen to her side.

She closed her eyes tightly before moving slowly to pull herself to her feet.

"Next time, I steal the fucking truck," she muttered.

Luc grinned as he rose as well, staring down at her.

"You have to steal the keys first. Want to know where they are?" He stuck his hand in his jean pocket and rattled the keys teasingly.

"Figures. Likely where your damned brains are, too," she snarled, heading back to the house. "Just my luck. All looks, nothing upstairs. Let's hope for the sake of your past lovers that at least you know what to do with the equipment a little lower, because my personal opinion is, that's all you have going for you."

Luc stilled his laughter. She was amusing. Had there been anything other than irritation behind her tone, then he would have likely been just a little offended. But her tone was teasing, a bit abstract. She was plotting another way to escape while hoping to piss him off enough that he wouldn't realize it.

"I've had no complaints," he assured her as he walked carefully behind her.

"Perhaps you should test it for yourself."

A less-than-ladylike snort left her lips. "No thanks. As difficult as I'm sure you think the decision is, I'll have to decline your lovely offer."

"For now," he grinned. But not for long, he promised himself.

She came to a stop, turning to him, and he was surprised by the icy look she gave him, the pride and haughty disdain that filled her expression.

"Save your lust for someone who cares, Mr. Jardin. I don't. And I sure as hell don't want my sister's used seconds. Please be so kind as to keep that in mind."

NINE

Her sister's used seconds? She was good, he had to give her that. Damned good.

Hell, he wanted to believe her and he knew better.

Nearly an hour later Luc was still fuming at the accusation as he dragged her into the house and up to his bedroom. She had fought him damned near every step until he had threatened to throw her over his shoulder instead. Her furious silence the rest of the way only edged his anger higher.

Fine. Maybe she hadn't really known what her friends were up to the day they had nearly killed him and Jack. She looked innocent enough. There were none of the signs of drug use on her and she was a hell of a lot more spirited than he had ever expected. She could make him feel like slime with one look out of those wounded, shadow-filled green eyes, and he wanted to cringe each time she turned them on him in accusation.

And she was always so ladylike. She even moved like a lady. Smooth and supple, teasing and tempting him in ways he wouldn't have imagined she could.

She was fucking classy, was what she was. Moving with grace and a regal bearing that had him watching her even when he didn't want to. But she didn't have to lie about who she was. All she had to try was the truth. Stupidity was forgivable; lying wasn't. He hated liars. And she didn't have to call him used seconds when he hadn't even had a chance to fuck her. Yet.

That could change quickly, though, he thought as he headed for his bedroom. He was on fire for her. Less than a week in her presence and his cock was like hot iron in his pants, so ready to fuck he could feel the seeping of the pre-cum from its slitted eye.

"This isn't my room," she finally yelled furiously as he pushed her into his room and slammed the door closed behind him.

Tension, thick and hot, filled the air. His body was hard and primed and she was soft, and he knew she would be so damned sweet to taste that it would send him over the edge of his control.

She looked more like a scared woman-child than a seductress, though, as she rounded on him, her eyes wide, her face pale, and her fists clenched at her side. So innocent. Damn her. She had sucked his dick like a pro and now acted like a virgin wronged.

"No. It's not," he agreed coldly as he wrestled the sacked cat from her and released the tormented little feline.

For his efforts, the little black demon took a swipe at him a second before disappearing under his bed. He would have chased it out if Catarina hadn't decided then to make a run for the door. The woman deserved a medal for sheer stubbornness.

He grabbed her arm, pulling her quickly to a stop before shoving her to the bed. If he had his hands on her for more than a second he feared he would lose any semblance of control. He was dying to take those lush, sweet pink lips in a kiss and see if her mouth tasted as hot and arousing as he knew it would.

"Since I can't trust you to stay put, you'll stay where I can keep an eye on you," he snapped as he jerked the blankets off the four-poster bed, fighting the hunger. "Now strip."

He turned back to her as her eyes widened in shocked outrage. "I will not."

She should be on stage, he thought furiously. She pulled off the innocent virgin too damned well. That was no virgin sucking his cock two years before. That was a well-trained, experienced woman who had swallowed every drop of semen spewing into her mouth.

"Stop with the damned act," he snarled back at her. "I'm tired and not in the mood for your snippy little protests of innocence. Strip your damned clothes off and get into the bed before I tear them off you."

His fingers clenched with the need to do just that, then to tear his own off and plunge his cock as hard and deep inside her pussy as he could. He could feel the blood surging through his veins at the thought of it. Of holding her beneath him, hearing her scream his name, her hips pumping beneath him as he fucked her past defiance.

"Adding rape to your crimes now?" she sneered,

surprising him. "Luc, surely there's enough dumb women around here to take care of the stupid cowboys in rut. Or do you have to wait for a season, like the other animals do?"

Luc held on to his control carefully. He couldn't blame her for being angry, for striking out at him with fury. But he'd be damned if he would allow her to push him much further. Further than he felt his own temper would allow. And that surprised him. No woman had ever touched that dark core inside him. The restless, hungry desire he had always been careful to keep hidden. She was doing more than tempting that pulsing, aching core, though; she was making it hunger, seethe. She was rousing a side of him that even he was wary of.

"You have one minute to strip and crawl into that bed," he growled softly. Even Lobo, who had followed them into the room, looked at him worriedly when he used that tone of voice. "Starting now."

Melina felt trepidation suddenly wrap around her senses. His tone was dark, dangerous, but the sudden shifting of the color of his eyes was even more so.

They darkened, became almost feral in intensity, and caused her to suddenly second-guess the belief she had formed that Luc Jardin was in any way safe.

He hadn't hurt her yet, she reminded herself. He wouldn't hurt her now. But damn if it wasn't hard to fight back the fear.

She felt perspiration dot her forehead as he stared at her, felt the aroused hunger leaping from him to wrap around her. Twisted, nightmare images of pain and cruel hands touching her body attacked her mind then. She fought the instinctive need to trust him. To believe in the fantasy visions she'd had of him since their first meeting.

"Please . . ." She backed away from him. "I won't do it again. I'll be good." She almost winced at the hasty words that suddenly flew from her lips. Dammit, she wasn't a child anymore. She swallowed tightly, steadied her voice, and whispered, "Luc, don't do this."

There was no mercy in his expression. If anything, he appeared harder, more determined than ever.

Tension thickened in the room. It became heavy with his sexual tension, with her fear.

"Undress." She flinched as his voice hardened. The wolf that lay in the corner of the room whined in confusion.

She wouldn't do it. Melina straightened her shoulders, knowing she would lose the fight to come, but she wouldn't stop fighting. She shuddered at the thought of how he could still her defiance, though—how it had been stilled once before—and she wanted to scream out in fury.

Melina held back her screams. She would need the energy for those later, she feared. She backed farther away from him, watching him carefully as she fought to breathe. She could feel the hard throb of her heart in her chest, the blood pounding through her veins, and the cold sweat that covered her body. She hated fear. Hated the weakness it brought and the sense of vulnerability that seemed to only intensify.

"No." She gripped the front of her shirt in defense as she defied him. He wasn't a man who would take that defiance easily.

They had gone for her shirt first, during that night of horror and pain in the cells.

They had torn it from her body and then ripped the loose jail-issued pants from her hips as she fought to cover herself. Every time she said no, the blows had only grown worse.

But she hadn't stopped, not until she lost consciousness, not until the pain had become so great that she knew death itself had come to rescue her. But it hadn't. She had lived.

And now she lived with the memories as well.

She was going to be sick. She could feel her stomach roiling, feel the fear washing over her as she stared back at his stony expression. It was a nightmare that she wasn't certain she could survive.

He took a step toward her and Melina jumped back, barely aware of the whimper that escaped her throat, or of Lobo's sudden, soft growl. But Luc stopped then. His piercing eyes turned to the animal at the side of the room before moving slowly back to her.

Melina swallowed tightly, forcing back the bile rising to her throat. Luc was tall, strong. Stronger than any man she knew. If he tried to force her . . .

"Catarina, I won't hurt you," he suddenly breathed tiredly, though his look was too intense, too knowing now for her to find any comfort.

He moved instead to his dresser and pulled out a dark T-shirt. "Take this to the bathroom and change. You will be sleeping in this bed. With me. Don't even doubt that. But I would never take anything from you that you don't willingly give me."

She was shaking. Melina hadn't realized how hard

she was shaking until she heard her teeth chatter as he came closer. She bit her lip, fighting the need to run, to flee as he advanced. She couldn't scream, she couldn't trust herself to utter a sound, afraid that if she did, the memories she had fought so hard to keep contained would pour out of her like bitter acid, scarring them both.

"Here." He pressed the shirt to her then caressed her cheek as she flinched away from him. "Get ready for bed, Catarina. Now."

She snatched the shirt. "My pajamas," she whispered as she fought to speak without stuttering. "Will you get me a pair? In my room."

The fleece bottoms would provide much more protection, more warning if he decided to change his mind. She needed that confidence more than anything else right now.

"No, Catarina." He shook his head, causing her chest to tighten in dread. "You have to learn to understand I won't hurt you. We'll begin tonight. No pants. Now go change. You have five minutes, and not a minute more."

She stared up at him, sensing the crisis had passed, though her mind refused to accept it. He seemed to surround her, to take up all the air in the room, all the freedom of movement.

Skirting around him, watching him carefully, she moved for the tenuous sanctuary of the bathroom and hopefully a locked door. She needed time to still the dark shadows that chased through her mind, time to repair the fragile control he had destroyed so easily.

TEN

He was shaking. Luc stared down at his hands as though they belonged to someone else, wondering at the trembling extensions. Suspicion coursed through him like a tidal wave, and he didn't like the conclusions he was drawing.

Catarina was like a light, fluid and bright whether she was angry or teasing, and hot as a damned firecracker. Until he had let the anger simmer to the surface. Until she had realized she would be in his bed—naked, at his mercy. And terror had swamped her. And there was but one reason for such overriding fear.

Had she been raped? Of course she had. He shook his head, fighting the rage that began to burn in his chest. There was no other excuse for it. No other way to explain her reaction to him.

If it hadn't been for Lobo, he feared he would have missed the sheer terror in her eyes as he fought her defiance of him. He had seen her beauty, his sudden arousal for her, but only at Lobo's warning growl had he understood the true cause of the desperation. The animal had sensed what he had been too stupid to see.

"Fuck," he whispered as he pushed his fingers restlessly through his hair.

His arousal had slammed to a stop the minute he realized how truly frightened she was. He knew the fear didn't come from his confrontation with her two years before. There had been no fear in her then, only anger.

Something else about her reaction now didn't make sense: confusion. She had been confused, wary, but resigned.

What the hell was going on? Joe wouldn't lie to him, he assured himself. He had spent enough time with the man to know he wouldn't willingly place his sister in danger. And he sure as hell wouldn't place an innocent sister in the line of fire.

He moved quickly to his feet as the doorknob turned slowly long minutes later and then opened. She left the bathroom, her shoulders straight, her head held high as she faced him, dressed in his T-shirt. Damn. He envied that shirt in ways he couldn't name.

It fell over full, luscious breasts and ended mid-thigh. Her legs were shapely, well-toned, and so tempting he could have spent hours touching them. Her eyes blazed, though. Green fire sparking with anger and the remnants of her fear.

"Lobo, keep her in here," he ordered the wolf as he watched Catarina carefully.

* * *

"Get in the bed. I'm worn to the bone and don't feel like fighting with you anymore, Cat. We'll talk in the morning."

"I'm going home in the morning," she stated quietly. "And my name is Melina, not Catarina, not Cat, not Maria. I am Melina."

Luc sighed roughly. "You're acting more like that damned spoiled cat than anything else. And you're not going anywhere tomorrow. Now get in the bed before I have to tie you in it. I'm not in the mood for theatrics or temperaments. I've had enough for the day."

He stalked to the bathroom before he did something stupid. Something like pulling her into his arms, holding her to his chest, and swearing he'd never hurt her, never let anyone else hurt her. Making promises he knew she would never believe.

As he slammed the bathroom door, he came to a startling, horrifying realization. He was starting to care for her, and that just would not do. He couldn't afford to care for this little wildcat. Not and survive with his heart intact. But damn if it hadn't already happened.

Shaking his head at his own foolishness, Luc prepared for bed. He stripped to his briefs, washed the dust from his face, hands, and arms, and quickly brushed his teeth.

Weariness dragged at him, as well as arousal, and he wondered at the sanity of having her sleep in his bed.

He could have set Lobo to guard her. Had actually considered doing it until he watched how the wolf merely played with her rather than displaying the aggression he should have in turning her back earlier. She had charmed the animal Jack called a demon beast, and

Luc wondered if he could trust him to do anything other than pant at her heels now. He snorted at that thought as he flipped the light out and left the bathroom. Lobo wasn't the only one willing to pant at her heels right now.

She was in the bed, hugging the edge as though her life depended on it, the sheet and comforter pulled up to her shoulders as she lay on her side, her back to him. When he got into the bed he was careful to keep the upper sheet beneath his body and used the comforter alone for warmth. He flipped out the light and settled in the bed, resigned to a miserable night.

For long minutes silence filled the darkened room as Luc fought every instinct in his body to turn to her. He needed her as desperately as he needed air now. His cock was throbbing, making him insane with the desire to fuck her, to fill her with every hard inch of it.

Finally, he sighed wearily. He could feel her wariness stretching between them, the nerves that held her body rigid and kept her from easing into sleep.

"I won't hurt you, you know," he finally told her softly. "I might paddle that tempting little ass of yours if you don't obey me, but I won't damage you, Catarina."

"You have no right to hold me here, Luc," she finally answered him.

He wondered at the thread of regret he heard in her voice. It was almost hidden, carefully held back, but the lingering echo of it had his eyes narrowing thoughtfully.

"Is prison preferable, Cat?" he finally asked her.

He couldn't imagine her in prison, her passion and energy restrained, the traces of vulnerability he had seen in her forever destroyed. She was too soft, too gentle for such an atmosphere.

Silence greeted his question, and though she didn't make a sound, he could feel the sadness that seemed to wrap around her as snugly as the blanket on the bed. He turned over on his side, staring at the fall of fiery curls that lay over her pillow and down her back.

"No," she finally whispered, and the sound of her voice had him frowning in confusion. It was rife with pain, with throttled rage, as she breathed in shakily. "Prison is not preferable."

ELEVEN

"Well now, aren't you a pretty little thing . . ." At the sound of a woman's coarse, spiteful voice, Melina opened her eyes and stared around in horror.

Where had the guards gone? There were supposed to be guards outside the cells. Her door was supposed to be locked at all times. She wasn't supposed to be harassed again. Not after the last time. The warden had promised.

"Why are you here?" She tried to sit up in the bed, to somehow put herself into a defensive position, but there was no place to go. Above her was another cot; there was no way out, no way to protect herself.

Dear God, where was Joe? His secretary had said he would come for her, that he would get her out of there. Why wasn't he there yet?

Panic welled in her chest, made her stomach roil in waves of fear as a cold sweat began to cover her body. For a moment, just a moment, the image of Luc Jardin flashed in her head. Luc Jardin who had come to her parents' home, fury throbbing through every inch of his body as he stared into her eyes, thinking she was Maria, and swore she would pay. Swore she would spend as much time incarcerated as he could manage.

But it was her sister, her cold, deceptive sister, who had made certain Melina was locked up in her place. Not Luc. Handsome, strong Luc. Oh God. She was going to die, Melina thought.

She would die and never know the chance to make up for what her sister had done to him. And she would die by the hands of the female rapist now staring back at her.

"Thought you'd get away from us, didn't you, pretty thing?" Bertha Saks was a towering woman, built like a man with long black hair and faintly almond-shaped eyes. Her lips were twisted in a sneer as three other inmates crowded into the room.

"Let's see if we can't teach you better than to run tattling to the nice warden next time I decide I want a little kiss from those sweet lips," Bertha chuckled. "Don't worry, sweet thing, it only hurts if you fight it."

Melina shuddered in distaste. The thought of giving the woman what she wanted nearly caused her to throw up.

"Bertha, leave me alone." She tried to keep her voice firm, reasonable. "You don't want to do this. My family can help you . . ."

A short, vicious laugh sounded from Bertha's lips. "Your family?" she sneered. "Darlin', haven't you figured it out yet? You don't have no family. They left you here all alone to my tender mercies. And I can be tender, sweet thing. You just lie back and spread those pretty legs and I'll show you how tender I can be."

Melina pushed herself deeper into the corner of the bunk, pulling her legs up in front of her, shaking, knowing there was no way to escape the other woman now. There were no guards, no sounds of movement outside the cells; there was only the echo of her own heart in her ears.

"I won't do it." She swallowed tightly.

"Oh, you will, bitch," Bertha assured her. "Before this night is over, you'll do that and more."

"Oh God. No." Melina tried to escape the suddenly grasping hands. Hands that tore at her clothing, ripping the cheap tunic and cotton pants off her body as others held her down.

"Now just settle down, sweet thing." Bertha's laughter echoed around her. "Oh, what pretty little tits. I bet they taste just as pretty as they look."

Cruel hands stretched her arms above her head as Bertha moved, her hands outstretched, fingers curling into claws as they lowered to Melina's breasts.

Enraged, terrified beyond anything she had known in her life, Melina began to fight. Her hands were restrained, but her legs weren't. She kicked out forcefully, catching the larger woman in the midsection and sending her flying back as Melina twisted against the others who held her to the small cot.

Bertha's curses echoed around the room a second before pain shattered Melina's body. A heavy fist had landed into her tender, undefended waist. Her body bowed as an agonized scream tore from her throat and her stomach began to revolt against the pain.

"Let the bitch go," Bertha ordered furiously. "I'll take her to my hand or I'll kill her."

Before she could find the strength to stumble away, the other woman was stretched on the cot beside her, staring down at her with an evil smile, her dark eyes malicious and determined.

"No, babycakes, you'll let me take you and you'll like it, or I'll make sure that sweet little body hurts real bad before you take your last breath."

Fighting to breathe, Melina stared back at her, seeing her own death in her eyes. Weakly, she sneered into the other woman's face. "I'd rather die . . ."

The next driving blow went into her stomach. As Melina's eyes widened at the pain, her mouth opening to gasp for air, cruel hands grabbed at her breasts, hard fingers pinching at her tender nipples as the order was given again.

Wheezing for breath, tears of agony streaking her face, Melina stared into the eyes of hell and repeated her preference. "I'd rather die . . ."

"Then die," Bertha sneered. "I'll fuck your cold body and make you like it . . ."

Melina's scream brought Luc instantly awake, his hand reaching automatically for the gun he kept beside his bed before he realized the agonized cry was one of sleep-induced terror rather than reality.

Turning to her, he caught her automatically in his arms as her body jackknifed, her eyes flying open, glazed with terror and pain as she stared back at him. A second later, she began to fight. Tears poured from her eyes as she screamed his name, yet her nails clawed at his arms, her body shuddering, sweat pouring from her as she fought against him.

"Catarina!" He yelled her name, his hands gripping her arms as she struck out at him, shaking her furiously before jerking her against his chest, holding her tight. "Goddamn, wake up, baby, please, wake up."

Her sobs were horrible to hear. Deep, gut-wrenching cries that tore at his soul.

"Oh God. A dream," she gasped into his chest as the cat suddenly jumped to the bed, wailing, his feline howls grating on Luc's nerves. "Let me go." She pushed against him, barely able to speak for her cries, barely able to function for the hard shudders ripping through her body. "Let me go. Let me go . . ."

He released her slowly, staring at her in shock as she grabbed at the fat little cat and hauled him into her arms. Her face buried into the fur of his neck as the cat's cries eased and glowing feline eyes stared back at him with a somber weariness that had him shaking his head in shock.

The fucking cat was meowing now, a low, soothing sound, a shushing sound, as Melina trembled, her arms holding the animal close, his fur absorbing the terror-ized sobs that were finally growing weaker.

"Catarina." He wanted to touch her, needed to touch her. God help him, but the sound of her cries was break-ing what was left of his heart. "Sweetheart, you're going to make yourself sick crying like this."

He tried to keep his voice soft, as soothing as the cat's meows had become.

"Go away." She was almost gagging as she fought for breath. "Leave me alone, Luc. Just leave me alone."

Like hell. He moved closer, his arms going around her despite the stiffness that suddenly seized her body.

"Do you think squeezing the life out of that cat is going to make it better, Catarina?" he asked her harshly. "That's not what you need and we both know it."

She quivered against him.

"Let me help you, baby," he whispered into her hair. "Come on, let poor little Mason go." He smoothed his hand down her arm, his hand covering one of hers as he tugged at it gently. "Come on, baby. Let's chase the demons back the right way."

He tipped her tear-drenched face up, surprised that she wasn't fighting with him.

Bleak, overwhelming pain filled her gaze, tearing at his heart.

"It's okay, baby." He lowered his head, sipping at the salty tears that fell from her eyes. "Come on, let me hold you. That's all. Just hold you."

She eased her grip on the cat slowly, allowing the animal to leave or stay as he pleased. Luc pushed at the fat little body; reminding himself to buy the animal a stash of tuna for the comfort he so obviously had brought her in the past. Catarina had turned too quickly to the cat for it to be anything other than habit. Mason comforted her.

The cat was aloof and cold at any other time, superior in his place in the world, until her screams had brought them awake.

"Come on." Luc pulled her against him more fully, hating the tremors that ripped through her. "It's okay."

His lips touched hers. Gently. Soothingly.

"Luc," she finally whispered. She drew in a deep breath and stared back at him with slowly dawning awareness. "I'm sorry. I'm so sorry."

She tried to draw away then. Tried, but he wasn't about to allow it. Luc didn't give her time to protest. His lips covered hers gently, his tongue licking its way past them into the velvet heat of her mouth.

He felt her still. Felt the shudders ease into a reluctant tremor as he moved his lips over hers gently. Cajoling, nipping playfully, watching her carefully through the fringe of his lashes as she stared up at him in the darkness.

"Nightmares are nasty little creatures," he murmured against her lips as his hands smoothed up her back, one moving to bury in the mass of silken curls that fell from her head. "You have to chase them back, show them that when they come callin', you'll fight dirty."

He smiled at the flicker of confusion in her gaze. He nipped gently at her lips, teasing her now with the threat of his kiss, keeping her waiting, watching.

"They don't come creeping out if they know something good is going to follow their harassment. So we just have to show them you'll fight dirty, huh? Do you like this, baby?"

His hands cupped her head as he lowered her back to the bed, coming down beside her, keeping his movements slow and easy, not threatening, not intense, just a silken slide of desire and pleasure to soothe and tempt her.

"I'm not Maria," she whimpered suddenly, causing him to still. "Don't hold me like this and think I'm Maria, Luc."

He frowned down at her as he moved one hand to allow his fingers to caress her cheek.

"Catarina," he whispered then. "All graceful and smooth like a little cat. Curious and tempting as sin. Come here, little Cat, let me show you how to chase away the nightmares."

He would figure out the thread of fear and longing in her declaration later. Right now, pouty, tear-swollen lips awaited him. He wanted them reddened with his passion, moving beneath his with hungry abandon. And they were.

A soft moan of surrender escaped her as he slanted his lips over hers and once again used his tongue to tempt her higher. Within seconds her arms were wrapped around his shoulders tentatively as she relaxed into the fiery embrace.

Control, Luc reminded himself. He couldn't take her now. Not while she was weak, frightened. He wanted to soothe her, wanted her to know he would hold her through whatever fears besieged her. He wanted—God help him, he needed—her trust.

"There, now." He drew back long seconds later and pulled her closer into his embrace. "See? It's all gone, baby."

A small grin suddenly edged her lips; he knew she could sense the sexual tension wrapping around them.

"I'm supposed to go back to sleep now?" she finally asked him, her voice hoarse, but thankfully without fear.

"Well," he finally said with no small amount of amusement, "unless you want to take care of this hard-on killing me. Otherwise, I'd advise you to go to sleep fast or I might be tempted to convince you to help me out with that matter."

She was definitely considering it. For a second his heart stilled in anticipation before going into overdrive and beating a fierce drumbeat of lust inside his chest. Then her eyes snapped closed, though the corners of her lips were still edging into a grin.

"I'm asleep," she murmured drowsily.

Luc snorted and settled deeper in his pillow, holding her to his chest and trying to fight back his own fears. Her screams would haunt him forever, he thought. What the hell had happened to her?

"You convince yourself of that, baby." He kissed the top of her head and sighed wearily. "Now go to sleep before my lust overrules my head and convinces me you're well able to handle a good old-fashioned tumble."

Her laughter was more relaxed now as her body softened against him.

"Thanks, Luc," she finally whispered.

"For what? Baby, I didn't do anything but make myself hard as stone with no relief in sight. You should feel sorry for me. Real sorry." He exaggerated his slow drawl, relishing her low laughter in the dark.

"Thanks anyway." She snuggled closer, sighed deeply, and within minutes was drifting back to sleep.

She left Luc staring into the darkness, a frown on his face and suspicion building in his head. If he weren't so certain of Joe, he would have sworn this couldn't be Maria after all. But one thing was clear. Whatever the hell was going on, she wasn't the type of woman he had been led to believe, nor was she the drug-dazed whore his information had hinted at. She was almost . . . innocent.

He wanted to shake his head to dispel that image. The woman who sucked his dick two years before wasn't innocent, not in any way. But strangely enough, the woman cleaning his house, and now sleeping in his bed, was just that.

TWELVE

Melina did her best to ignore Luc the next day. It wasn't that the nightmare had left her frightened. Strangely enough, it had left her more comforted than she had ever been after such an episode. No, she was avoiding Luc because that single act of comfort had suddenly shifted the balance of her emotions. What had been simple lust, a desire for that tough-as-hell body, was turning into something she didn't understand, something deeper, something more intense. Something that was almost frightening.

He had held her through the night. His arms, so muscular, strong and warm. God, he was so warm.

She paused as she loaded the washer with dusty jeans and closed her eyes at the thought of it, remembering the feel of him holding her. A shudder raced down her spine. Like live bands of flexible steel, his arms had surrounded her, wrapping around her and holding her close to his chest.

And his chest . . . She sighed. She was a lost cause. One of those silly, insipid females who caved for lust. She stuffed his jeans into the washer as she grimaced at the very idea of it. It was bad enough she had been a doormat for her family her entire life; this was a new level of ridiculous. She despised women who caved so damned easily.

"But it's just for a little while," she muttered to herself as she stared into the depths of the washer as though it could actually hold answers.

He would realize his mistake soon. Luc wasn't a stupid man, just a determined man. And when he did realize what he had done, he would pack her up and take her back to her empty apartment and her empty life.

It wasn't that she couldn't find a lover, if she wanted one. It was, unfortunately, a matter of having only wanted one man. Luc. Silly wimp, she berated herself. Take one look at six-feet-plus of hot cowboy and what do you do? Good-bye, common sense; hello, hormones.

She slammed the washer lid closed.

"I am not this insane," she mumbled to herself. "God, I have to have more self-control than this."

"I don't know, Cat. If you start answering yourself, I'd worry if I were you."

Melina swung around, her eyes widening in mortification, her body flushing in embarrassment as she stared back at the object of her insanity.

Luc leaned casually against the frame of the laundry room door, his gray eyes glinting with amusement, a smile quirking those eat-'em-up lips. That full lower lip was as tempting as chocolate, and she knew his kiss was anything but sweet. It was hot and wild and mind destroying and she wanted to feast on it.

"I thought you were outside," she snapped, turning quickly away from him to check the clothes in the dryer before turning it on with a quick flip of the switch.

"I was." She could hear the shrug in his voice.

A second later she heard him move closer. She tensed, though her pussy began to weep in serious distress. That particular part of her body was not pleased with her reticence in jumping his bones. It really wasn't fair, she thought. Men like Luc Jardin should seriously be outlawed for the good of all females.

He was too close. She could smell him. She straightened the containers of fabric softener, laundry detergent, and various stain removers as she fought the racing of her heart, the tightening of her nipples. Why did he have to be so damned gentle last night?

If he had been a bastard, she could have resisted him, could have reminded herself how mean and rude and totally irrational he was.

"Cat." His chest brushed her back as she drew in a long, hard breath. "You feel it, too, baby. It won't just go away."

She shook her head, denying him, denying herself.

"Do you have any idea how difficult it was to just hold you last night?" he asked her. "Your hard little nipples burned holes in my chest, even through that shirt. I bet I have the singe marks to prove it."

She couldn't stop the smile that begged to curve her lips, but she kept her back to him, trembling, jerking in response when he kissed her bare shoulder. The sleeveless tank top was no defense against him. The gauzy slip-skirt she wore with it suddenly seemed too heavy, too restricting. She wanted to get naked with him. Wanted to roll across beds and floors and tables and scream in pleasure as he fucked her sillier than she must already be.

"I have half an hour before a buyer shows up," he murmured, his lips brushing over her bare skin once again. "Plenty of time, baby, to show you how good it could be."

Oh hell. Like he had to tell her anything. Even her womb was rippling with pleading little tremors. Her panties would have to be changed. And she didn't dare turn around because her nipples were about to pop through the cloth of her shirt, they were so damned hard. Yep, she was in trouble here.

"I have to clean . . . something." She rolled her eyes at the betraying squeak in her voice. Silly twit, she accused herself.

"Hmm." The soft hum against her neck had her shuddering in response.

"Luc, please . . ." She licked her suddenly dry lips as she fought to hold on to her control. "This isn't the wisest course of action here."

"Do you know how sexy that little skirt looks?" He ignored her statement as his hands gripped her, one smoothing down her thigh. "I've denied myself all day, Cat. Turn around, baby, and tell me why I shouldn't raise that flimsy excuse for a covering and push my cock as deep inside your sweet pussy as I can get it."

Why he shouldn't? There was a reason why he shouldn't?

Twit.

She flipped around, opened her mouth to say . . . something, she was certain, though she quickly forgot what as his lips covered hers. He lifted her against his chest, his arms coming around her, causing her to whimper at the warmth, the security of being enfolded so snugly against him.

Her lips opened to him, her tongue meeting his with a speed and hunger that she knew should have shocked her. Her hands went to his hair. All that long, thick black silk hiding beneath his Stetson. The Stetson was pushed quickly out of the way—who the hell cared where it landed?

Could fingertips have orgasms? Her fingers flexed; the flesh covering them rioted with pleasure at the feel of the cool, incredibly soft strands they suddenly gripped.

His lips ate at hers, but she dined in return. Hard, deep kisses that drew the breath from her body and left her dependent on him alone for survival. His head tilted, his lips slanting over hers as he growled into the kiss and lifted her further.

"Luc . . ." She tore her lips from his, crying out his name in dazed pleasure as she felt the cool metal of the washer beneath her bare butt. Thongs were no protection.

Her head fell back as his lips moved down her neck. His tongue was a demon. It licked as his lips created a delicate suction along the sensitive points of the column of flesh. One hand smoothed beneath her skirt, spreading her thighs, drawing ever closer to the hot center of need that tormented her.

"God, you're like a flame," he groaned as his other

hand, sneaky, diabolical, gripped the hem of her shirt and jerked it over her swollen breasts. "Sweet heaven," he muttered harshly. "Cat, baby . . ."

Melina opened her eyes, staring into his flushed, lustful face, and she swore she nearly came in that second. Had any man ever looked at her with such hunger and need? Never, she quickly answered herself. Not at any time.

"Bad idea . . ." She trembled as his hand cupped the full curve, his thumb rasping over the sensitized tip. She wasn't about to make him stop.

"Good idea," he denied. "Best damned idea I ever had."

His lips covered the engorged peak and Melina lost the last bit of common sense she might have originally possessed as the heat of his mouth surrounded her needy nipple.

Could she bear the pleasure? She arched to him, a thin wail escaping her lips as her fingers sank deeper into his hair, holding his head to her as he suckled at the tight flesh deeply. Her legs tightened on his hips as he jerked her closer, grinding the hard ridge of his cock against the swollen mound of her pussy.

Ah God, it was too good. His teeth nibbled at the hard peak his mouth surrounded, his tongue lashing at it with fiery demand before he sucked at it firmly once again. She couldn't stay still. Couldn't stop her hands from holding him closer, her hips from moving, rubbing her cunt against the hot wedge of flesh behind the tight fit of denim.

Her clit was swollen, throbbing, so agonizingly sensitive she knew it would take very little to send her exploding into orgasm.

"God. I'm going to end up fucking you blind on this damned washer," he muttered as he drew back, despite her attempts to hold him to her.

She was supposed to protest that? She shuddered as he pushed her skirt higher, his thumbs edging around the elastic at the side of her lacy panties. She was dying with anticipation, her pussy saturated with it as she stared back at him in dazed awareness of exactly where this was heading.

"I want to taste you," he whispered as his fingers delved beneath the lace slowly, pulling it to the side as his other hand rose to press her back until her shoulders touched the wall behind the washer. "Just like this, baby. Just a taste . . ."

His tongue swiped through the hot slit of her cunt, curled around her clit, then traveled back down to suddenly plunge into the entrance of her vagina as he lifted her legs over his shoulders.

"Oh God! Luc!" He would kill her. She didn't have the experience to combat this, didn't have the self-control to deny it.

"Mmm." The sound of male pleasure, the feel of his tongue fucking inside her was nearly too much. She was reaching, desperate . . . oh God, she was so close. Her hands were in his hair again, holding him to her as he ate her with such sensual abandon that she felt lost in the headlong flight to wherever he was determined to push her. Insanity, she imagined. Complete, hedonistic mindlessness.

His tongue was a weapon of sensual torture. It flickered in and out of her vagina, licking up the shallow cleft to torment her swollen clit, his lips covering it, suckling it, his tongue rasping over it. She was seconds from an orgasm. She could feel it building in her womb, her nerve endings gathering themselves for the explosion to come.

"Hey Luc, where the hell are you?" She froze at the sound of the unfamiliar voice echoing through the house. "Dammit, boy, thought you wanted to sell those horses."

Luc jerked back. As he looked up at her in surprise, Melina felt her womb contract in vicious need at the sight of his lips glistening with the proof of her arousal.

"Fuck." His voice was brutally rough with lust, his eyes nearly black as he straightened quickly.

He pulled her shirt down quickly, then her skirt. Grabbing a clean cloth from the rack over the washer, he quickly dried his lower face, his expression rueful as he stared back at her.

"Sam August," he muttered. "Hell. Get presentable, baby. That's one ol' boy you don't want to tempt."

"Well hell, no wonder you didn't answer." Amused and blatantly confident, the laughing male voice was like a splash of ice water to Melina's hormones.

The big cowboy suddenly framed in the doorway was breathtakingly handsome.

Laughing blue eyes watched them in amusement as sensual lips curved upward in response to Luc's curse. "Should I come back later?"

"You should get your ass back in the kitchen until I get there," Luc snapped, frowning at Melina's surprised look.

Sam August laughed quietly. "That's okay, Luc, Heather would have my balls if I even considered it. Do what you have to do and get out here. I brought her with me and she gets a mite impatient if she has to wait too long."

Melina looked between the two men in astonishment as Luc helped her from the washer, shielding her body with his as though trying to hide her from the other man.

"Maria Angeles, right?" Sam craned his neck to see around Luc. "Hell, son, she don't look tough enough to be a criminal . . ."

The kick Melina delivered to Luc's shin was anything but weak as she pushed past him and moved for the doorway. Fury engulfed her. Damn him to hell and back.

"What the hell . . ." Luc stared down at her with a glimmer of his own anger. "What was that for?"

Rather than answering him, she turned back to his friend.

"Maria Angeles, my ass," she informed Sam heatedly. "Try Melina or I'll take your head off right after I get finished taking his off. Now excuse me while I go try to find my sanity. I'm sure it's floating around here somewhere."

She stalked from the laundry room past a surprised Sam August, her head held high as she mentally kicked herself for ever believing, for even a second, that there was a chance in hell that Luc Jardin could have even suspected she wasn't Maria.

Hell, he had even told his friends about her. And only God knew what he had told them.

Twit, she accused herself again. And it wasn't like she didn't deserve it. She had fallen into Luc's hands like the silly ninny he thought she was. And this time, she couldn't even blame it all on him. She had done everything but beg for the humiliation.

Twit.

THIRTEEN

Melina had every intention of rushing straight upstairs as she cursed herself for her lapse in common sense. And she would have, if she hadn't nearly run over the slender redhead who had her head buried in the depths of the nearly empty refrigerator.

"Oh. Hello." The other woman straightened and flashed Melina a bright smile before glancing back at the cavernous interior of the appliance. "I'm convinced Jardin is a vampire. The man has to exist on some sort of nourishment, but you never see anything in his fridge." She gestured to the half-empty gallon of milk, a few jars of pickles, and a full package of lunch meat.

"That's because his cooking abilities are zero." Melina reached up and jerked open the upper freezer to display the myriad TV dinners and frozen entrées he kept stored there.

"Oh." Her expression seemed to drop as she sighed

in disappointment. "I knew I should have made Sam stop at the hamburger joint in town." She closed the door and stuck out her hand. "I'm Heather August. You must be Luc's kidnap victim. You know, it's against the laws of the Geneva Convention to starve prisoners. You should mention this to Luc."

Melina shook her hand automatically as she stared back into the amused green eyes regarding her. Heather August wasn't much taller than Melina. She had a healthy, wholesome appearance, clear creamy skin with only a scattering of freckles across her nose. Long red hair, pulled back from her face and bound into an intricate braid that fell past her shoulder blades, hinted at a temper that was nowhere in sight at the moment.

She was dressed in jeans and a loose, dark-blue silk blouse.

Her hands were propped on her hips as she regarded Melina curiously.

"Amazes me how everyone knows and yet I'm still stuck here. Kidnapping is against the law," Melina grunted as she stood aside for Luc and Sam to enter the room.

"So is drug running," Luc retorted as he passed her. "Beats prison. Remember?"

Heather laughed softly before Melina could snap out a reply to Luc. "If I thought you were in any danger, I would kick his ass myself. But I have to admit, you're not what I expected. You're definitely not the drug-runner type."

Melina felt like rolling her eyes. "Could be because I'm not a drug runner." She cast Luc a hateful glance as he followed her into the kitchen. "Exactly who all have you told anyway? If I find out the law enforcement in this godforsaken . . . wherever I am . . . knows about this, I'm not going to be happy."

Luc arched his brow mockingly as his dark-gray eyes filled with amusement.

"I haven't seen the sheriff in a few weeks, actually. I didn't get around to telling him about it."

"Why not just take out a damned newspaper ad?" Melina snapped temperamentally. "Then you wouldn't have to remember to tell anyone."

Luc chuckled, though Sam and Heather both seemed to watch her curiously.

"A newspaper ad isn't nearly as fast as some people's wagging tongues," Sam laughed. "Luckily for Luc, we're trustworthy." He turned to Luc then. "Let's go do some horse trading. Maybe your woman will have pity on mine and fix something edible. Those frozen dinners are gonna kill you, boy."

Melina crossed her arms over her chest and stared at the two men furiously. "I am not his woman. He didn't court me, he kidnapped me."

"The best marriages in the West started that way." Sam shrugged, then chuckled when his wife's fist landed on his thick shoulder. "That's my cue to go." He turned to Luc. "Let's go check out some horseflesh, Luc, before I get myself in trouble."

Melina watched Luc, her eyes narrowing as he struggled to hide his own grin and followed Sam from the house. She wanted to hate him, wanted to blame him, but the more time she spent with him the less she looked forward to him learning the truth of who she was. And that only made her madder. Though the anger was directed more at herself now than at Luc.

"He's a hard man, but he's a good man." Heather's voice suddenly interrupted her musings. "And I think he's a little bit fonder of you than perhaps he's letting on."

Melina sighed and looked over at the other woman. "You're hungry?" She ignored Heather's observation.

"Not really." She shrugged. "I just like to hassle him over it. He never eats properly."

Melina snorted. "The man can't boil water safely. Thankfully, he kidnapped someone who does know how to cook. How about some coffee and cinnamon rolls instead?"

"Sounds great. Can I do anything to help?" Heather asked as Melina moved to the coffeemaker and began brewing a fresh pot.

"The rolls were baked this morning and coffee won't take but a few minutes."

Melina shrugged. "Go ahead and sit down. I'll have it ready soon."

Silence filled the small room as Melina finished preparing the coffee, removed the cups from the cabinet, and set out the fresh rolls. It took only minutes for the coffee to brew; during that time Melina laid out small saucers, sugar, and cream and endured Heather's narrow-eyed perusal.

She wondered what Luc had told the couple about her. Of course, they would have known about Maria's part in the shooting two years before. Luc seemed rather close to the other man, so she had no doubt that Sam August knew about it. There had also been a glimmer of resentment in the other man's eyes when he watched her. He was polite, a bit mocking maybe, but she could tell he was concerned about Luc.

* * *

Heather seemed more direct, though she had yet to say much. She merely watched as Melina prepared the coffee, poured it into oversized cups, and then returned to the table.

"You're the sister," Heather finally said softly. "You're not Maria."

Surprised, Melina stared over at the other woman.

"Luc swears there isn't a sister," she said sarcastically. "So you must be wrong."

Heather laughed gently. "I would say Luc spent very little time researching his subject. The minute Sam told me what Luc had done, I got on the computer. I have to admit, I'm glad he didn't kidnap Maria. She would have made certain he went to prison for it."

"And you think I won't?" Melina asked coolly as she stirred sugar into her coffee.

Heather tilted her head to the side and regarded her for long moments.

"I don't think you will. I think you're more likely to fuck him silly than you are to see him behind bars."

Melina could feel the heat filling her face and knew she was flushing in both embarrassment and acknowledgement. The other woman was far too perceptive.

"I'm more likely to kill him myself." She sighed. "Do you intend to help me convince him he has the wrong woman?"

Heather leaned back in her chair and watched her silently. Melina found that those green eyes could be uncomfortably focused as she stared back at her.

"Why not just let him hang himself?" Heather finally shrugged. "I've rarely seen Luc smile as he did today.

He's more relaxed—almost happy. And I don't sense a burning desire in you to be free."

She was much too close to the truth.

"I should be desperate to escape." Melina shook her head at that knowledge. "I think I'm a failure as a kidnap victim."

The episode on that washer earlier proved that. She would have begged him to take her then and there if Sam hadn't shown up. And she wouldn't have regretted it, she thought. She would have gloried in it.

"I think maybe you're just what he needs right now." Heather leaned forward again and picked up her coffee cup. "Teach him how to cook while you're here. Maybe he won't kill himself with frozen dinners after you leave . . . that is, if he lets you leave."

Melina wondered at the smile that played about the other woman's lips as she lifted her coffee cup and sipped at the hot brew. Heather seemed much too convinced that leaving wouldn't be an option.

"He has to let me go soon." Melina glanced out the window to her side, watching as Luc led one of the huge horses from the barn for Sam to examine. "He won't keep me forever."

No matter how much she wished he would. For a moment, shock vibrated through her system. This wasn't what she wanted, was it? It wasn't a question she could answer right then.

"Stranger things have happened." Heather shrugged. "But what will be, will be.

"Now tell me about your sister and how the hell you ended up being kidnapped in her place. I'm dying of curiosity."

FOURTEEN

Heather and Sam hadn't stayed long, but by the time the two men had concluded their visit, Melina knew she had made a friend. Not that Luc seemed comfortable with the idea, nor Sam. But both men seemed smart enough not to comment on it.

Besides, as the evening wore on, Melina could tell that Luc had something much more serious on his mind.

He kept watching her silently. His dark-gray eyes were reflective, his expression too serious to suit her. She had a feeling she knew what was coming, but when the question was voiced, she found that she still didn't have the answers that would have placated him.

"What happened to frighten you last night?" Luc's softly voiced question finally came after dinner.

Melina stood in front of the sink finishing the last of the dinner dishes and staring through the window at the steadily darkening backyard. She lowered her head, focusing on the thick mass of suds that covered her hands, and wondered what to tell him.

The truth can often hurt, and Melina had no desire to hurt Luc. The fact that he had been the catalyst that ended with her in that jail cell that week had been forgiven long ago. Her own foolishness, she realized, was the reason she had landed there. She had trusted her parents, had trusted Maria, when she knew better.

She flinched as she heard the chair he was sitting in scuff across the floor. Her gaze rose to the window, her heart speeding up in her chest as he approached her. His expression was somber, his black hair falling over her brow, his lips compressed into a controlled line as his eyes met hers in the reflection.

"Wouldn't any woman be frightened at the thought of being tied naked in a stranger's bed?" she finally snapped in defense.

He was getting too close. She could feel the heat of his body along her back now, the intensity that was so much a part of him wrapping around her with gossamer threads of emotion.

He stared at her in the glass until she finally dropped her eyes, covering her retreat by letting out the water and rinsing her shaking hands with a quick motion.

"Catarina?" He touched her.

Melina stilled, wanting nothing more than to close her eyes and escape the merciless perception in his gaze. She felt trapped by his look, drawn into it, captivated by the dark clouds of concern that shifted within as his hand settled on her hip.

She swallowed tightly.

"I have to finish the kitchen . . ."

She was not giving in to him. Not again. She couldn't let herself forget who he thought she was. She couldn't let herself forget who she was. Despite her desire for him, despite the hunger that sped through every cell in her body, she couldn't forget what they had both suffered at her sister's hands.

"Fuck the kitchen, Catarina." A frown snapped between his brows as he turned her to face him, both hands gripping her hips now, holding her so close that a breath of air would have had trouble passing between his body and hers. "I want answers. Do you think I didn't see your terror? That I wouldn't suspect what's behind it? What happened?"

Melina breathed out with a short angry burst of air.

"I don't owe you answers, Luc. You've kidnapped me. Refused to listen to reason once you were informed of the mistake you made. And you push and prod at me every chance you get to force admissions that are no more than lies to appease you. You have no right to be concerned about anything."

Melina pushed away from him, stalking across the kitchen to replace his chair beneath the table and straighten the small, cloth place mats. The old oak table gleamed with its fresh coat of wax, a testament to her hard work that day.

"Catarina, freedom comes with a price." His voice was gentle, but the meaning was clear. "You can't change if you don't learn from your mistakes."

Amazement filled her. How gentle and concerned he sounded. It was almost enough to make her sick.

"God, can you get any more pompous." She rounded on him furiously. "Listen to yourself, Luc. I've told you at every opportunity what a fool you're making of yourself here, and still you aren't listening. You know what?" She propped her hands on her hips, tired of the arguments, sick of dealing with his determination to believe she was Maria. "You just believe what you want to. Everyone else has. You want to believe I'm Maria? Knock yourself out, asshole, but don't expect me to cooperate. I grew sick of wearing my sister's shoes quite a while ago. I won't let you force me back into them."

The situation would have been laughable if it weren't for the fact that she was aware she was losing her heart to the knucklehead.

"This isn't about your refusal to admit who you are," he retorted, his voice harsh, dark. "I don't give a damn who you want to pretend to be. Dammit, Catarina, have you considered the fact that the drugs could just be an escape from whatever happened? If you admit you're frightened, wouldn't it be easier to accept you have a problem? Now, I want to know why the hell you looked at me like I was within an inch of raping you last night, when you should have known damned good and well that's not a danger you face. If I don't know the problem, then I can't help you fix it."

Some men were just too damned stubborn for their own good.

"Oh, you know the problem," she snapped. "You just won't admit it. Dammit, Luc, when are you going to admit that maybe, just maybe, I'm not Maria?"

"Catarina, do you think I didn't make certain before taking you?" he growled in frustration.

"Evidently you didn't." She shrugged, lifting her brow mockingly. "Listen to you, you don't even call me

Maria. You call me Catarina. Why, Luc? If you're so insistent you know you're right, why not call me Maria?"

He grimaced, male irritation filling his gaze as he stared back at her with a determined glint in his eyes.

"You're deliberately trying to change the subject," he said darkly. "You're good at that, Cat, I have to commend you. But I won't let it continue. Why were you so frightened of me last night? You knew I wouldn't hurt you."

"Oh, did I?" She arched her brow with mocking inquiry. "And how am I supposed to know this, Luc? You threaten things when you don't get your way. You threatened Mason's safety before I admitted to who you thought I was. You made me lie to you." It still infuriated her. "But I let it go." She threw her arms wide to indicate her former surrender. "I wasn't about to strip naked for you so you could tie me down and do whatever the hell you wanted with me."

He stared at her. He didn't argue with her, didn't answer her accusations. He merely tucked his thumbs in the waistband of his jeans and watched her for long, nerve-racking minutes. She could see a storm brewing in his eyes. Melina stilled. He looked dominant, forceful; he looked like a man unwilling to accept the answer she had given him.

She wasn't afraid of him. She was wary of the threat he represented to her heart, but last night, as darkness closed around them, she had admitted, to herself at least, that Luc would never harm her. He might infuriate her. He might drive her insane with his complete confidence in what he thought he was doing, especially when he was wrong.

But he would never force himself on her.

"Who raped you?" He finally asked the question she had been dreading.

God, why did this man, of all men, have to be the one her heart had set itself on? If it had just been lust, maybe it would have been easier to handle. But the moment she met him, despite his fury, she had been drawn to him. In the months after that, all she learned about him had only increased her fascination with him. Now, spending the days with him, seeing his quiet humor, and dealing with his stubbornness was turning her into a fool. A fool because she could feel her emotions peaking, edging toward him, yearning for him.

"Because I'm not ready to spread my thighs and invite you in, then I've been raped?" She crossed her arms over her chest, praying now for an intervention. Any kind of intervention would be nice.

He advanced on her. There was no way to retreat. The table behind her came against her rear as Luc pressed against her front. This time when his hands gripped her hips, she knew there would be no escape from him.

"Catarina." His head lowered, his gaze dark, deliberate, as his lips stopped within a breath of hers. "Tell me why I care," he whispered, staring at her somberly, his voice filled with his own confusion, his own need for answers. "Tell me why the thought of your terror last night has driven me insane to find an explanation for it. And tell me why in the hell all I can think about is how to ease those fears long enough to get you beneath me and show you I would never hurt you."

Lust slammed into her womb. Melina's eyes widened at the hard, convulsive shudder of hunger that rippled through it. She swallowed tightly, fighting for breath.

Fear was the last thing on her mind. All she could think about now was the sheer, unbridled hunger glittering in his eyes and the liquid heat pooling in her vagina.

And he knew it. He knew what he did to her. Knew how damned hot he could make her.

"You're imagining things." She cleared her throat nervously, trying to push away from him, desperate to escape the building desire.

"I watched you wax this damned table," he whispered, his lips glancing hers, freezing her in place. "Bent over, that tight little ass bouncing around, and all I could think about was stretching you across it . . ."

He lifted her. Melina gasped, gripping his hands as he set her on the table and quickly moved between her thighs.

"Luc." She meant for the word to come out as a protest, not the plea it seemed to be.

"I wanted to make a meal out of you on this damned table," he growled, baring his teeth in a tight grimace. "And all I could think of was the fear in your eyes last night and how much I hated knowing you were frightened of me. That, and cursing myself for letting my own lust interfere in what should be a punishment rather than a vacation for you." His voice deepened in self-disgust and bemusement.

"Yeah, us naughty girls definitely shouldn't have any fun." She meant it to come out with a wealth of sarcasm, not the sultry tone it was wrapped in.

She couldn't forget the episode in the laundry room.

Couldn't get it out of her mind and couldn't make her body accept that this man was the wrong man for her heart. Her hormones just didn't give a damn. This was the one they wanted.

His eyelids lowered, giving him a drowsy, sensually dangerous appearance as his hands tightened on her hips.

"Don't tempt me," he whispered.

Tempt him? What the hell did he think he was doing to her? He was killing her.

There was no fear of him, which left only the need. She wondered if she would be safer being frightened of him. Because she was just confident enough of her safety, and his desire for her, that her own need to tempt him in return surged ahead of any caution she may have displayed.

"Hm. Admit who I am, Luc, and I might help you with that," she murmured, almost shocked at the impish impulse to torment him now. "Come on, big boy, tell me what I want to hear."

His eyes flared, his cheeks flushing as his breathing began to match hers.

"You're playing a very dangerous game, sweetheart." The rough warning only made her braver.

For a moment, she wondered at her own daring. Never would she have attempted to spar with another man in this manner, especially not in the past two years. But this was Luc. She had dreamed about him for years, lusted for him, ached for him.

She licked her lips slowly, staring back at him sensually.

"Who am I, Luc?" she asked him, her thighs softening against his hips as she fought a whimper of longing. His jean-covered cock settled tighter against her pussy, a hard, thick wedge of heat that made her clit swell in need and her vagina ache in emptiness.

His eyes narrowed. The cloudy gray was nearly black now, his expression slack and filled with hunger as he stared at her moist lips.

"A minx," he growled, though a smile edged his lips. "One who's going to end up spanked if she isn't careful."

"Hmm. Hurt me so good." She licked her lips, pushing her luck and knowing it.

But damned if he didn't look hot as hell. He was staring at her as though he could consume her at any minute. Lust and perhaps even a shade of confusion filled his expression.

"You like pushing your luck, don't you?" he asked her softly as he moved away from her.

Nothing could dispel the heat that wrapped around her, though, as he watched her.

She could feel it licking over her flesh, stoking the fires in her pussy and leaving her almost weak with arousal. She wanted to touch him more than he could ever know. But she would be damned if she would let him kidnap her and break her heart.

"Actually," she stated a bit regretfully, "pushing my luck has been my choice, Luc. At least, until now."

Flashing him a saucy smile she moved quickly away from him, aware she was only delaying the inevitable. She knew she couldn't hold out much longer against the sensual promise he represented. She only hoped that when the time came, he didn't whisper Maria's name. That would be one insult she didn't think she could bear.

Luc couldn't push aside his certainty that Catarina's fear had somehow been rooted in sexual violence. Though her good humor restored itself quickly, he could glimpse the shadows in her eyes, the lie spilling from her lips. He knew she was evading him.

Going to bed with her was hell, though. Dressed in another of his shirts that night, she pulled the blankets to her chin and went quickly to sleep. Luc was left to stare into the darkness, aroused and confused by the woman he was sharing his bed with. He was convinced by now that she wasn't taking drugs. Withdrawal was a son of a bitch and impossible to hide. Catarina wasn't in withdrawal. And she sure as hell wasn't taking anything.

He didn't like being confused. And he sure as hell didn't understand the strange emotions that were beginning to fill him. He wanted to believe she wasn't Maria. He found himself daily attempting to come up with reasons why Joe might have lied to him. He was attempting to fool himself, and it wasn't sitting well with him.

Confirming his suspicions would have to wait until he could talk to the other man, though. Each time Luc had called him in the past few days he had been unavailable, which only roused Luc's suspicions that much more.

He sighed tiredly, thumped his pillow, and closed his eyes. Sleep would have to come soon; if not, he would drive himself insane trying to make sense of it all. But one thing was for certain: This was not the Maria he had expected. If she was Maria.

FIFTEEN

Melina woke in the least likely position. She had grown used to waking up draped across Luc's chest, but never like this.

One of her legs had crossed over his, her knee bent, resting uncomfortably close to the center of his thighs. His leg was pressed firmly to the mound of her pussy and as she woke, she realized in mortification that she had been slowly rubbing herself against him.

How did she get herself out of this one? Better yet, how had she managed to get herself into it?

She tried to keep her breathing slow and steady, to ignore the heat building in the depths of her cunt. She had never felt so moist, so on fire there. Her clit was sensitized, swollen, and when Luc shifted against her she caught her breath at the sudden pleasure that whipped through it.

His hand tightened in her hair, the fingers of the other smoothing against the bare flesh of her side where it had burrowed beneath her shirt. The pads of his fingers were calloused and warm; the feel of them pressing lightly against her skin had her fighting to control the shiver that raced up her spine.

She could feel excitement sizzling over her flesh, pleasure and need mixing in her bloodstream until she could barely breathe for it. One of her hands lay flat against his hard abdomen only inches from where the bulbous head of his cock had risen past the soft elastic of his briefs. A small, pearly drop of pre-cum glistened on the tip of it as it throbbed erotically.

Melina knew the minute he became aware of their positions. His stomach tensed; his heart began to race furiously beneath her ear. She could feel the sexual tension heating his big body now and the careful control he used as his hand flattened against her hip.

"Better move," he whispered with drowsy amusement. "I'm about two seconds from doing something stupid."

Melina lay still. How long had she fantasized about him like this? His arms wrapped around her, his hunger heating the air. It hadn't made sense, even before she met him, and it made less sense now. But she couldn't deny the incredible pleasure or the desire that sang through her blood at his touch.

His fingers moved, playing lightly with the band of her lacy, French-cut panties as she stared at the dark head of his cock in fascination. The feel of it against her lips that first day had been a temptation that only her fury had allowed her to deny. He had no idea how much she wanted to open her lips and take him inside her mouth. Taste the thick moisture that had gleamed on the tip, and lick the rounded head slowly.

She moistened her lips in hunger.

"Catarina," he warned her tightly as her fingers flexed against his hard abdomen. "This is a dangerous game, baby."

His voice was tense, his big body almost vibrating beneath her.

Melina turned her head a fraction, her lips pressing beneath his breastbone as her tongue peeked out to taste.

"Fuck." He tightened as though he had taken a lash rather than a small warm lick.

Fascinated at his response, she let her fingers caress the flesh of his lower stomach as her lips and tongue caressed him again. All the while she kept her gaze on the thick erection below.

The mushroomed head had darkened, rising toward her as his hips jerked, and she imagined it was pleading for attention. The little slitted eye spilled another lush drop of creamy moisture, tempting her to taste.

There was no fear as she felt the leashed arousal in his body. He was careful, controlled. And she was hungry for him. There was none of the previous anger or male dominance; there was only hot, thick need filling the air now. The same need she had dreamed of—ached for—for the past two years.

"Cat," Luc groaned, the sound vibrating against her body as his breathing accelerated. "You have two choices, baby. You can move or accept the consequences."

The consequences being his touch, his passion.

Her hand slid lower, her finger reaching out hesitantly to slide over the moist, turgid head of his cock.

A throttled groan slipped past his throat, a sound of excruciating sensation. His hips lifted, pressing his erection closer as her tongue flickered out to once again taste the flesh below his breastbone. She watched as her finger smoothed over the hot male erection, feeling the heat and hardness that awaited her there.

Her clit throbbed in demand, a piercing sensation of unbearable need streaking into her womb. Melina pressed against the hard leg, her eyes nearly closing at the rasp of pleasure.

"Catarina," he growled. "Sugar, if you don't want to be fucked, you'll stop now."

She smiled slowly. She did want to be fucked, though. Maria had only taken his cock into her mouth; she knew that from her sister's snide comments. But Melina wanted so much more. She wanted all of him, every inch of his hard body covering her, taking her, making her scream with pleasures she had only heard about.

Shudders of sensation worked over her body as she let her finger slide idly around the crest of his erection. It throbbed, darkening further as she pressed her pussy tighter against his knee.

"Cat, what do you want, baby?" His voice deepened as one hand tangled in her hair, the gentle pressure against her head encouraging her to go lower, to draw closer.

"Luc," she whispered beseechingly.

"Whatever you want, baby," he whispered as the bulging head came closer, his hand urging her down the hard muscles of his stomach as she whimpered in a hungry desperate need she hadn't known she was capable of.

She wanted to taste him. She wanted to know how hard and hot his cock would be within her mouth, feel the hard pulse of life beneath the tight flesh and know it was for her.

Melina was but a breath away, fighting to control the hard tremors of response quaking through her flesh as her tongue reached out and licked slowly over the small eye that pierced the head of his cock.

Oh yes. Hot. Hard. He was all male, huge and ready for her.

"Catarina . . ." The hand at her head grew heavier. "Take it, baby. Put that hot little mouth over my cock before I die for it."

She could have denied herself. But Luc? She had dreamed of him for too long, lusted after him through too many of her own darkest fantasies. There was nothing he could do to her that she would object to. Nothing that he would want that she could deny him. Not here. Not now.

Her mouth opened, drawing the bulging head of his erection between her lips as her tongue began to stroke and caress, tasting the small drops of semen that escaped it.

"Oh hell . . ." His hips lifted as a sound of sharp surprise left his lips. "There you go, baby. Ah yes, Catarina, suck my cock, baby. Take everything you want."

She was going to kill him. What the hell had happened? This was not the experienced little cocksucker who had swallowed his dick like nobody's business two years before. This was sensual, sexual—a hungry little vixen consuming his erection.

And she was destroying him. No experience here, but none was required. Only hot, wet suckling strokes that drove him to the very edge of his control.

Her cool, silken hand cupped his testicles, tested their weight gently a second before her mouth slid lower, the flared head of his cock nearly touching her throat as she began to suck him with hungry abandon. Small, lusty mewls escaped her and vibrated on his erection, nearly sending him over the edge.

"Catarina. Baby." He clenched his teeth as he fought to hold on to his control.

His hands tangled in her soft hair, holding her to him as he pushed his cock deeper into her mouth, glorying in the sounds of the pleasure she was taking from an act that drove him steadily closer to ecstasy.

She moved, though her mouth never left the shaft throbbing heatedly beneath her touch. She came to her knees, moving between his thighs as he lifted the curtain of hair to see his cock disappearing between her tightly stretched lips. Her eyes glittered up at him with drowsy sexuality, her cheeks flushing, and any control he may have had was shot in that second.

"I'm going to come," he growled as she worked his flesh with moist hunger. "Catarina." He could feel the fire arcing up his spine. "Baby. I'm going to lose it."

His cock flexed and her eyes darkened further. His hands tightened in her hair as his balls drew up against the base of his shaft and he felt his semen surging from the very depths of his soul.

"Fuck." His lips drew back, his eyes threatening to close, but he didn't want to miss so much as a moment of this.

He felt his seed erupt from the tip in hard, jetting pulses of release. Her eyes widened; her lips paused for a bare second before she shuddered, moaning wildly, swallowed, and began to draw on him again as each pulse thereafter was greedily consumed.

"Luc." She licked her lips as she drew back from him long seconds later.

She was wild; her eyes glittered feverishly, the flush of arousal on her face now spread to her hard-tipped breasts, making him insane to fuck her. If he didn't get his cock inside her, he would go mad from the desire.

SIXTEEN

Had anything ever been so wild? So impossible to deny? Melina gasped as Luc bore her back upon the mattress. Each inch of his broad, callused palms smoothed over her flesh before he stretched her arms above her head and came over her slowly.

"I keep telling myself to wait." His voice rasped over her nerve endings, sending a shudder of pleasure down her spine as her womb convulsed in need.

His body was taut, glistening with perspiration as he braced himself above her, his thighs on either side of hers, his hands moving slowly back down her upraised arms.

Melina couldn't control her breathing or the response surging through her. She was trembling with the need to have him fill her tormented cunt. Her clit was a pulsing knot of painful desire now, the slick heat coating the curves of her mons, intensifying its sensitivity.

"Why wait?" She was panting, staring up at him,

shuddering as his hands slowly framed her swollen breasts.

His expression was drowsy, his black hair falling over his forehead as his gray eyes darkened to almost black.

"Because I want to make you as hot and as crazy as I am right now," he whispered, his voice so sexy, so sensually dark and deep that she whimpered at the sound.

She could almost climax from the sound of his rough voice alone. It was powerful, hinting at forbidden secrets and ecstatic pleasures only guessed at.

"You mean I'm not yet?" she moaned weakly, her fingers clenching in the sheet above her head as he continued to stare intently at her firm, peaked breasts. "Luc, if I get any hotter, we're both going to go up in flames."

He raised his eyes. Pure carnal hunger reflected in his gaze.

"Yeah." He bared his teeth in a tight grimace. "We just might at that."

Her breath caught in her chest, pushing her breasts closer to him as his thumbs raked over the sensitive tips. Pleasure shuddered through her. It was exquisite, the sharp, racing spears of sensation that pierced her nipples and sped to her womb. She caught her lower lip between her teeth, fighting to hold back the cries that threatened to erupt from her throat.

She could feel the pleasure from that simple touch swirling through her body, building the growing band of tension in her womb tighter. He watched her as his thumbs rasped the tender peaks again. His eyes gleamed in satisfaction as she flinched from the extreme sensations.

"So responsive," he muttered as his head began to

lower, his tongue moistening his lips a second before it curled around one taut peak.

"Luc," she almost screamed as her hands loosened the sheets and flew up to grip his damp shoulders.

Melina arched involuntarily; sizzling excitement bowed her body as he drew the tip into his mouth, applying a firm, strong suction that had her writhing beneath it. It was too intense, too much pleasure. Her eyes closed, her hips straining toward the length of his cock lying against her lower thigh.

A second later, he freed her from the exquisite torture, his gaze rising as her eyes opened drowsily.

"God, you're beautiful," he whispered as his lips moved to hers. "So beautiful you take my breath away. But you know that, don't you, Catarina?"

Guttural and intense, the words didn't matter as much as his lips smoothed sensually over hers, creating a rasping pleasure that had her begging for more.

"Please, Luc," she whispered as he kissed the corner of her lips while his hands cupped her breasts, his fingers plumping and stroking her nipples, sending arcs of diabolical pleasure straight to her aching cunt.

He licked her lips as she opened for him, her breathing hard and erratic, need slicing along her nerve endings as she fought against his strength. He held her still, arched over her, his bigger body controlling her smaller one easily.

"Let me pleasure you, Catarina." His lips caressed hers as he spoke. "Let me show you how much I love hearing your cries and your pleas. Let me show you how good it can be, baby."

He was going to kill her. The kiss, when it finally

came, was greedy, hot, and hungry as his lips and tongue tore through any resistance she may have thought she had. His hands roamed over her body, one smoothing along her tummy as he shifted her legs and spread them slowly.

Melina gasped for breath as her hips rose. His eyes, shielded by thick lashes, watched her with heated lust as his fingers slid between her thighs. Melina's eyes widened as his fingers circled her swollen clit. The touch sent her system into a riot of sensations as she fought to breathe through the pleasure exploding along her senses.

"Will you taste as good there as you do everywhere else, Catarina?"

A sharp detonation of pleasure exploded in her womb at his question. She jerked, whimpering against the intensity of it. Her hands clenched on his shoulders as he spread her thighs further, moving lower along her body.

"Let's see if you are as good here, baby."

His tongue swiped through the bare, plump curves then curled around her clit an instant before he drew the little nubbin into his mouth. He hummed against it, a sound of lust and satisfaction as her hips surged closer to his hot mouth.

Tightening his hands on her hips, Luc held her in place as he began his campaign to drive her crazy with the slow, hungry licks and carnal sips he took from her weeping pussy.

"So good . . ." he muttered as he traveled lower, his tongue rimming the entrance to her vagina. "So sweet and hot . . ." He invaded her slowly as Melina's tumultuous wail echoed around them.

She scrambled to hold on to the last shred of control.

Fought to hold back, to enjoy without losing herself in his touch, but from the first caress she had been a goner and she knew it. When he lifted her thighs, opening her further, and plunged his tongue into the snug cavern of her cunt she gave up the last measure of sanity.

She had never been loved like this. Had never been taken with such carnal intent as Luc was taking her now. His tongue fucked deep inside her burning pussy, pumping into her with fierce strokes as he threw her higher, deeper into the maelstrom awaiting her. Whipping arcs of heat flickered through her, heating her flesh, sensitizing each nerve ending as she strained closer to the inferno building in her womb.

"Luc. Oh God. I can't stand it . . ." Melina thrashed beneath him, her voice rising in reaction to the extreme pleasure rushing through her. "Luc . . ."

She was terrified, exhilarated, yearning, and yet desperate to draw back. The conflicting impulses were shattering her sense of reality.

"No." She nearly screamed the word as he jerked back from her, moving quickly between her thighs as he bent across her and opened the small drawer in the table beside the bed.

"Condom," he gasped.

At the same time, the thick head of his cock nudged into the snug entrance of her pussy. They froze, breaths rasping, lust sizzling around them.

"Fuck," he seemed to wheeze as his hips jerked, only to bury him marginally deeper.

Melina felt the convulsive clenching of her vagina, the hungry milking motion of her muscles as Luc's flesh stretched them tight. Bare, hot flesh buried inside her.

A danger. She panted, fighting not to tempt the control he was trying to impose over his big body. But it was so good.

"Luc . . ." She jerked as she felt the head throb within her, driving him deeper.

"Condom," he rasped again, jerking one free of the drawer a second before he drove deep inside her gripping flesh.

Reality no longer existed in any way, shape, or form. There was only this. Luc buried within her, hot and steel-hard, fucking her with deep driving strokes as she screamed out beneath him. Melina's legs wrapped around his pounding hips, her hands gripping his shoulders as he held her close, lunging forcefully into her wet sheath.

Each stroke sank to the very depths of her cunt, caressing sensitive tissue, rasping delicate nerves until with a final, weak cry Melina fought the final battle with the orgasm overtaking her and lost. She exploded beneath him, the white-hot streaks of ecstasy surging through her body as her pussy tightened spasmodically around his plunging cock.

A second later she felt Luc's release; hot, hard jets of semen spilled into her as he groaned her name roughly, his voice tortured, dark, and hungry. The heated warmth shattered her again, sending her plunging headlong into a smaller but no less destructive orgasm that left her weak and terribly frightened that she had just given this man more than her body. She had given him her heart.

She wasn't Maria Catarina Angeles. Luc held her close in his arms, feeling her soft breathing against his chest, her body relaxed in exhaustion, and admitted the truth she had been trying desperately to tell him. She wasn't Maria. She was Melina.

Which meant Joe had lied to him. But why?

He smoothed back the fall of red-gold curls and stared down at her sleeping face somberly. What the hell had he done? He had somehow managed to fall in love with a woman and not even know who she was. It was terrifying. It was—Hell, he was in deep.

He drew in a deep breath and ignored the erection pleading for another dose of rapture. Nothing had ever come close to the pleasure he had experienced as he plunged his cock inside her snug pussy unprotected. He had been a goner the minute he had unintentionally buried the head of his erection inside her. He had tried, though, he assured himself. Hell, he had been clutching the condom in his hand even as he spurted his seed deep inside the hot depths of her vagina.

What now?

God, she was pretty. Now he understood the innocence in her eyes, the unlined, unblemished skin of her face. Her laughter, unaffected and so often freely given. Her joy in that black mouse catcher she gave so much affection to.

He doubted she had ever taken a drug in her life. There were no tracks on her arms, no furtive behavior, no withdrawal. There was none of it, because she wasn't Maria.

What the fuck was Joe trying to pull on him? Luc frowned heavily as he gently disengaged himself from his sleeping lover and pulled on a pair of loose pajama bottoms before leaving the bedroom quietly. Joe had called several times the first two days to check up on Maria. Luc snorted. The other man knew what the hell he had done; now Luc wanted to know why. And the reason had better be a damned good one.

He slipped downstairs and into his study, his anger building with every step. There had been times that he had been unjust in his treatment of her. He hadn't gone easy on her. The house was spotless, dust was now afraid to enter, and the place smelled like her. The tempting subtle scent of woman seemed steeped into every nook and cranny of the house.

Sighing wearily, he picked up the phone and quickly dialed Joe's number. Several rings later, the other man answered.

"You have two minutes to tell me why you fucking lied to me. If the explanation isn't satisfactory, then your voice will rival Melina's for soft feminine sweetness."

There was a long silence on the line. Shock and sudden comprehension filled the line.

"Fuck," Joe finally said. "No matter what you do to me later, Luc, don't let her out of your sight right now. She's in more danger than you know . . ."

SEVENTEEN

Every time she said no, they hit her again . . .

She was beaten so badly we didn't think she would make it . . .

The doctors doubt she'll ever conceive due to the internal injuries . . .

She was tricked, Luc. Maria didn't spend that week in jail that you demanded, Melina did . . .

Luc pushed shaking fingers through his hair as the words replayed through his mind. His fault. It had been his fault that an innocent woman had nearly died. The same woman who had called him, apologizing for what had been done to him, her voice whispering in regret and sadness.

The woman he had confronted in her parents' living room hadn't been Maria. He remembered his fury when he had faced her, seeing the confusion and fear in her eyes when her parents introduced her as Maria. The memory of the awareness that had sizzled between them that day had haunted him over the years. For some reason, his cock had strained in urgent demand when her soft lips had trembled into a self-conscious smile that day.

He had allowed his rage free. His voice hard, harsh, his words damning as he watched her face drain of color.

You'll pay for it, Ms. Angeles, he had warned her furiously. *By God, I'll make sure you spend time in jail if it's the last thing I do in my life.*

At the time, he had ignored the bleak pain that filled her expression. Her gaze had dropped, her soft lips pressing together a second after a betraying quiver had shaken them. He had wanted to haul her into his arms and apologize, which only made him madder at the time.

Now he knew why. Some instinct, some primitive part of his mind, had recognized the fact that he was punishing the wrong woman. That he was punishing his woman.

Damn. Where had that thought come from?

Shaking his head, Luc rose to his feet and paced from his office through the darkened house and back upstairs to his bedroom. She was still sleeping in his bed, curled in the middle, her hair tumbling around her head and shoulders like a fall of silk.

She hadn't been raped. Thank God. Out of all the horror she had faced, at least she had been saved the destructive pain of having been raped by her own sex. His fingers clenched as pain threatened to swamp him. He had put her there. Unintentionally perhaps, but he had been to blame all the same.

He sat down in the wing-backed chair beside his bed and stared at her. He simply watched her sleep, realizing he had never done that before. He had never watched a woman sleep nor would he have thought he would have gained any pleasure from it.

But he did. Seeing the steady rise and fall of her full breasts, the way her lips parted just the tiniest bit, the small shadows her light-colored, surprisingly lush lashes cast on her cheeks.

She was exquisite. In admitting that she wasn't the shell of a woman he had thought she was, he was able to look beyond what he thought was there to the woman beneath. There was no longer the conflict that had warred between his head and his heart where she was concerned. Now if only he could find a way to keep her safe.

Maria was missing and, with her, two of the dangerous drug runners she associated with. According to Joe's information, she was looking for Melina. There was only one reason for Maria to be searching so hard for her sister. To find a way to ensure that Melina endured the coming prison sentence rather than her.

God, what kind of monsters raised a child to believe her sibling could always stand in front of trouble for her? What hold did Maria have over her parents' hearts to have allowed something like that to happen? How did a sister—a twin—turn so dark and black against the other? It made no sense to Luc.

He knew twins—the August twins, especially. Men whose battles had left them, for a while, scarred and almost broken. But they had always protected each other, and their older brother, Cade, had protected them all.

They were brothers; there were no questions of loyalty or determination to help each other. It was a part of them. How had Maria managed to be born without that innate love for her sister?

And Melina. How had she endured it? To be betrayed, not just by her twin, but by her parents? They had left her in that fucking jail cell while they vacationed in the Bahamas, accepting Maria's word that her sister had been released. Accepting, without question, the word of a known liar, thief, and drug addict.

Melina had nearly died. He stared at her, horror streaking through his system as he noted the almost fragile build of her slender body, the delicacy of her bones. She had been beaten so badly that she had suffered two broken ribs, internal bleeding, contusions, and scarring that might never heal. She had been only minutes from death when Joe had carried her into the emergency room of a local hospital. For days, it had been touch and go.

Hell, what had made her even fight to live? What did she have to hold on to at that time?

One of the inmates heard her scream your name . . . It had surprised Luc when Joe told him that. Why would she scream for him? It had been his fault she was there to begin with. But she had screamed his name, cried out for him.

He wiped his hands over his face as fury consumed him. God help him, he prayed he never had a chance to wrap his hands around her father's neck, or her sister's. He feared he'd kill them himself for what they had done to Melina.

Rising to his feet, he shed his pajama bottoms and

returned to the bed. He pulled her gently into his arms, surrounding her, holding her to him. She moved against him with a murmur of satisfaction, pillowing her head on his chest as he pressed his lips to her hair.

She was where she belonged. In his arms. His bed. His life. He'd be damned if he ever let her go. She might as well get used to being his captive, because she had stolen his heart and there wasn't a chance he was going to let her leave with it.

EIGHTEEN

Melina slipped out of bed the next morning, aware of Luc's stormy eyes opening, his silence as she gathered up her clothes and headed for the shower. He didn't speak and she was thankful for that. She wasn't entirely certain she could handle a conversation with him right now.

Never in her life had she experienced a pleasure as astounding as what she had felt in his arms the night before. Sex had never been one of her favorite pastimes, even before she met Luc. Her few experiments into it had left her disappointed, wondering why she bothered. Last night had shown her why she should bother with Luc.

She shivered beneath the pounding force of the hot shower, her eyes closing as she fought the sensitivity of her own body. She ached in places that she didn't know could ache. Her breasts were tender, the snowy globes marked here and there with the reddened proof of his passion. Even her hips carried one of the rosy brands from his mouth.

Her thighs clenched as she felt her pussy ripple in remembered pleasure. His mouth had lingered there, kissing her so intimately she had thought she would die from the sensations. If she wasn't extremely careful, she could become addicted to his touch, his kiss.

She shook her head, attempting to dispel the memory of his touch, and quickly finished her shower. She had to figure out what to do now. She hadn't expected things to progress to this point. She had never imagined she would be so weak as to allow Luc to actually take her while he still believed she was Maria. Yet she had.

Rinsing quickly, she turned off the shower and dried her body roughly, wondering if there was any way to erase the feel of him from her flesh. The heat and hardness; the strong thighs parting hers; his cock, so hard and thick, working inside her.

Melina sighed before dressing in one of the soft cotton summer dresses Luc had packed, then drying her hair. She was so screwed, and she knew it. She was falling helplessly, hopelessly in love with a man who thought she was her sister. Who believed to the very core of his being that she was a thief, a drug addict, a woman who would stand by and allow murder to be committed.

Her fists clenched at the thought as she stared back at the image reflected in the mirror. She didn't even look that much like her sister anymore. The basic coloring was the same, but Maria's lifestyle had hardened her, had shaped her face and tightened her mouth until there was little left of the woman she could have been.

The little enforced stay on Luc's ranch had been nice. It had given Melina a chance to think, to find her bearings after her parents disowned her. It had given her precious days to find a balance between the child she had been and the woman she was. Time to figure out the chaos that had existed in her heart and in her mind.

She loved Luc Jardin. She had known, two years ago, that she could love him.

When she had first stared into the dangerous depths of his stormy eyes, saw the flicker of pain and rage that chased across his expression, she had known she could love him.

Had known he could become the most important person in her life. If she wasn't who she was. If Maria hadn't gotten to him first.

But she wouldn't let her love turn her into something or someone she wasn't.

Taking a deep breath she opened the door, stepping into the bedroom with every intention of confronting Luc. Instead, she drew up stock-still. He was still in the bed, the sheet pulled to his hips, and on his chest sat Mason.

"This black mouse chaser of yours is holding me prisoner." She saw his banked smile, heard the amusement in his voice as his fingers ruffled the cat just under his wide chin.

Could any man look sexier than he did at that moment?

"Thought you didn't like cats, Mr. Hardass," she grunted as she walked over to the bed and lifted Mason into her arms.

The animal purred in contentment, settling into her

hold as he stared back at Luc with a hint of feline arrogance.

"I don't." There was that controlled quirk to his lips
again. "I hate the little beasts."

He stared up at her, his gaze becoming drowsy, suggestive. "Put him down and come here. You can make
it up to me for being nice to him."

She couldn't help the flicker of her gaze to where the
sheet began to tent at his thighs. Melina swallowed
tightly at the knowledge that he was becoming aroused
right before her eyes.

"Don't you have work to do?" she finally asked, back-
ing away from the bed and the temptation he represented.
"I thought you had horses to train or something."

He sighed heavily, though the amusement in his eyes
only grew. "Or something," he agreed, though she had
a feeling he wasn't talking about the horses.

"Then maybe you better get to it." She turned away from
him, trembling, wanting to lie back in that big bed with
him so badly she couldn't stand it.

She took a step away from the bed, desperate to escape him and the carnal hunger rising inside her. She
wasn't expecting him to move so quickly. His arm
wrapped around her waist, and before she could do more
than squeak and release a startled Mason she was flat
on her back on the mattress, staring up at him.

Just that fast the blood was racing through her body,
excitement and exhilaration thundering through her system as he stared down at her with a lazy sexuality that
had her toes practically curling.

"Maybe I should get to it then," he agreed, his husky voice washing over her nerve endings and sensitizing them further.

With her hands braced against his bare chest, she could do little about the bare expanse of her thighs that his hand revealed as he smoothed the soft material of her skirt further above her legs.

"That wasn't exactly what I meant, Luc." Her fingertips curled against the hard pad of muscle beneath them as she felt his other hand move beneath her head.

"Do you know how good you felt last night, Cat?" he asked her, stilling the objections rising to her lips. "I wasn't even able to protect you, you stole my control so quickly."

Melina stared up at him, seeing a softening in his eyes that hadn't been there before last night. As though he had eliminated some barrier that had been there previously. He watched her in a way she had thought he never would. There were no hints of accusation, no shadows of suspicion. There was amusement, arousal, and a heat that blazed between them like an inferno rushing quickly out of control.

"Luc, this isn't going to work." She was not going to arch closer to him. She fought the need to rub against him in a sensual imitation of Mason begging for attention. But it was so hard not to. His body was sleek and hard as he lay against her, holding her to the bed.

His hand rested on her lower thigh, fingertips smoothing an intricate design into the flesh above her knee and slowly upward. Her thighs parted, though she was certain she meant to keep them tightly clenched.

"Sure it's going to work, baby." His head lowered, his teeth catching her lower lip gently as he stared back at her, the hunger in his gaze growing.

When he released her, his tongue smoothed over the curves. Melina parted her lips for him. She wanted his kiss, wanted his touch. What was the point in lying to herself or to him? She was weak and he was so damned tempting. Her time here would come to an end soon enough, surely there was no harm . . .

"No, Luc." She shook her head, pulling back. There was more harm awaiting her if she gave in to him. He already held her heart; soon he would hold her soul.

"Hmm. Captives aren't allowed to say no," he told her, his voice rumbling playfully in his throat as he moved closer to her.

His hard chest raked over her cloth-covered breasts. The cotton did nothing to stop her nipples from peaking, growing hard and tight as they pressed demandingly against the bodice of her dress.

"Aren't you taking this too far?" She tried to still the weakening desire that flooded her pussy. God, she needed him.

"Nope." His fingers clenched in her hair as his lips moved to her neck, smoothing over the sensitive flesh just beneath her ear. The shudder that rocked her body would have been embarrassing if Luc hadn't groaned so roughly. "Taking it too far is tying you to the bed and listening to you beg while I paddle that sweet ass until it's rosy."

Her thighs clenched. This should not be turning her on. "Then parting the pretty little red curves and watching as I work my cock inside your tight little ass."

She could feel her pussy creaming, her anus clenching. This was perverted, she told her traitorous body.
Not that it cared. She was fighting to breathe now, panting beneath the fingers that had moved to unbutton the
bodice of her dress.

"Maybe that wouldn't be going too far, though," he
mused as he folded back the material and bared her
swollen breasts. "Do you know how hot, how hard, the
thought of that makes me, Cat?"

No one had ever talked to her so explicitly. Especially
not while they watched her face, hands moving over her
body, gauging the depth of her arousal.

"Would you beg me?" he asked her as his fingers
gripped a hard nipple, working it between them, tightening to the point that pleasure and pain blurred and
sent her body rioting into a plane of sensation that she
had never known existed.

"You're killing me." Melina was well aware she didn't
have the experience to combat the sexuality he was turning on her. "You know you are, Luc."

His smile was sensual, tight, a grimace of extreme
lust and hunger.

"Tell me what you want," he whispered, his fingers
tightening on her nipple again as she gasped and arched
to him. "You like it, baby. See how much you like it."

He repeated the move and Melina swore she was
going to orgasm from that sensation alone.

"Yes," she moaned brokenly. "You know I like it."

"What else do you like?" His head lowered, his
tongue curling around the reddened peak of her breast.
"Tell me, baby. What else do you like?"

He didn't give her time to answer. His mouth covered

the tip of her breast, drawing it deep inside his mouth and suckling at it with sensual abandon. His teeth rasped the delicate point; his tongue licked until Melina dug her fingers into his hair, holding him to her, arching closer as he insinuated himself between her legs.

Traitorous body. She whimpered as her thighs parted for him, her hips rising, a keening cry of need echoing around her as his cock pressed full-length against her pussy.

"This isn't fair," she panted, but she arched her neck as his lips moved around to her throat, then her collarbone, growing inexorably closer to her swollen breasts. "You're supposed to hate me. You can't hate me and want to fuck me."

He stopped then. His entire body stilled for several long seconds before his head raised, his eyes blazing into hers.

"Oh baby, hatred is the last thing I feel for you," he said, the dark cadence of his voice throbbing with lust and something more. That something more, undefined and yet hidden, had her senses reeling.

How could he do this to her? Was it fair that love should weaken her even as it made her feel stronger, taller, more able to face whatever she must to hold his heart? Even when she knew his heart would never be hers.

"You're dangerous," she whispered, her hand moving to touch the swollen pad of his lips as she stared back at him, knowing she couldn't turn him away, knowing she couldn't do any more than love him while she could.

His tongue swiped along her fingers an instant before he gripped them with his teeth.

"Let's see how dangerous we can get together, then."

His hand reached down, gripped the side of her panties, and ripped them from her body. Melina's eyes widened but before she could snap out a derogatory comment about cowboys and manners he was sliding his cock inside her.

Melina stilled, her eyes closing as she fought to breathe and to concentrate on the slow, sensuous glide of his flesh. Inch by inch he pressed his cock inside her, stretching the sensitive tissue, searing her with a heat and hunger that stole her sanity. It was a pleasure unlike any she had ever known before. A pleasure she couldn't deny.

"You're killing me." She was fighting to breathe, to survive the white-hot lash of pleasure streaking through her.

"Then I'm killing us both," he growled. "Damn, baby, you're so hot, so fucking tight it's all I can do to hold on."

He was buried in her to the hilt. A hot throbbing presence that filled her pussy to overflowing and sent her senses spinning. Then he was moving. Thrusting hard and deep, his hard breaths echoing around her as she held on to him with desperate fingers.

Her senses were spinning, her body blazing.

She wrapped her legs around his hips, crying out beneath him as the tension began to tighten, the conflagration threatening to destroy her.

"Luc!" She screamed his name as he nipped at her shoulder, almost growling against her flesh.

"I have you, baby," he groaned, his voice rough, hard hands holding her to him, his lean hips moving harder, faster, plunging his erection through the tight muscles and delicate gripping tissue that enclosed his cock. "Fuck. Fuck. I have you, baby. Always. Always."

She shattered. Every cell in her body exploded in a fury of ecstasy at his words. Her pussy convulsed around him, clamping down to hold him deep, tight, as he began to jerk with his own release.

"Sweet Cat." He lowered his head to her breast, his big body trembling with pleasure. "Sweet. So perfect. So fucking perfect."

And it was. Perfect.

The aftermath was a gentle easing, a soft glide from chaos to the peace of Luc's bed where he had rolled to his side and pulled her into his arms. One hand held her head against his chest; the other clasped her hip. His heart was still racing, but so was hers.

"It can't last forever," she said aloud, a somber sadness threatening to disturb the cloud of pleasure that enfolded them.

"It can." He sighed. "But only if you want it to, baby. Only if you want it to."

NINETEEN

Now that he knew the truth, Luc found it harder and harder to hold back from Melina. He could see her emotions clearly in her beautiful eyes, in her soft face. She was falling in love with him; he refused to accept any other alternative. But he also knew the time was swiftly approaching when he was going to let her know that he knew the truth. He would have already, but he had a feeling she would pack her bags and head out just as fast as he had kidnapped her to begin with. That, he couldn't allow.

Whatever the hell Maria was up to, it couldn't be anything good. Joe was worried sick, more concerned with Melina than with the threat Luc had made to rip off his damned head for lying to him. Had Joe told him the truth, he would have been more than willing to help. But not like this. Not in a way that threatened every shred of happiness Luc had ever dreamed of.

He sat on the wide front porch, watching as Melina

tried to stand between Lobo and Mason. The wolf hybrid was amazingly patient with the feline invader to his home.

Not that he didn't harass the fat-assed cat. He did, on a daily basis. But only if Melina was around.

Mason was growling from Melina's arms, staring down at the huge canine with a smug feline expression. Luc almost believed the wolf just wanted Melina's attention rather than a chance to harass the cat. Not that he blamed him.

"Lobo, you're as aggravating as your owner," Melina laughed as she pushed the animal back when he made a mock lunge at the cat in her arms. "Mason is not lunch. How many times do I have to tell you that?"

Neither was warm, willing woman, but Luc had taken her for lunch before he ever got around to the sandwiches and soup she had fixed. She was addictive, he thought, watching the bunch and sway of her sweetly curved ass beneath her jeans.

Her laughter echoed around the ranch yard as Lobo grabbed at her jean leg, growling playfully as he stared up at her.

"Luc, call this monster off." She turned to him, laughter sparkling in her gem-bright eyes as she tugged back on Lobo's hold. "He's going to snack on Mason."

Her laughter was like an echo of light and beauty. Luc couldn't help but grin at the sappy thought. He got to his feet, intent on joining the play, when Lobo suddenly released her, his body going instantly alert as he stared down the road.

"Get in the house." Luc moved quickly for Melina, ignoring the confusion on her face.

"What?" She stared down the curving ranch road before turning back to Luc.

"Get in the house now." He gripped her arm lightly and drew her to the porch as anger began to glitter in her eyes.

"Don't want anyone to know you kidnapped your houseguest?" she snapped, jerking away from him and stomping to the door. "Don't worry, Luc, I have a better revenge planned for your arrogant ass." She slammed the door behind her as Luc breathed out roughly and moved quickly to where Lobo stood in a guarded stance at the road.

He breathed a sigh of relief when the vehicle came into sight. The unfamiliar Jeep was the reason Lobo had reacted so quickly, not the driver behind the wheel.

"Luc, dammit, I was within a day of a killer sale." Jack jumped from the new vehicle, his long blond hair tied at the nape with a strip of leather, his white silk shirt clinging to his shoulders. "What the hell could be so important that you called me back on an emergency?"

Irritation flashed in the other man's brilliant blue eyes; his tall, corded body was tense with it.

"Good to have you home, Jack." Luc grinned. "Let's go to the barn and we'll talk."

"The barn?" Jack didn't move from where he stood. "Fuck the barn. It's over a hundred in the shade here and I need a cold drink. What the hell is wrong with the house?"

Luc adjusted his Stetson carefully. "This involves an explanation." He sighed. "If you want to get out of the sun, we'll go to the barn. But you're not stepping into that house until we talk. So are you coming or not?"

Jack's eyes narrowed. They had known each other for a lot of years. Hell, they had nearly died together. There was a trust, a bond that flowed between them when danger threatened the other. They weren't brothers but they might as well have been.

"Hell. Fine." Jack sighed wearily. "But this one better be good, Luc. Damned good."

"You did what?" Jack's question rose in volume until he was almost yelling the last word.

Luc leaned back against the frame of the barn's entrance and restrained his smile.

For a man who had been in more scrapes than Luc could ever hope to dive into, Jack was amazingly incredulous at Luc's daring.

"Are you aware kidnapping is a federal crime?" Jack growled furiously. "Doesn't matter the reason . . ."

"Yeah, well, so is stealing cars, but I remember helping your ass when you decided to try your hand at it," Luc reminded him.

Jack's eyes narrowed. "It was my fucking car," he snapped. "They stole it from me."

Luc shrugged. "They had the papers; you didn't. That makes it grand theft."

Jack grunted in irritation. "I can't believe you got messed up with that damned family again," he finally snarled. "Son of a bitch, a fucking twin sister. Just what the hell we needed."

Luc frowned at his friend's tone of voice. Jack could

rage over Maria for hours and Luc would be more than happy to listen, but Melina was another matter.

"She's my woman, Jack," Luc said softly, his voice deepening. "Watch what you say."

A frown snapped into place over Jack's eyes as he stared back at him. That was Jack. He could be a mean gutter fighter when he had to be, but he could also be a hell of a strategist. Right now he would be carefully considering the information he had, as well as the fact that Maria was currently searching for her twin.

"So we protect her." Jack sighed. "Have you managed to locate the bitch yet?" he asked, obviously meaning Maria.

"Joe's working on it." Luc shrugged. "My main concern is Melina and keeping her safe. She's spitting mad at me right now, but she seems to like the ranch well enough. Until her sister is apprehended, my main concern is keeping Melina undercover here."

Jack released the leather tie that held his hair back while sighing again, roughly.

"This one could be a mess." He shook his head tiredly. "Maria is a viper, Luc. We both know that. I've kept up with rumors over the years, too, and there are a lot of them. The woman doesn't have a conscience. All she has is a hunger for drugs. She won't be easy to catch. And if she suspects her sister is here, it might not be that damned easy to keep her away."

Luc smiled coldly. "As long as I catch her," he said softly. "That's all I care about, Jack. Keeping Melina safe and making certain her sister never has a chance to use her again. These are my top priorities. Now, are you in?"

Jack stared back at him in surprise. "Of course I'm in, dammit. I don't have to like it to go along with it. I just have to be able to bitch about it. And don't you think I won't be bitching later, ol' son. Hard and long. You can take that one to the bank."

And likely draw interest on it, Luc thought in amusement. Jack wasn't a man who kept his thoughts to himself until the situation required it.

"Come on to the house then. I'll introduce you. Remember, you don't know she's not Maria," he reminded Jack.

Jack grunted. "Like I could have made that mistake. I think you just didn't want to know. You weren't yourself after that meeting with her and her parents after the shooting. I had a feeling something was wrong then. I think, my friend, you might have known all along."

Luc restrained his smile. He might have. He knew damned good and well that even before the plane landed that day he had no intention of taking Maria Angeles up on her sexual offer. The desire to do so just wasn't there. She was a mean little cocksucker, but that was about it.

Melina was pure sweetness, though, head-to-toe. Soft and delicate, passionate. His.

He stepped to the porch, heard pots and pans rattling loudly, and chuckled before opening the door. She was pissed, too, which suited him fine. If she stayed a little mad for a while, then she wouldn't catch on nearly as easily to the fact that he had fallen so completely beneath her spell that he knew he would never recover. Now all he had to do was convince her that she shared the madness with him.

TWENTY

Jack's arrival was a surprise to Melina. She stood in the kitchen, fighting back a sense of guilt as she watched the amused friendliness in his eyes.

"You're a sight prettier than the last time I saw you," he said, his blue eyes crinkling at the corners as he smiled down at her. "Being sober is good for you, Maria."

She clenched her teeth and shot Luc a hateful look. "I guess you neglected to inform him of exactly who I was," she snapped.

Luc grinned back at her. "No, I didn't. I told him exactly who I thought you were."

Melina sniffed sarcastically before turning back to Jack. "I don't answer to that name. You can call me Catarina or Melina, your choice. But call me Maria and you'll be taking your life into your own hands."

Jack scratched his ear thoughtfully. "Hell, darlin', I think just being around you would be a danger. But you're damned sure worth looking at."

"Cool it, Jack." Melina glanced over at Luc, seeing the irritation that filled his expression.

"Sorry, Jack, Luc thinks he's the only one who has the right to be ill-tempered and rude," she said with wide-eyed innocence. "Personally, I've decided it's just a part of being a cowboy. I mean, neither of you is actually sporting any manners." She stressed the last word sarcastically before turning away from them and heading toward the living room.

"Cat, you're forgetting dinner," Luc growled.

She turned back to him, smiling sweetly. "No, Luc, I didn't forget, I just decided to quit. Fix it your own damned self."

He caught her before she left the kitchen, his lips quirking as he fought a smile, his gray eyes hooded, but the amusement in them wasn't hidden.

"You can't quit. I kidnapped you, remember?" he reminded her.

"Then you better reconsider not just the crime but the punishment." She jerked her arm from his grip, furious with him now. "Because I'll be damned if I'll put up with this much longer."

His brows lowered to a frown as he blocked her way, his hands gripping her hips, jerking her to him, ignoring Jack's covered laugh as he lowered his lips to her ear.

"Punishment, my love, definitely comes later," he growled. "And I promise, you won't forget it when it does."

He nipped her ear, smiling into her furious face before looking over at Jack.

"Come on into the living room and we'll discuss

those sales you made. I think Cat might need a break from us irritating cowboys."

"Hmm," Jack murmured. "Maybe it's just you. You go pout in the living room and I'll keep her company."

"In your fucking dreams," Luc growled, frowning heavily at Jack. "Get your ass in here and tell me how cheap you sold my horses for. And keep your damned eyes off her. Not to mention your hands."

Jack sighed as though disappointed. "One of these days, I'm gonna bring my own woman. You're starting to get downright unfriendly, boy."

Men were just strange, that was all there was to it. Luc had to be a Gemini. The alternating personalities of the zodiac sign made perfect sense. It was the only explanation for . . . this. He had gone from surly jealousy that evening to one of the most amazing lovers she could have imagined later that night.

Melina clenched her teeth to hold back a scream of pleasure as she felt Luc's cock sink slowly inside her well-lubricated behind. She had never, ever, been taken anally. She had never considered it. But there she was, on her knees, her butt in the air, her shoulders to the mattress as the big cowboy pumped his dick up her ass.

Her pussy was sizzling. She could feel her juices literally dripping from her vagina as he held her tight, fucking inside her with slow, careful strokes that stretched her impossibly, sending streaks of fire blazing up her anus as pleasure tore at her very core.

"You're so tight." His voice was rough, so deep and dark she shivered at the sound.

"So hot and tight around my cock it's all I can do not to come inside you now."

Melina moaned in rising lust. Yes, that was what she wanted. She wanted him to come now, to feel him shuddering against her, pumping his seed inside her.

"You like this, baby?" he asked her; the eroticism of his voice had her pulse rate jumping. "God, I wish you could see the way your tight little ass stretches open for my cock, sucking me in . . ." He groaned roughly. "I'm going to come up your ass, baby. I'm going to fill it so deep with my cum that you'll never forget the feel of me inside you."

She never would anyway.

She had to be in shock, she thought as she moved against him, taking him deeper inside the forbidden little hole, glorying in the pleasure/pain tearing through her. She had woken to his fingers smoothing through the cleft of her ass, his hot voice whispering his intent to fuck her there.

She had shivered at the threat, believing he only meant a bit of hot foreplay. She had more than a bit of the foreplay. She had more than an hour of it. And each touch, each lick, each nip was designed to drive her higher, make her hotter as his fingers stretched the nether hole. Until finally, she was begging him to fuck her there. Pleading with him to drive his cock inside her, take her, anywhere, she didn't care. Now she was within a second of begging again.

Her clit was a swollen mass of torturous lust; her pussy was sobbing in its need and she could feel . . . something. An edge of dark coiling need gathering in the pit of her stomach with each stroke of his cock up her ass.

Melina's fingers tightened in the already bunched sheet beneath her, a mewling whimper escaping her throat as he ground his erection deeper inside her. She could feel every inch of his cock boring through her sensitive flesh. Every throb, every pulsing vein as it tunneled through the tender tissue.

"Luc, I can't stand it." She could barely speak, the need was so great. "Fuck me harder. Do something, please."

She was writhing beneath him, or trying to. His hands held her hips tightly, keeping her in place, refusing to allow her to increase the pace of his thrusts.

"Easy, baby." He was fighting for breath; his voice was deepening further. "Patience. Just a little more. You're so fucking tight I can't stand it much longer."

He felt as thick as a baseball bat, as hard as iron, but each long thrust inside the tender channel was making her crazy for more. She wanted him driving inside her, plunging as hard and fast inside her ass as possible. She was dying for it.

She clenched the muscles of her ass as he thrust inside her again, thrilling to the moan that tore from his throat. He was moving faster now, shuttling in and out of her anus as he gasped for breath and she whimpered in longing. She could feel the pleasure building inside her. It was unlike anything she had ever known before. The hot fist of sensation gathering in her womb was tightening, burning.

"Luc, please." She tried to scream out the demand,

but it sounded more like a sob. "Fuck me. Fuck me harder. Please."

He came over her then, covering her smaller body with his own, one elbow bracing her shoulder as his hand moved beneath her body. Before she had any idea of his intention, two broad fingers plunged inside her cunt as he began to fuck her ass in earnest.

Deep, driving strokes, a dual pleasure that shocked her senses and turned her into a creature of sensation, of lust and need so powerful that she was helpless in its grip. Her hips bucked into each driving thrust as the knot of need built within her womb. Tighter, tighter . . .

"Luc. Oh God. Luc . . ." She was dripping with sweat but so was he. He groaned, a thick, harsh sound at her ear that caused her to shudder as his fingers plunged deeper inside her weeping pussy.

It took no more than that. Helplessly her mouth opened to scream, but the sound that emerged was a low, keening cry as she erupted. Her orgasm exploded through her system. Radiant, blistering with heat and a pleasure so intense it was nearly painful.

Muscles tightened, locked, holding him inside her as he growled her name and began to pump hot jetting bursts of semen deep inside her anus.

She was shaking in the aftermath. Never had she known anything could be this intense, this incredibly erotic. She moaned in regret as she felt him slide free of the grip she had on his flesh and fall into the bed beside her. The dark entrance he had so thoroughly fucked still tingled almost violently from the possession he had taken of it.

Her body was sensitized, exhausted. She didn't think

she could drag herself from the bed if her life depended on it.

She could jump in shock as a fist pounded on the door, though, her eyes rounding in surprise at Jack's querulous voice. "If you two are going to fuck like minks all morning the least you could do is throttle the fucking sound effects."

Her face flushed a bright crimson as she heard Luc chuckle tiredly.

"Oh my God." She buried her face in her pillow as she remembered her screams. "Oh my God. This is terrible." There was no way she could ever face that man again.

Not that facing him had been easy the first time, of course. He was the most mocking, sarcastic creature she had ever laid her eyes on. And he had nearly been killed because of Maria. One thing about her sister that she could count on: She knew how to make enemies.

Luc grunted. "Come on, get up. All this exertion makes me hungry. I need breakfast."

"Well, have fun," she muttered. "I'm not facing him this morn—dammit, Luc." He hauled her out of the bed, laughing at her shrieks as he flipped her over his shoulder and carried her to the bathroom.

"Barbarian," she accused him when he set her on her feet by the shower.

"Wench." He leaned down and kissed her quickly. "Now shower. I need breakfast. If you're not downstairs in half an hour, I'll come carry you down."

She frowned up at him mutinously. "Don't you think you're taking this captive thing just a little too far? I mean really, even the worst prisoner gets time off for good behavior."

The fact that she was naked and his eyes were darkening in lustful appreciation wasn't lost on her. Just as the knowledge that he was naked and his cock was slowly taking notice of her once again wasn't lost on him. He frowned darkly. "Damn, you're going to kill me. I'm too old for 'round-the-clock sex. Shower." He pressed her toward the cubicle. "I'll use the guest bath. And hurry. I'm hungry."

He was always hungry. Melina shook her head in amusement as her heart clenched in longing. Damn, he was sexy. Sexy and fun and so hot he made her toes curl with the heat. He made her heart break with emotion, too.

She quickly shook away the somberness of that thought. She would enjoy this while she could, she promised herself. Reality would come all too soon, and when it did, it was going to bust her ass hard. For now she wanted to revel in his touch, enjoy his laughter, and just be a part of him. Even if he didn't know she wasn't Maria, he knew she wasn't the woman he thought Maria was. She would content herself with that for now. It was all she had left when it came right down to it. All she had to sustain her in the future when, she was certain, Luc would no longer be a part of her life. Then she would allow herself to hurt.

TWENTY-ONE

Melina's breakfast of fried eggs, hash browns, sausage, and homemade biscuits was consumed quickly, and within an hour both Luc and Jack were out at the barn with the horses. Several had been sold, Jack had told Luc at breakfast. The two mares were exceptionally beautiful, graceful despite their size, and even-tempered. Melina had watched from the porch for a while as the two men went into the corral and began to go over each of the animals.

Summer was in full swing, and the East Texas weather was damned hot. It was a dry heat, though, one that warmed the bones and made her think of the sultry night to come. There was no doubt in her mind that as long as she shared Luc's bed, there would be no lack of physical exertion. The man had enough testosterone for three men.

Turning back into the house, she entered the kitchen, determined to get the dishes done quickly so she could get the rest of the house cleaned. Luc had mentioned taking a few of the horses out later if she felt up to it. It had been years since she had ridden, and never an animal as large and graceful as the Clydesdales he so loved.

It was easy to convince herself that the situation could continue indefinitely. Easy to let her heart and mind push back the problems that would await her when she returned home.

Her parents had disowned her. She likely didn't have an apartment now and she definitely didn't have a job. All she had was a fat cat, a fairly nice car, and a nursing certificate that she hadn't used in two years.

But when Luc's arms went around her, when his lips touched hers, none of those problems existed. There was only here and now, his touch, the heat, and the hard wash of pleasure that surged through her body. It was becoming harder, daily, to imagine being without him. A sigh of longing escaped her at that thought. She didn't want to be without him—that was her problem.

"Why the sigh, little sis, missing home?" The voice from the doorway made Melina freeze in shock. She stood still before the sink, desperately trying to convince herself she hadn't heard that voice.

"Maybe missing me." The coarse roughness of the other female voice had Melina swinging around in fear.

Melina blinked warily, certain it wasn't possible that the two women she was staring at were actually there.

"Oh look, Bertha, we surprised her. Doesn't she look so cute when she goes all pale like that?" Maria clapped her hands together like a child, an expression of malicious amusement twisting her face.

"Yeah, just makes the juices flow." Bertha smiled in

anticipation, her dark eyes glittering with an unnatural lust. "Wonder if she'll be as hot as you are, Maria? I bet once she gets worked up, she'll be better."

Maria grimaced distastefully as the back door opened and two unfamiliar men entered. For a moment, just a moment, she had hoped it was Luc, until she saw the men. There was no doubt these were friends of Maria's. They had eyes like snakes, cold and devoid of emotion as they stared at her.

"These are friends of mine, Mellie," Maria told her cheerfully. "You don't need to know their names, but they've come to help me take you home. Poor baby. I'm sorry you were kidnapped in my stead, but I'm sure I can take care of your big old cowboy.

"Besides"—she glanced at Bertha—"your good friend Bertha has really missed you. I think she's looking forward to greeting you properly."

Maria was high; her eyes were glazed, the unnatural smile on her face too wide.

"God, Maria." Melina shook her head as she faced the sad waste of the sister she had once loved. "What the hell are you doing here?"

Maria frowned back at her, a flicker of anger in her gaze. "You refused Papa's plan, Melina. You aren't supposed to do that. I came to bring you back so you could reconsider." She smiled like a child proposing some wonderful adventure. "Papa has it all worked out this time, honey. And Bertha here . . ." She motioned to the large-boned woman lazily. "She came along with us to remind you of what happens when you refuse to do what she wants. And she really wants you to help me." The beatific smile that filled Maria's face shouldn't have looked so twisted and sinister, but it did. It terrified Melina.

"I nearly died last time, Maria," she reminded her, fighting to remain calm as Bertha's eyes traveled over her body. "Do you really want to see me dead?"

There was no compassion, no hesitation in her sister. "Better you than me, sweetie. You know I'm the favorite. The best. Papa wouldn't want to lose me, Mellie, you know this. And it would break Momma's heart. They don't love you nearly as well as they do me, so you're really protecting all of us."

It was no more than the truth, but it sliced across her soul like the sharpest blade.

"I won't do it, Maria." Melina breathed in roughly. She wasn't alone, she reminded herself. Luc and Jack were at the barn; they would be back soon. Luc wouldn't let Maria take her. He couldn't.

"Now, see, sweet thing, there's where you're wrong," Bertha spoke as Maria giggled gaily. "You will come back, and you will stand in her stead and pray to God you do it right. Otherwise, the rape you would have gotten at my hands will look like a Sunday picnic when I get finished with you."

Her arm went around Maria. Melina watched in sick fascination as Bertha's head bent, her lips covering Maria's as her sister responded with such unrestrained passion that Melina wondered if this wasn't another nightmare rather than reality.

"Cut it out, Maria," the bigger of the two men on the other side of room ordered her harshly. "We need to get the hell out of here before those two head back. We don't need any trouble here."

The two women disengaged slowly. Maria cuddled against Bertha's breasts as the other woman smiled over at Melina viciously. "Ready to go, sweet thing?"

Melina stared at her sister. In that moment she realized that there would be no saving her twin. She was horribly thin, her skin pasty, her mind so corrupted by the drugs that there was likely no hope of ever bringing her back.

"I love you, Maria," she said softly as she watched her pitifully. "I hope you always know that I love you."

Maria blinked, her gaze flickering before going dull and cold again. "Then you'll have no problems going to prison for me." She reached up and fondled one of Bertha's breasts, humming in approval as the other woman's nipple hardened.

Melina shuddered in revulsion.

"I'm not going anywhere." She stood still, her hands gripping the counter behind her as all eyes turned to her.

"Sorry, lady, but you are coming," the bigger man sighed roughly. "Sucks, huh? Having a sister like that? But she's pretty damned useful to me. You aren't, so you lose."

He wasn't a handsome man; he was cold and she knew he wouldn't hesitate to kill.

The gun he pulled from beneath his jacket proved that.

"Let's go."

She gripped the counter harder. "Once I start screaming, Luc and his men will be here. They won't come unarmed."

A flicker of unease passed across his expression.

"Then we'll just have to make sure you don't scream."
Bertha pushed Maria aside and jumped toward Melina.

She did scream. Luc's name reverberated through the
house, but she knew he would never hear her at the barn.
A second later a hard blow landed against her head as
she attempted to shove past the larger woman.

Melina could hear her sister's laughter as she fell to
the floor.

"Luc!" she screamed again as she scrambled beneath
the table, kicking out at Bertha and the man who grabbed
her legs.

A hard blow went into her kidneys a second before a
savage howl sounded and the sound of breaking glass
over the table was heard. Screams, curses, and feminine
laughter echoed around Melina as she fought the pain
sweeping through her body. As always, Bertha knew exactly where to aim when she used those brutal fists.

Lobo's snarling growls were followed by the sound
of Luc and Jack. Melina struggled to regain her breathing to see more than the dim, blurry shapes struggling
across the kitchen. But Maria was no longer laughing,
and if she wasn't wrong, the still form lying across the
room was Bertha.

"You killed her," Maria suddenly shrieked. "You
killed her, you bastard."

Melina cleared her vision in time to see her sister
dragging the gun from her purse and pulling it up. Luc
was struggling across the room with one of the men;
Jack had the other on the floor, and the gun was pointing at Luc's head.

"No . . ." Gathering the last bit of her strength Melina threw herself at her sister, her hand gripping Maria's wrists as she fought to take the weapon.

"Damn you, Mellie." Maria's knees went into her ribs, sending pain exploding through her body as she went to her back. "You can die first."

The gun turned on Melina; her sister's eyes were cold, hard, as her finger tightened on the trigger. Then Maria jerked, shuddered, the gun dropping from her hand as red began to bloom across her chest. Melina watched the horrible stain in shock as silence seemed to fill the room.

"Joey?" Maria whispered bleakly. "Joey, you hurt me. You hurt me . . ."

She toppled across the fallen figure of her lover, a last gasp heaving from her chest as she stilled.

"Melina." Luc lowered himself beside her, his hands going over her ribs as she cried out weakly.

The pain was terrible, just breathing was agony.

"Fuck, they broke her rib, possibly two. Jack . . ."

"Calling the sheriff and ambulance now," Jack called back, though the words barely penetrated the shock in Melina's mind.

Maria was dead. Melina stared up past Luc, seeing her brother's tear-ravaged face as he gazed down at Maria. In his hand he carried a gun. The gun he had used to kill his sister.

"She wouldn't have stopped," he said wearily, his voice tear-choked as he knelt beside his dead sister. "She would have never stopped."

"Easy." Luc eased her against him as she fought to sit up, pain streaking through her. "Lie still, Cat. The ambulance will be here . . ."

"No. I'm not Maria." He called her Cat. Surely he didn't think she was Maria now.

"No, baby, you're not." He kissed her forehead gently. "You're my little Cat, though. That won't change."

"You hate cats." She stared up at him miserably.

"I love you. I've always loved you.

"But you hate cats."

"I've learned to tolerate one in particular." He smiled then, a weary curve of his lips as he smoothed her hair back. "The other, I can't live without. I love you, Cat. Now rest easy. Everything's going to be okay. It's all going to be okay."

But would it? She gazed over at her brother, his lowered head, the stoop to his shoulders, then stared back up at Luc. His faced was creased with concern, his eyes black, his shirt torn.

"I love you," she whispered again.

Gently he smoothed the tears that fell from her eyes, from her cheek. His touch was gentle, tender, but his gaze was fierce.

"No more than I love you, little Cat. Never more than I love you."

TWENTY-TWO

Maria's funeral was a small, quiet affair. Melina had been forced to miss it. Two broken ribs and a bruised kidney canceled any flight plans she might have wanted to make. She knew Joe had gone, despite her parents' formal request that he not attend.

The media circus had nearly destroyed the family.

Her father's brief visit to the hospital had resolved nothing. His grief and the clear indication that they blamed her for their favored daughter's death had been abundantly easy to see.

All she needed was your love, Melina. You never understood, Maria just needed more love and never received it. She only had her family to understand and lean on . . . It made no sense, but then, it never had.

Joe, as always, was enduring most of the anger, though. He had been formally disowned rather than verbally. Had he not suspected Maria had learned where Melina was, then Maria wouldn't have been killed. She wouldn't have been lost to them forever. It hadn't seemed to sink into them yet that Maria would have gladly killed Melina. They refused to accept it.

Luc brought her home after a small stay in the hospital. Their home. And there he had kept her, pampering her, caring for her until her ribs had healed completely. She still had nightmares sometimes, visions of her sister taunting and laughing as she pointed the gun in her direction. But Luc was always there. His arms surrounded her, holding her close, whispering his love to her. And throughout the night he would pleasure her, driving all thoughts of nightmares, death, or sadness from her mind.

Three months later, after just such a night, he surprised her by going to his dresser, pulling a small velvet box from a drawer, and nearing the bed. There he dropped to one knee, took her hand, and pushed an outrageously expensive diamond on her finger. The engagement ring glistened with shards of color and heat as she stared down at it for long minutes.

Then she looked up at Luc in surprise as he rose to his feet. "No proposal?" she asked him archly.

He stared down at her arrogantly, though the effect was spoiled somewhat by the glint of amusement in his eyes.

"Captives are not given a choice. Remember, Cat? I decide, you follow."

She arched a brow as she allowed her hand to trail slowly up her silk-covered stomach before circling her swollen breasts. She sighed deeply.

"Is that how it works now?" she asked him huskily as her thighs shifted to allow him a glimpse of the plump, bare curves of her pussy. His cock responded immediately.

"Some captives get stubborn, you know? They do all sorts of things to get back at their captors. Things like finding another bedroom to sleep in."

And she wasn't joking. She'd be damned if she would wait that long for a proper proposal just to have him try to slide out of it.

He stared down at her for long seconds before sighing roughly. He went to one knee once again, took her hand, and stared back at her.

"Marry me," he whispered. It sounded more like an order than a proposal, but she had learned a lot about her cowboy, including his fierce arrogance, his determination, and his love for her. His love for her still amazed her.

"Of course I will." She shrugged. She wasn't finished with him yet. "Who's going to explain to our son, though, when he asks why we're sleeping in separate bedrooms?"

"Separate bedrooms? Dammit, Cat, I love you past hell, but if you think they'll be separate . . ." He stopped. His eyes widened. "Son?"

Her hand smoothed over her still-flat abdomen. "It seems some of the scarring healed," she said softly. "We're pregnant, Luc."

He trembled. She hadn't seen him tremble since the day Maria had nearly shot her.

"Pregnant?" He licked his lips almost nervously, his hand moving to flatten on her stomach. "You're sure?"

"Positive," she said softly. "The doctor ran the tests twice just to be certain."

He swallowed tightly, staring back at her, his eyes darkening like a summer storm as he watched her with such emotion it clenched her heart.

"You steal my breath," he said simply. "You're my heart, Melina Catarina Angeles. My heart and soul. Please say you'll marry me."

Melina blinked back her tears then.

"You're my world," she said tearfully. "My life. Of course I'll marry you."

He moved quickly, coming over her, his lips covering hers as he moved between her thighs, opening her, his cock sinking slowly, gently inside the sensitive depths of her pussy.

Melina's breath caught at the pleasure. It always did. He was hers. Her heart and soul breathed for his touch, his kiss.

There were few preliminaries. Emotions seemed to strip Luc's control as nothing else could. The depth of her love for him still seemed to amaze him, just as his amazed her.

Her legs clasped his hips as her lips moved hungrily beneath his. His thrusts were gentle, tender, but no less fierce than they ever had been. Within minutes her orgasm swept over her, shuddering through her body as she tore her lips from his, crying out his name as she felt him erupt inside her at the same moment.

"I love you, Cat." She heard his gentle whisper as sleep began to overtake her.

"I love you, Luc. Forever . . ."

COWBOY

AND THE

THIEF

PROLOGUE

Be watching for him, Joe. Our girl is dependin' on ye now. Ye may not know fer sure when ye meet him. Ye may not know for a time after ye've known him. But the time will come when ye'll talk to him and he'll tell ye that love is but a fairy tale and a search fer fools. He'll say he's traveled this grand world and he's found no lass that wasn't easily forgotten. And then, my love, ye'll remember my words . . .

Joseph Manning stared at the portrait of his wife where she looked down on him from her place above the fireplace and wondered that he hadn't remembered her words before now.

How could he have forgotten even one precious memory from those final days with his beloved Megan? Especially one such as this? Now, as his gaze met her laughing violet eyes, he realized she had warned him that he would forget her words. And how right she had been.

He couldn't help but grin at the thought. Fiery and strong-minded she'd been, that was for sure. And always so certain she knew the way of things, no matter how unbelievable he sometimes found it.

She was descended from a long line of powerful Druids, she'd laughingly tell him, didn't he think she'd know these things? And what pride she found in that lineage, and rightfully so. The lass had always known things, things he could never explain. Things such as the call he'd taken this eve.

He frowned at her now though, because he wasn't so sure of the lad who had him remembering the words he was told to wait for by his Megan.

"That one's a charmer, he is, Meg," he worried, slumping in his seat as he stared up at her, frowning. "A heartbreaker, he is. Our wee lass will take one look at him and those eyes of hers will blaze with violet flames, they will. The banshee from her youth will reemerge." He shuddered at the thought.

But how often had Megan cried when their fiery, fightin' lass had returned from that school, vanquished, no longer fiery, but so calm and quiet that even now, years later, her brothers would berate him for the change.

They'd done wrong by her, and they'd known it. Still, ah, how wild she had been. How wild she would be when she met Jack. She didn't take much to charmers.

Da, I've no doubt you've lost your mind, she'd say.

His wee lass didn't question anything. She stated. Remarked. She was known to observe. But asking questions she'd told him, merely gave others an excuse to lie.

There was a reason why he'd never invited that young

lad to Ireland. His wee girl had already had her heart tweaked a time or two and he'd feared Jack could do far worse than bruise her tender feelings.

"Ah well, we shall see, won't we, my love?" He grinned up at her.

Then his gaze slid to where a much younger him stood behind his Meg. And there, around his neck, gleaming of gold and age, was the ancient Wolf's Head Torque that had so drawn him when he'd first seen it in her da's study, when he was but a young lad.

The torque will draw the heart destined to hold the lass, descended from the first of ancient magic, Megan's da had told him. *A gift he gave to his daughters, and to the lads that would merge their hearts with them.*

A silly legend, he'd always told his beloved. But for as far back as her line went the marriages of their lasses were always strong, blessed, and always fiery.

Just as his marriage to his Meg had been.

As he had hoped his wee daughter would one day find.

Perhaps the legend was true, perhaps it wasn't. But the words he'd been told to watch for had been given him, and the invitation he'd given in response accepted.

Now, well, now they'd just have to see.

ONE

It wasn't the first castle he'd ever stayed in, it wasn't even the finest he'd ever been invited to, but Jack Riley had to admit, it was the most interesting. And the scenery was simply stunning.

Leaning against the natural stone wall at the entrance of what Joe Manning called the family room the night before, he stared at what couldn't be less than a bewitching sight. And there weren't many sights that he'd ever considered bewitching. At least, not until this morning.

"Da, Mrs. Mulhaney called a bit ago," the vision stated from where she sat at the elegant little wood writing desk, going over the papers lying in front of her. "She claims there's an American wanderin' around the village. Do ye have friends visitin' again?"

Jack looked around but didn't see a sign of his host.

He grinned as she trailed graceful fingers down the side of her neck, calling attention to the classy little "do" her hair was pulled into at the back of her neck. It was like a neat, intricate braid that created an oval roll from the back of her head to the bottom of her graceful neck. It pulled the glossy black strands from the peaches and cream flesh of her face to reveal the delicate planes and angles. Wide violet eyes surrounded by sooty lashes and an aristocratic little nose above pouty pink lips. If she was wearing make-up, then she was damned good at applying it because he couldn't see it.

Dressed in a dark skirt that ended right below her knees, white silk blouse and a loose creamy colored unbuttoned sweater, she sat at the table, graceful legs crossed from knees to ankles in a perfect display of innate elegance and feminine modesty.

Cool, polished, dispassionate until one paid attention to the stroke of her fingers against her neck. The movement was absent, almost lazy. The concentration on her face was intriguing. She didn't even realize she was showing the world, men in particular, just where she longed to be touched. And he was a man who wouldn't mind a bit to show her just how good he could make it feel.

"While you're thinkin' on the matter could ye also be thinkin' on exactly how ye intend to convince Haverly to be takin' care of the . . ." Her voice trailed off as she lifted her head and caught sight of him.

Pretty violet eyes widened just a little in surprise as her hand stilled at the curve of her neck and shoulder. She didn't blush, flush, or stammer. She simply stared back at him with mild interest.

"Good afternoon," she greeted, rising unhurriedly from the upholstered little chair she sat in. "I assume you're the American Mrs. Mulhaney called about."

It wasn't a question and that cute-as-hell brogue was exchanged for a classic boarding school tone. Cool, perfectly polite, without a hint of an accent.

"Ah, there ye are, Jack," Joe Manning's familiar voice greeted as the other man stepped into the room and looked between Jack and his daughter. "I see ye've met Angel, then?"

With his gray hair, steel-gray eyes, absentminded scruffiness and more relaxed dress he was a sharp contrast to his picture-perfect daughter.

"Actually, Father, he has yet to introduce himself." She stepped from behind the little desk and walked unhurriedly to her father. "And you should check the mirror before leaving your room." Patient, gentle, her tone with her father softened from the prissy voice of moments ago. "Your collar is turned down again."

She straightened Joe's collar as he stood quietly, staring down at her with fatherly love.

"There." The smile she gave her father was filled with warmth as Joe gave an amused little grunt.

"Well then, I'll take care of introductions," Joe decided, turning to Jack as his daughter followed suit.

Jack did have a few manners, he told himself as he straightened from the wall and stepped closer.

"Jack, meet my lovely daughter, Angel." Joe all but glowed with pride as he looked down at his offspring. "Angel lass, meet a good friend, Jack Riley. He was visitin' Ireland so I invited him to stay with us for a spell."

"Angel." He took her much smaller, fragile hand in his.

"Mr. Riley." Cool, impeccably mannered. "I'm always pleased to meet Father's friends. I do hope you enjoy your stay. Father didn't say how long you'd be staying."

Like hell she was pleased to meet him, and she wanted to know exactly how long she was going to have to put up with him.

"I haven't decided." Staring into those pretty violet eyes, he grinned at the flash of fire he saw in them. "My plans are open-ended for the moment."

"I see." The words were accompanied by a flare of disapproval in her gaze.

A lazy smile curled his lips. Disapproved of him, did she?

"Jack's from Texas, dear. In America." Joe beamed down at his daughter.

"So I heard from the accent, Father," she assured him, linking her hands gracefully in front of her. "And what does Mr. Riley do in Texas of America?"

He really wanted to say beach bum. It was right there on the tip of his tongue.

"Import/exports, of a sort, isn't that right, my boy?" Joe asked as Jack slid him an amused look.

The older man was fiddling with the sleeve of his sweater as he frowned down at it, obviously avoiding Jack's gaze.

Angel's delicate brow lifted with mocking curiosity.

"Of a sort," she repeated. It wasn't a question.

"Of some sort." He didn't bother hiding his grin.

Imports/exports was a very loose term for the single-cargo plane he used to pick up and drop off deliveries for international clients. Though that was only part of the business he co-owned with his partner and friend, Luc Jardin.

"Very well then," she murmured, turning back to her father. "I'll leave the two of you to enjoy your morning, Father." She turned back to Joe. "Please take care of the issue with Haverly. I understand the situation's becoming quite dire."

"O'course, ma dear, o'course," Joe agreed soberly. "I'll take care of that directly."

"Of course you will." Her smile was patient but knowing. "Be certain to actually do so this time." She kissed his cheek fondly. "We'll talk later." She turned back to Jack. "Good day, Mr. Riley."

With a graceful incline of her head she walked past him, moving with a fluid, restrained sensuality that his cock was far more interested in than it should be. *And just look at the pert, round globes of that delectable ass beneath the dark silk skirt.*

Turning to his host after she left the room, he arched a brow as he grinned. "You didn't mention you had such a pretty daughter, Joe."

"Yes, well." Joe tugged uncomfortably at the lobe of his ear, a sheepish look on his face. "Angel can be a bit prickly, doncha know? She's not fond of men with the . . . uh . . . appreciation you have of all things feminine."

Jack couldn't help but grin at the description. "Is that what you call it?"

Joe's look was a bit chagrined. "Well now, Jack, ye've a bit of fondness for the ladies," he pointed out. "A charmer they're of a mind to call ye, I believe."

"Are you calling me a playboy, Joe?" he drawled, amused.

"Perhaps, but fondly, lad. Always fondly."

TWO

Angel was used to her father inviting friends to stay at the estate, but two days later, she found herself wondering exactly why he'd invited the American, Jack Riley. Not that the two didn't get along. They did. And Jack was indeed a charming person when he had a mind to be. Unfortunately, he seemed more inclined to anger her than to charm her.

Relaxing in one of the two wingback chairs that sat facing the warmth of the fire Haverly had started as evening fell, she stared into the flames, frowning at the attention she was giving each sound of movement outside the family room. As though she were awaiting his arrival. Which she absolutely wasn't doing.

No matter how much he fascinated her. He was a playboy, her father had already warned her of that. A hellion he'd even said. The type of man who would break her heart and never think of her again once he left, she had finished silently. But he'd be the type of man who knew a woman's body and exactly how to touch it, how to maximize the pleasure.

Returning her attention to the book she was reading, she let her fingers stroke along the side of her neck as she settled into the corner of the chair and tried to once again pay attention to the words on the page she'd begun more than an hour before. She'd had no problem whatsoever with the novel until Jack's arrival. Now it was all she could do to concentrate on the highly suspenseful adventure she'd once enjoyed.

Because all she could imagine was that American heartbreaker in her bed. And she knew she had better sense than that.

"And here's our lovely hostess." The Texas drawl had her head jerking up, tearing her eyes from the page to stare up at the man who had obviously tiptoed into the room.

"So I am," she answered, her tone measured and quiet despite her disconcertment at his stealth. "Is there something I can do for you?"

Hospitality, manners, a cordial demeanor. Her mother had taught her how to be a lady.

That slow lazy smile assured her his mind went straight to the gutter. Unfortunately, hers had already been there.

The bastard.

"Joe suggested I find you and ask for a tour of the gardens," he informed her a bit quizzically. "Are the gardens that difficult to navigate?"

She couldn't help but smile at the question.

"For Father perhaps." Sliding the bookmark in place, she laid the book aside. Again. "Come along then. He'll never forgive me if he has to worry about you wandering into the maze and becoming lost. One of his hunting buddies spent several hours searching for a way out. I still have yet to understand why he didn't just push through the evergreens . . ."

Jack followed her, his attention on that cute little butt as she very politely questioned the intelligence of Joe's hunting buddy.

She was wearing another of those prim little skirts that made his mouth water. The straight cut of the dove-gray garment with its little slit in the back was driving him crazy. Three-inch black heels and a long-sleeved black and white block silk shirt, sleeves rolled a few inches up her arms, completed the lady-of-the-manor look.

"Will you need a jacket?" she asked as she paused at a small closet outside the ballroom and, after opening it, pulled free a cream-colored sweater.

"I'll be fine," he promised, taking the outerwear from her hand and holding it politely as she slid her arms into it.

Hell, helping a woman put clothes on rather than take them off was something new for him. His friend Luc would be rolling with laughter if he could see him.

"I understand Texas can get quite cold in the winter," she commented. She rarely asked questions.

"Parts of it," he agreed, following her through the ballroom to the double glass doors on the far side. "Snow-fall last year was great though. We had about three feet in that last storm that hit."

"What a grand sight that would be," the soft hint of

a brogue slipped past as she stepped aside to allow him to open the doors.

"It was beautiful," he agreed, realizing it had been a damned pretty sight. He hadn't thought it until he saw the little glow of excitement in her violet eyes.

"Father lived in Russia once. He tells me often of the snowfalls there, the cold and the beauty he found in it," she told him as they stepped outside. "I found it to be far more than just cold and the snow quite frigid."

The irony in her smile caught his attention.

"Your father was in Texas one winter during one of the worst blizzards I've seen hit the area. He was out in shirt sleeves, slacks, and those expensive black boots of his, exploring the town. Every major highway shut down, the wind so cold it sliced through the heaviest winter coat, and here he was, walking around like a damned tourist in the Florida sunshine." That memory still had the power to amaze him.

"That's Father," she agreed, the sound of her laughter stroking over him.

His lips quirked as he followed her into the gardens, listening to the history of the place, which went back centuries, according to her. When they entered the maze created by the closely grown evergreens and the soft carpet of grass beneath their feet, with the shadows of evening lengthening along the tall hedges, he could see why her father's hunting buddy hadn't wanted to push his way through the prickly green growth.

Until she pointed out the breaks in it, just in case a solitary explorer were to get lost within it.

She seemed to know where she was going though. As

they walked and she answered the few questions he could come up with, he found himself moving to her side, his hand settling low on her back.

"And here is the center of the maze," she said softly as they entered the sheltered garden. A covered marble portico sat in the center, surrounded by trailing roses and a variety of other plants he had no clue how to identify.

He had no problem identifying the wide, cushioned bench and fire pit within it though. Private, sheltered. Entering the vine-and-flower-covered enclosure, he watched as Angel sat on the wide stone edge of the fire pit. A second after she tucked her fingers beneath the ledge, flames rose above the small lava rocks that filled the pit, warm, inviting in the evening dusk.

Damn him, she was pretty sitting there, the glow of the flames reflected beside her, the looped braid at the back of her head so prim and proper, the elegance and tamed sensuality was driving him crazy.

"Do you come out here often?" he asked her, sitting beside her, staring down at her as her head lifted slowly.

"Sometimes. To read," she answered, her gaze meeting his, her gaze softer, almost wistful.

"Just to read?" This place was made for sex.

For laying her back on that cushioned bench less than two feet away and watching that prim and proper melt away beneath some hot, dirty sex.

"Just to read," she answered, and if he wasn't mistaken that was regret in her tone.

He was just the man to show her some of the other activities that could take place in her secluded little reading nook. And he'd make sure she enjoyed every minute of it.

Angel knew he was going to kiss her.

They'd spent two days as though neither of them was certain if they were going to bicker like children or behave like adults. He had a way of making her irate despite her best intentions.

As his head lowered though, she decided at this moment, that acting like an adult could be more beneficial. It could be quite pleasurable perhaps. Exciting, if the speed of her heart beating was an indication. It was racing out of control, making her feel a bit lightheaded, perhaps a little drunk as his lips covered hers.

Oh.

He wasn't the least hesitant. He wasn't asking permission to kiss her, he was showing her in no uncertain terms what he had to offer her with a kiss.

One hand cupped the side of her face, the other slid to her hip, and his lips demanded compliance, pliancy, submission. They covered hers, parted them and his tongue swept inside like a conqueror, instantly claiming her response. Pleasure exploded through her senses like fireworks and stole her breath as she found herself being pulled to her feet, his lips never releasing hers, and a second later she was being eased to the bench next to them.

Her back met the cushion and Jack came over her, a warm, heavy weight, his touch certain and knowing as his fingers traced down her neck and sent sparks racing through her bloodstream. The caress was similar to the stroke of her fingers used to calm her nerves or settle her thoughts. There was nothing calming or settling in his touch though. His fingertips rasped against her neck, brought alive nerve endings she didn't know she possessed, and awakened a hunger she had no idea lurked inside her.

Just as she was certain she would feel those rough, heated kisses along her neck, he stiffened against her.

"Jack?" Her father's voice sounded from the other side of the path leading into the small grotto. "Jack? I found the name of that barmaid you were asking about."

Barmaid?

Jack's head lifted and her eyes sprang open.

And all it took was a single look at his expression. The rueful amusement, the air of male wickedness and certainty that seducing one woman as her father searched for another for him was perfectly acceptable.

"Move." She formed the words with lips stiff from anger. It was definitely anger she told herself. It had nothing to do with that flash of hurt that tore through her.

"Yeah, I figured that one." Easing his weight from her, he grinned back at her. "I guess you wouldn't be willing to listen to an explanation?"

Angel sat up slowly, her breathing still erratic, her pulse pounding through her veins.

"I was unaware there was another woman you were concentrating your efforts on," she stated. She never asked, nor questioned. She'd be damned if she'd give anyone permission to lie to her by asking.

"Baby, the world is full of women," he told her with charming amusement. "Concentrating on a single one is a mistake I don't make."

A mistake.

She rose slowly to her feet.

"Ah, there you are." Her father stepped into the grotto, his gaze taking in the fire, Jack's seat on the bench, and Angel before his expression turned somber.

In that second she knew he was aware of what might have nearly happened.

How foolish she was to have given into the illusion that there might have been more . . . She pushed the thought back. She was just foolish.

"Yes, Father, here we are," she agreed, keeping her tone low, unaffected. "And now that you're here you can see your friend back to the house. Excuse me, I have things to do."

She stepped to the path and strode calmly away from them when she wanted nothing more than to run, to race back to the castle and up to her room. To hide beneath the blankets of her bed and pretend she hadn't just experienced a kiss that burned through her senses from a man more than willing to share the same with another woman as soon as he left her.

Whoremonger, her wounded pride raged. He was no more than a whoremonger and she was the foolish little twit she'd once been called by another of his ilk. A mistake she'd sworn she'd never make again.

THREE

He was kicking himself and he didn't even know why. Irritable, out of sorts, or put out over a woman wasn't how Jack normally allowed any affair to affect him. There were too many women in the world to be put out over one, he'd always told Luc. So it was no surprise that finding himself in all three of those states at once only made it worse.

The fact that he wasn't looking for the barmaid to seduce wasn't the point. It was that instant assumption that he was doing just that while seducing her that pissed him off. There might be too many women in the world to tie himself down with just one, but only a stupid man thought he could actually seduce two at once and keep his sanity for long.

He didn't play games either. Had she just given him the chance, then he would have explained that the barmaid he was searching for had inquired, through one of Joe's friends, if he was willing to give her an estimate on delivering a crate of housewares to New York on his flight back for her sister who had married an American serviceman. There was room left on the plane, so he'd been willing once he had the information he needed.

Angel hadn't been willing to wait for that explanation though. And he sure as hell wasn't going to beg to give it to her.

What the hell was it about her anyway? What drew him to her when he'd never been drawn to one of those uptight boarding-school prisses before? Women like that were more trouble than they were worth. Too much time and effort for too little return.

Until Angel.

Fuck, she might have singed his toenails with that kiss. And his toenails had never come close to being singed before.

"Father, if there's nothing you need, then I'll be going to my room." Frosty as hell she was, he thought, glaring at her as she stepped into the family room.

"So soon, dear?" Perplexed, Joe looked at his daughter over the reading glasses he'd put on to go over the contract Jack had given him for the barmaid and her family for the shipment of the goods.

"I'm rather tired." That stiff upper lip drew his gaze.

He could see her on her knees, all prissy-dressed, face flushed, eyes burning with lust as he fucked those pouty lips. He narrowed his gaze on the curves as his cock throbbed, beating in wild hunger at the thought of watching her take him so intimately.

Joe frowned. "I was rather hoping you'd go over this contract a bit for me first. You remember Alice Gilroy, married that young Army man from America? Her sister

and family are wantin' to send a crate of housewares
back to her when Jack flies home. They've asked me to
go over the contracts for 'em, but you understand these
things much better than I."

For a second the statement didn't penetrate. When it
did, Jack kept his surprise to himself.

That old bastard had nearly negotiated him and Luc
out of a single penny of profit when he was in Dallas
five or six years ago. They'd barely skinned by with
enough to cover their time and fuel on that deal.

Her lips tightened and his balls tightened along the
base of his dick. Yeah, he could fuck that pretty mouth
and enjoy the hell out of it.

"I'll take it to my room . . ."

"Come, lass," her father chided her. "The evenings
are all the time I have with ye," Joe complained. "You'll
be back with yer phone calls and meetins this week with
barely a moment to spare for yer da. Come sit a spell.
Look over the papers for me and visit with Jack while I
find Haverly to fuel the fire, then we'll share a bit of Ireland's finest."

Rising from the chair across from Jack in front of the
fireplace, the one he'd found her in earlier that day, he
stared back at her expectantly.

"Come now, Angel. It took me more than a few hours
of work to find the lass tryin' to contact Jack for her
sister. All Haverly told us was that she tended the bar.
The least ye could do is go over the papers for me," he
chided her gently while giving her the reason for his
search for the barmaid.

What the hell was that old geezer up to? He'd known
damned good and well what had been going on when

he'd stepped into the center of that maze and saw Jack and Angel together. He wasn't a fool.

Her nostrils flaring, violet eyes spitting fire at him despite the explanation, she tried for a smile when she looked at her father. There was no doubt she was fond of her father, and he clearly adored her.

"Very well, Father," she relented, though he swore she pushed those words between clenched teeth. "Do hurry with Haverly though. My day begins early tomorrow."

Walking sedately across the room she took the papers, but when she moved to turn to her little desk her father all but pushed her into his chair. For the first time Jack saw surprise round her eyes as she stared up at her father.

"Stop being so antisocial, girl," Joe demanded in exasperation. "Yer mother taught ye better now, I know she did."

"Of course, Father," she answered rather suspiciously, or perhaps warily as Joe huffed before straightening his sweater, nodding and stalking away from them.

She shot him an accusing look, as though it were somehow his fault that her father was acting strangely.

Lifting a brow, he sipped at the Irish whisky Joe had pressed into his hand when they'd returned to the family room. And he couldn't help but be amused by her predicament. She would have preferred to be anywhere but sitting there with him.

Pressing her lips together firmly, she turned toward the light on the small table next to her and began reading over the contracts, blatantly ignoring him.

Being ignored wasn't something Jack normally allowed.

"Are you normally antisocial, or is it just me?" Jack asked, grinning at the irritation in the look she flashed him.

"I believe I'm being quite social, Mr. Riley," she answered, her gaze returning to the papers. "All things considered."

Oh, there it was. "All things considered," that one unneeded little phrase and a hint of a brogue accompanying it. Now he had her.

"What are we considering?" He frowned, as though he were confused.

He wasn't in the least confused. She was so put out over the comment he'd made that there were too many women in the world to concentrate solely on one, that she could barely stand to hold back her anger.

"The fact that yer no more than an alley cat," she stated, those violet eyes spitting flames of wrath over the papers she held.

"Sweetheart, there was only you there," he reminded her. "You had only to give your father a moment to explain."

Contempt curled her lips. "I needed no explanations," she assured him. "I should have known better than to find myself in such a position to begin with. You've no loyalty to anyone but yourself, have ye, Jack?"

Well, that wasn't exactly true.

"I have friends," he assured her, though he was certain that wasn't what she was talking about.

"By yer own admission ye've no family, an orphan ye called yerself," she reminded him, not quite as calmly as she would have before. "No wife, ex-wife, nor children.

Ye've only friends," she said a bit sadly now. "And lovers."

"And lovers," he agreed softly.

"In the plural." The word sounded dirty with that little bit of brogue behind it. It made his dick harder. "No loyalty tae even one at a time. No one waitin' for ye when ye return to her home. Not even a maid to greet ye when ye enter. What a lonely life it must be."

The more she talked, the thicker the Irish came out in her, and the more he felt the lash of those softly spoken words and the truth of a life he rarely allowed himself to consider.

"No ties," he agreed. "You only live once, sweetheart. Live it to the fullest."

"Yer living life to the fullest and how grand that must be for ya." She gave him a pitying look. "Ye also only die once, Jack. I've a mind not tae not die alone. Men such as yerself die in seedy motel rooms regrettin' life as they've lived it, and missin' what they've never known."

"And that would be?" he growled before tossing back the rest of the drink. "What am I missing, Miss Manor?"

She smiled with the same patient tolerance she used on her father when he'd lost his glasses the evening before and she had to find them for him.

"Yer missin' that smile that love would give ye when ye return from yer travels. Yer missin' the smell of a fire in the evenin' that ye can share, the warmth of one that knows ye well. Not just yer body, as well as ye know how to use it, I'm sure. But one who knows yer desires before ye know 'em yerself." She stopped, swallowed, and shook her head. "Forgive me, Jack." The lady of the house was back, damn her. "Your life is no concern of mine. Your future loss is no concern of mine." She rose from her chair and laid the papers in the seat. "Please tell Father I'll meet him for breakfast in the morn."

When she would have walked past him he reached out for her, gripped her hips, and had her on his lap, in his arms, and his tongue in her mouth before she could do more than gasp.

Heat, fiery and intense, spilled from her kiss and the little cry she made as her hands clenched at his shoulders, short little nails flexing against the material of his shirt like a little cat. Holding her against him, he plundered her lips, drew from her kiss and growled at the hunger tearing through him unlike anything he'd known before.

He wanted to lay her down in front of that damned fire and come over her, push inside her, and hear her screaming in pleasure. He wanted to watch the lady melt, see the woman emerge and reap the bounty he knew no other man had known. She might not be a virgin, but he bet his last dollar she'd never burned as he knew they'd burn together.

"Jack, lad, I'll be there in just a bit," Joe called from outside the room. "I thought I'd have Cook get us a nice slice a that cake I saw her bakin' earlier . . ." His voice trailed away.

How the fuck long would cake take anyway?

No way in hell it would take as long as he needed to sate his need for this damned woman.

"Enough." She was the one to break the kiss, to put

a halt to the mind-numbing pleasure he knew she was feeling as well. "Let me go, Jack."

"Let me go up with you, Angel." He wondered if he was finally reduced to begging a woman. "I'll pleasure you. I swear it."

She pushed herself from him, her lips red and swollen, face flushed, hands trembling as she slowly straightened the blouse he'd been pulling from her skirt.

"Of course ye would," she snapped, glaring at him. "I've no doubt when ye left my bed I'd well know that ye'd been there. Just as I'd know I was no more tae ya than all the others that had gone before me."

"You're saying no because you want to be the one that got away?" He snorted at the thought. "No man my age hasn't heard no a time or two, baby. You'll not be the first." He smirked. "Maybe not even the last."

"No doubt." Her chin lifted, her voice turned frosty, but her eyes raged. "There's no doubt in my mind, Mr. Riley, that I'll be just one of many women you've known in your life. But what I'll not be is just one of many lovers that you've cast aside when it came time to protect that frozen heart of yours. Good night."

She walked away from him, but she didn't do so unhurriedly. The heels of her shoes snapped against the wood floors and might have even been close to a run as she went up the stone steps leading to the bedrooms. And she left him sitting there, looking into a future he didn't want to see.

Sleepless nights never failed to make Angel cranky, and she knew it. And this was but another sleepless night among those since Jack had been in the castle, disrupting her schedule and her life.

Hours after she heard him retire to his room, she pulled on her robe and slipped from her room, intent on making her way to the kitchen and perhaps a glass of warm milk. Instead, she stepped into the family room as she glimpsed the glow of the fire still burning. The crackle of the flames, the gentle flicker of the light against gold drew her gaze to the glass-enclosed relic resting beneath the picture of her mother and da over the mantel.

The torque was curved to fit about the neck, the open end to rest just at the male's collar bone. To one side was the shape of the wolf's head, to the other an open ring that fit over the head of the wolf. The ring was the female, enduring and inescapable, the wolf the male she would give her heart to and bind to her forever.

The legend of the torque was that so long as it remained with the female descendants of the Druid's line, then they'd always know happiness in their marriages and security in the arms of their mates. The male would always know the warmth of her love and the prosperity the torque would bring.

A silly legend, she reminded herself, but still, she reached out and touched the glass, the familiar warmth she knew wasn't due to the fire alone, meeting her fingertips.

Her mother had once told her that the torque would accept only one, that it would know the mate born to capture her heart. The tales her mother had told her of the torque's adventures were as much a part of her life as the castle itself. She was raised on the legend of it, and as a child believed in it.

As a child.

Drawing her hand back she sighed heavily. The torque was indeed ancient though. And more than once others had attempted to steal it, only to meet with a bitter end. It was considered both blessed and cursed by the Druid who created it. What it was was a beautiful piece of workmanship belonging to a family that had been smart enough to create the legends and the curse to ensure it remained forever within the castle.

"There ye are, lass." Her father stepped into the room, his heavy robe tied snugly at his middle, his feet pushed into warm slippers. "I thought I'd check the fire to be certain it was banked for the night."

"The fire's fine, Father," she assured him, looking up at her mother and seeing the gentle regard she so missed. "She loved us too well, Father," she said softly as he came beside her. "We've not left this place for fear of losing our memories of her."

Perhaps it was time for her to leave, to see the world as her friends kept urging her to do.

"Do ye think that's why?" He chuckled at bit at her musings. "No, lass, I don't believe that's why. She but ensured only happy memories graced her home, is all. That is not what holds us here though."

"What holds us here then?" She frowned up at the younger version of her parents, seeing their bond in the way her father's hands lay on her mother's delicate shoulders, the way one of Megan Manning's fingers lay against one of those broader, stronger hands. Or did she merely wish to see it?

"Tis home, lass." He sounded faintly confused by the question. "Ye don't seek to leave the place yer heart calls home. Yer happy in it, content in the air of it, the beauty ye find in it. Tis all," he said gently. "Are ye not happy here? Do ye find ye've a need to leave, Angel?"

"Would you be angry, Father?" she asked, pushing her hands into the pockets of the robe she wore. "Would you wish to hold me here if I didn't want to stay?"

"Such questions ye ask, girl," he chided her, smiling as she looked at him. "I'd no' be angry. I'd miss ye, but I'd understand. Will ye be leavin' then?"

She pursed her lips for a moment. "When Mrs. Mulhaney's pigs fly perhaps," she laughed softly. "I was merely curious." She leaned her head against her father's arm. "I'll never find a husband though." And she did feel a twinge of sadness at that. "But as I've found, there are none that would love this place, this land as I do."

She couldn't imagine living anywhere but Ireland. To see the storms sweeping in from the sea, to stand at her bedroom window and watch the waves crash against the cliffs below. To hear the winds howling about in the winter storms and know there was nothing to fear there.

"Yer mother said the torque would ensure your wolf arrives, child," he told her. "And ye may travel the world, but ye'll return here before the birth of your first child. Yer mother and I lived in America close to my own family, until your brother was conceived. We agreed to return so he'd be born in the walls of this castle, and we never left. A decision I was happy with every day once it was made."

"The torque is but legend, Father." No matter how much she wished it was more. "Very pretty and very dear. A piece of history I shall always treasure myself, but legend nonetheless." Turning, she stood on tiptoe and kissed his scruffy cheek. "Good night, Father. I love you."

"As I love you, ma dear," he replied, kissing her brow before she turned and left the room to make her way back to bed. "Sleep well."

Jack stared at the piece of jewelry Joe still stared up at, remaining silent where he stood next to the bar, hidden in the shadows from where he'd watched and listened in interest.

Joe sighed, gave the torque a final look, then turned and headed for the doorway.

"Poor lass," the old man said softly, obviously talking to himself. "Ah well, she'll not be so upset if I were to sell it then, would she?"

Jack stared at the piece of jewelry and wondered why the thought of Joe having to sell it bothered him so damned much.

FOUR

The torque was no longer on the mantle where it had sat for most of her life. The dull gleam of gold, the comforting presence of it was gone. For as long as she could remember it had never been moved but to clean the case, until now.

"Father?" she questioned him as he sat before the fire with Jack. "Where's the torque?"

She could only stare at where it had once sat, her heart struggling to beat, the blood pumping sluggishly in her veins as she tried to make sense of its absence.

"Well now, lass, Jack and I were discussin' the price on it as Haverly cleans it up properly for him. I thought it time to let the past go, since we agree it's no more than a pretty piece of jewelry . . ."

She turned slowly, staring at Jack, with an implacable expression as he sat in the chair before the fire with her father and tossed back the rest of his drink and rose to his feet.

"He'll not be buying it. He's no deservin' of it." The fury that shot through her didn't just shock her and her father, but it seemed to surprise Jack as well.

His eyes narrowed on her, the blue hardening, growing cold.

"Undeserving of it?" he asked her then, his tone only faintly curious.

"Yer no' but an alley cat," she snapped. "Mr. Too-many-women-too-little-time," she sneered. "That torque is not fer the likes of you, Jack Riley, and ye'll not have it."

It was hers. It was always meant to be hers. The legacy of it was all she had of hope for her future.

Jack bent and placed the glass on the small table next to the chair he'd been sitting in.

"The money will be transferred to your account this evening, Joe," he stated. "I agree to the price as well as the terms. I'll collect the piece from Haverly and be on my way. I thank you for your hospitality." The look he shot Angel was cold, unemotional.

"No!" She grabbed his arm, the anger and hurt burning in her like a flame out of control. "What do ye need of the torque? Tis nothin' to ye."

His lips quirked mockingly. "Maybe I decided this alley cat deserved it," he said softly. "The deal has been made. The torque is mine."

Carefully, gently, he removed her hand from his arm and stepped back.

"Ye'll no keep it." She was shaking from the inside out, terrified, knowing she had lost the legacy she'd dreamed of for so long and had no idea how to stop it.

And just as she had before she'd learned to control

her emotions, her temper was controlling her, making her rash, and she knew it.

"I always keep what I make mine, Angel," he assured her. "Don't worry, I'm sure I'll find some use for it."

The negligent shrug, the cruel words. They were more than she could bear.

"I'll make sure ye no keep it, Mr. Riley," she sneered. "On my oath I swear it to ye, one way or the other, I'll have it back if I have tae steal it back."

"Angel!" Shock filled her father's voice. "Child . . ."

"Try something so stupid and the first thing I'll do is paddle your ass," Jack promised her. "Then, I promise, you'll find a reason to regret it. No one steals from me and gets away with it. You don't want to test me on that."

"And ye'll no scare me," she yelled as he strode from the family room. "Damn you. Ye won't have it . . ." Her voice broke as she tried to race after him, only to have her father catch her arm and pull her around.

"Angel?" Concern, regret, worry. They flashed across his expression as he reached out, his fingers brushing her cheek. "Lass, yer cryin'?"

"What have you done, Da?" she cried out, aware, so aware that she'd lost the torque her mother had so loved, a legacy of a thousand years passed from mother to daughter gone. "How could you do that? How could you sell the torque?" A sob tore from the depths of her soul, ragged and lost as she stared up at her father. "How could ye do this to me?"

"Tis but a pretty piece of jewelry," he reminded her gently. "Remember your mother's words, lass. Remember the conditions to attainin' the torque. Twas by your own lips that ye lost it, and now, no matter my wishes, or the mistake I may 'ave made, it's too late to call it back."

The conditions to attaining it?

Her mother had warned her: She had to believe. She had to trust the torque to find the man whose soul was of the wolf. A man who would mate for life, and love beyond forever. She had to believe, or risk losing it forever.

"No," she whispered, shaking her head. "Da, no." She grabbed his arm, holding to him desperately. "Don' do this. I beg ye, Da. Please . . ."

"Lass, the deal tis done," he whispered, grief echoing in his voice, his eyes. "May God forgive me, the deal is done."

She jerked her hands back from him.

The hell it was done. It wasn't done, she wouldn't allow it to be done.

"May God forgive both of us then," she heard her own voice and would be shocked by it later, she thought distantly. "Because I vow to ye, Da, he'll no' keep it!"

She was the one who sounded like an animal. Enraged, perhaps irrational, but that torque twas hers. A thousand years of women who had known only happiness in marriage, who had found the man whose heart was like the wolf, whose love would see her through her life, always untainted, that was the legacy of it.

A girl could be forgiven for having doubts.

Just because she doubted didn't mean she didn't hope.

It didn't mean she would allow the dreams of an old Druid, who'd wanted only happiness for his daughter and all her line, to be wasted on a man who knew naught of love, of loyalty.

He'd not have her torque.

Not without her, he wouldn't . . .

Joe watched his daughter all but run from the family room, all that prissy schoolmarmishness stripped away by her fury, by her knowledge of what she was losing. And hadn't her dear sweet mother been just like her?

Still, guilt, and even fear, squeezed at his heart. He'd promised his Meg he'd do what must be done when the time came. He'd vowed it. But had he known what it would do to his precious Angel, perhaps he would have tried to find another way first.

Jack was a good lad though. No matter what the girl tried, he'd not hurt her. Megan had sworn it to him, and she'd vowed to him that she had the second sight. That she had glimpses of their daughter's future with the one she'd gift her torque to and it had been filled with many children and a long happy life.

Unlike his wee Megan who had succumbed to that horrible lung infection she'd contracted.

Their Angel and her wolf would live to see their grandchildren grow strong and true, and together they'd guide their daughter to the wolf awaiting her.

And even knowing that this was his Angel's possible future, still, he worried.

There was a reason Megan had chosen to send their daughter to that fancy school and to teach her to control that temper that ran so deep, so hot.

Aye, there was a reason he worried now.

FIVE

Sometimes women just amazed him, Jack thought pensively as he hid in the shadows of his ranch house and watched the cute little bit of nothing slip through the opened living room window not more than hours after he'd returned to his Texas home.

They shouldn't, not anymore, but he had to admit he hadn't really expected Angel to keep her very rash promise. Especially considering the fact that her daddy knew damned well what she would be getting herself into if he caught her.

Let your daughter even attempt to steal what's mine, Manning, and I'll show her a party she'll never fucking forget.

Manning hadn't appeared too worried. He'd actually seemed rather amused. But then, only God knew what that horse-trading, calculating son of a bitch knew, or was up to.

A smiled slowly curved his lips as Angel pulled

herself into the house, her long black hair secured in a tight braid, her rounded little body poised cautiously like a doe in hunting season. Damn, she made his cock hard. Even during a spot of breaking and entering, pissing him off in the worst way, she turned him on.

Angel. Why anyone would name that bundle of carefully restrained fire and energy, Angel, he had no idea. One look into those dark-violet eyes, the first glimpse of wild, impetuous passion in her gaze, and it wasn't angels you were thinking about. It was wild steamy sex. Hot, naked, sweaty bodies tangled together as feminine cries of tortured pleasure echoed around your ears. That's what you thought about when you saw Angel. Hard, deep fucking. Watching her eyes widen, her body arch, the soft folds of her sweet little pussy stretching open as he impaled her with his steel-hard dick. That's what hit his mind.

He stood silent, motionless as she looked around the dimly lit room, obviously searching for the lights. Lights that weren't going to work for her. He had thrown the breaker the minute he realized someone was attempting to break in. God only knew who it could be. He had made several enemies over the past few years, none of whom he wanted to meet up with in a dark alley, or his normally well-lit home.

Now he only shook his head mentally. He was going to have to remind her that cat burglars did not turn on the lights. It was an arrest waiting to be made.

He may not have been expecting Angel, but damned if he didn't know what to do with her now that she was here. Jack wasn't a fool, and he knew she wasn't averse to his touch. But how easily would she settle into the more perverted hungers he could unleash on her? It might not be easy for her, he thought in satisfaction, but she would do it. He knew her, and knew jail wasn't an option for her.

He watched as she pushed her hand into the small satchel she wore at her hip. A second later he ducked as a beam of light swept across the room.

"Of course, he couldn't just make it easy for me, now could he? Damn him." Her voice was faintly accented, the soft Irish cadence stroking his flesh like a physical touch. He couldn't wait to hear her screaming his name.

No, he wasn't going to make anything easy for her. She had made certain of that the minute she attempted to steal from him. It didn't matter that she considered what he held hers. He had bought it in a fair deal, and though it meant little to him, Jack kept what he considered his. It was a lesson he had learned during a particularly nasty episode years ago. When a man faced death, things changed inside him, whether he wanted them to or not.

He shifted carefully, staying hidden in the corner, moving a bit to the left as the beam of light came too close. His naturally blond hair was covered by a dark, woolen cap. Blond hair was like a beacon in the dark and he wanted to hide, not make a target of himself.

She checked the room carefully before proceeding through the rest of the house. Jack stood back quietly and let her have at it, knowing there wasn't a chance she was going to find what she was looking for. He would let her look, though. Sooner or later she would have to head upstairs. When she did, he would make certain he was right behind her.

She wasn't in Ireland anymore. This was Texas, his home turf, his hometown, and she was about to learn he wasn't as easy to control as she might believe.

He shook his head. It shouldn't be so easy. He had actually been considering flying back to Ireland, his prized torque in hand to offer her, for the chance of bedding her. It wasn't as if prized Irish antiquities were his passion or anything. He'd liked the piece and when Manning had offered it to him, he'd intended to pass. The gold neckband had piqued his curiosity, but nothing more. Until Angel had deemed him unworthy of it. Furious. Commanding. She had stared up at him with those raging violet eyes and informed him in no uncertain terms that he had no right to it. That he was in no way good enough to possess it.

He had bought it then and there without even haggling over the price.

Now the pretty little sprite was out to steal it back. He would have chuckled if she weren't within hearing distance, cursing like a sailor and heaping insults on his ancestors. Damn, she had fire in her, she'd just been determined to hide it. A fire he was anticipating tapping quite soon.

Finally, he heard her near the stairs, her soft footfalls moving to the upper story before he moved. He stayed well behind her, moving up the staircase as she disappeared into the first bedroom. It would take her several minutes to check it well, which gave him plenty of time to slip past the closed door to his own room.

It was in his room that the torque rested, still packed in his luggage, nearly forgotten amid the rush and bustle of ranch life after he returned home that morning. His partner Luc had sold the last of the Clydesdale horses and taken up training mustangs for rodeos. The man was as mercurial as spring. The business seemed to change with the seasons where he and his new wife, Melina, were concerned. Not that they didn't make money. They did. But Jack never seemed to be certain if he was selling Clydesdales, mustangs, cattle, or dry Texas dust.

"Men should be neutered." The soft voice approached his bedroom as Jack flattened himself against the wall. "Jack Riley should be neutered. Too much testosterone making decisions for him."

Her soft mutterings were amusing, if insulting. He shook his head, watching as the bedroom door opened, the little penlight sweeping out in front of her as she stepped into the room.

Jack moved then. Silently, swiftly, he slid across the distance, coming behind her, his arms going around her, one hand locking at her throat as a frightened gasp left her lips.

"Testosterone can come in real handy at times, little girl." He pressed his hips against hers, grinding his erection against her lower back as his lips lowered to her ear, his teeth nipping at the silken lobe as he felt her tense in his hold. "Especially when it comes to punishing pesky little kitten burglars with smart mouths."

Oh hell! Angel stilled, tensed, feeling the thick wedge of Jack's erection pressing into the small of her back as his big hand circled her throat. And she should have been frightened. She should have been terrified and fighting for her life and she would have been, if she didn't know him so well. He was undoubtedly going to piss her off, but he wasn't going to hurt her. He wasn't going to let her go, either—the snug hold he had on her assured her of that.

"You're a goon, Jack," she snapped as her hands rose to the fingers locked on her throat.

The position tilted her head back, angling her head on his shoulder as his teeth played at her ear, sending shivers of pleasure racing over her flesh. And the sensation wasn't one she wanted to feel right now. She didn't want to become weak with arousal when she knew the man holding her wasn't the keeping kind.

"Oh, it's goon now?" he purred at her ear. "Not nearly as brave as you were moments ago, are you, sweet thing? I think the last insult I heard in Ireland was much better. Stinking dirty cowboy with an attitude." He snorted. "I do not stink, Angel-mine."

Angel-mine. He had called her that every time he caught her away from her father on the Manning estate in Ireland. The possessive tone had sent small flutters of pleasure attacking her stomach as an insidious weakness attacked her limbs. Just as it did now.

"I told you not to call me that," she retorted through gritted teeth as she strained against his hold. "Now let me go, dammit."

"Oh, I don't think I want to let you go, little Angel," he crooned at her ear, his tongue licking playfully at her lobe as an unbidden shudder raced through her body. "You've been a very bad girl. Stealing is against the law here, you know. Maybe we should give the sheriff a call."

Her eyes widened. He wouldn't. Surely, he wouldn't dare call the sheriff. If she was arrested for breaking and entering and attempted theft, it would ruin her father.

Not to mention what it would do to her. She would lose everything she had worked for in the past six years.

And her brothers would be positively horrified. Their careers would be ruined.

Surely he wouldn't.

"You wouldn't dare!" she gasped, unable to hold back the shocking thought that he would indeed.

"That's what we do in America, Angel-mine." His fingers stroked her throat as his teeth raked the sensitive flesh of her neck. "We put them in a cell and reporters crowd around for all those incriminating little pictures to flash in their trashy tabloids. It's all damned amusing while it's going on."

She heard the threat in his voice, but also a suggestiveness that had her eyes narrowing in suspicion.

"So what do you want in exchange for not calling the sheriff and the trashy tabloids, Jack?" Manipulative bastard; she knew he was up to something. And she knew she wasn't going to like it.

She felt his overnight beard rasp over her shoulder then. The prickly caress had her breathing in deep, fighting to maintain her composure as well as her sanity while pleasure threatened to swamp her.

"What do you have to bargain with?"

Bingo.

"You dirty bastard!" She twisted out of his hold, growing angrier at the thought that she had escaped him only because he allowed it.

Facing him in the dim light of the moon that pierced the thin curtains over the window, Angel clenched her fists at her side and stuck her chin out challengingly.

"I should have known ye wouldn't play fair," she

snapped. "Do ye expect me to trade sex for your silence? To believe you'd do anything so underhanded as have me arrested for attempting to reclaim my own property?"

"I bought it." He shrugged his broad shoulders, crossing his arms over his chest as his blue eyes gleamed from within his ruggedly dark face. "It's mine, Angel. Not yours."

"He had no right to sell that torque." She felt like throwing something at him. "It's mine."

"The papers he had said otherwise." He moved from the doorway, closing the door as he stepped over to the opposite wall.

Seconds later the lamps on the bed tables glowed to life, and she was certain the downstairs lights that previously didn't work were now blazing brilliantly, just as they had been the past two nights.

"His papers are a mockery." She faced him fully now, her lips thinning at the arrogance, the supreme male confidence that surrounded him like an aura.

His tilted grin was knowing, his stance—thumbs hooked in the pockets of his low-riding jeans, legs braced apart—was one of sexual assurance. He believed he had her exactly where he wanted her. Unfortunately, as much as she hated it, he might not be too far off the mark.

And as sad as it was to admit, he was turning her on. He had turned her on from the first moment she'd met him, had made her long for a touch she knew she shouldn't crave, a man she knew she couldn't hold.

He was like a wild wind, blowing in, ripping past defenses and tearing asunder denials, stroking with a devil's touch, only to blow away again, leaving what was left behind lost and broken. He would break her heart in just such a manner, if she allowed it.

"The papers are completely legal. I made certain of it, Angel-mine." His voice was a caress, stroking over her senses despite the male mockery in the tone. "They'll stand up in any court."

"You had no right to buy it, knowing it was to be left to me." And that hurt worse. That he had bought it, despite knowing that her father was selling it unfairly.

"If I hadn't bought it, someone else would have." Those wicked, wicked blue eyes stared back at her with a hint of laughter and a flame of arousal.

The very valid, logical argument did nothing to sway her.

"Then sell it back to me," she demanded roughly. "You've no need of it, Jack. The torque is nothin' to ya. It's everything to me."

She watched the frown that creased his brow as she faced him and prayed she was finally getting through to him. The man was such an enigma you could rarely tell what he was thinking. The most you could be certain of was that he was horny. She had rarely seen a time that the bulge in his pants wasn't fully engorged and stallion-hard.

"I doubt you would meet my price," he finally mused pensively. "And if you did, I'd be more than upset to realize how easily you could be had. How easily can you be had, Angel-mine?"

She flew at him. Teeth bared, nails extended, she went for those damned laughing eyes. The bastard dared to think she would whore herself for him. For anything. And in doing so, he blocked any desire she had to give in to him. Just as he had done when he bought the torque, placing between them obstacles that her pride could never surmount.

His laughter echoed in her ears as he caught her, swinging her around and holding her nearly immobile as he pressed her into the wall, her cheek pressing into the cool dry wall as she screamed out in impotent rage.

"I'll cut your devil's heart out of your chest," she snarled furiously. "Blackhearted, evil wretch. I'll gut ye myself."

"Bloodthirsty little vixen," he growled at her ear rather than releasing her. "If you had been a little less confrontational and demanding, you might have had the torque before I ever left Ireland. But you had to play the shrew instead."

He released her quickly, moving well away from her as she turned on him with rage in her eye.

"Ye say that now," she snapped heatedly. "But I know better. I did all but go to my knees and plead with you not to buy the piece."

She was breathing harshly, fighting not just her fury but also the unaccountable pleasure she had felt as he restrained her, held her immobile, and pressed his hard body into her own. Never had she known such weakening arousal and desire as she had each time he had done that.

"As I said, if I hadn't bought it, someone else would have. Your best chance was to convince me to sell it back to you before breaking into my home and attempting to steal from me. I don't like thieves, Angel."

"Ye should," she snarled. "Birds of a feather and so forth."

His eyes narrowed. "You're pushing your luck, baby."

"And I'm no' your babe." Her hands were clenched at her side, her nails biting into her palms. "Go ahead, ye coward, call your precious sheriff and have me arrested. Do your worst. I'd expect nothing less from a bastard such as yourself."

"You think that's my worst?" His voice was a rough growl, proof that she had finally pierced that amused exterior. Let him get angry. Damn him, it wasn't possible for him to become any angrier than she was herself.

"I think you're a coward with no more honor than an alley cat skulking through the shadows," she charged, heedless of the darkening of his eyes, the way his expression tightened. "Only a man with no honor would steal such an heirloom for the paltry price you paid, despite my pleas," she accused him rashly.

"I'm going to tan your hide." He lifted his lip in a snarl, his body tense, his eyes narrowing on her dangerously.

"I've no doubt you'll try," she sniped. "It sounds like something you'd attempt to cover your own shortcomings. Does it make ye feel like a big man, Jack Riley, to overpower little women? To show them who ye think is boss?"

She ignored the fact that it had turned her on like nothing she had ever known when he had done just that.

"Actually, it does." The smooth, dark tone should have warned her. She should have known better than to be taken in by his playboy image, his attitude of calculated disinterest. In that moment, she knew she had made a grave tactical error, and now she would pay for it.

SIX

"Now, there is a damned fine sight. Angel-mine, that has to be the prettiest little ass I've ever seen."

Angel screamed out furiously, the sound muffled by the black gag secured over her lips as she fought the strong hands that held her wrists behind her back as he stretched her over his lap.

She had fought him like a demon, attempting to rake his flesh with her nails, to kick out at him with her feet. He had laughed, a rough, sexy sound that she had liked entirely too much. And though fury raced hard and fast through her bloodstream, outrage that he would attempt to actually spank her rioting through her system, still, the flares of excitement were singing through her veins.

That didn't mean she had to let him live. No man would spank her and live to tell the tale. She was going to kill him. She was going to slice his heart out and feed it to the wolves. She would . . .

She screeched in humiliating surprise as his hand

landed on her upturned rump with a stinging little slap that was more startling than painful. And much too pleasurable. It wasn't supposed to be pleasurable. It was supposed to be humiliating. Infuriating. Painful. It wasn't supposed to tear into her womb and leave it convulsing in erotic hunger.

"Stay still," he ordered lazily. "Let me at least admire my handiwork here. If you're going to go to the trouble to spank a spoiled little witch, then you should at least have the pleasure of viewing the soft little ass you're reddening. I warned you, didn't I? Try to steal from me and I'd paddle your ass."

Her cheeks flamed in mortification as his hand smoothed over her nearly bare rump. What had possessed her to wear the silken little thong rather than the less-revealing panties she had packed as well? Sexy lingerie and playing cat burglar didn't go well together, but she realized, in one startling moment, that she had worn the softest, sexiest undergarments she possessed.

Bits of silk and lace she had bought months before, imagining how they would tempt the shadowy lover she often dreamed would come into her life. The one who would make her feel courageous enough to be a woman, to take what she hungered for, to live out the fantasies she admitted to only in the darkness of the night.

This wasn't one of her fantasies, but it was making her hotter than anything she could have envisioned.

Jack had managed to not only wrestle her across his knees, but to lower her pants as well, leaving her nearly bare to his lust-filled gaze. And she knew it was lust-filled. She could feel the heat of it stroking her bottom even as his fingers smoothed over it.

"You have the most delightful little ass," he crooned, the sound striking a bolt of pleasure straight to her cunt.

How she hated that response to him. Hated the knowledge that what he was doing to her was unlike anything she had known in her life, yet it was likely commonplace to him. A ragged whimper of shameful need escaped her lips at the admiring tone of his voice. She had never considered herself particularly pretty. She had rarely felt sexy or as sexual as she did at this moment.

She struggled against him again, fighting his hold, determined to break free before the dampness leaking from her pussy began to wet the dark silk of her panties. Before he realized the erotic pleasure she was gaining from her helplessness. Who could have known? Surely she hadn't imagined that such dominant extremes could destroy her defenses in such a way.

"Bad girl." He smacked her bare rump again, causing a throttled scream to tear from her chest. One she prayed he thought was no more than fury.

Velvet heat rushed through the warmed cheek of her ass and struck her pussy like a sword of erotic fire. Mercy, she screamed silently. Have mercy on the helpless pleasure tearing through her.

She wasn't a bad girl, but at his accusation she realized how much she wanted to be one. To be a wicked, wanton. To take him as she had only dreamed of taking a man before.

"Soft and sweet." His hand smoothed over the curves again. "Do you know what I'd like to do, Angel-mine? I'd like to put you on your knees, part these pretty curves, and watch my dick slide deep inside that tight little entrance to your ass."

Her eyes widened in shock as his words tore through her at the same time he delivered another heated strike to her ass. Her anus clenched, and her pussy began to drench her panties. Black silk panties that she knew would show the proof of her arousal.

Her breasts swelled instantly, her nipples hardening to the point of pain as he delivered another slap to the opposite side, heating her backside repeatedly as she began to shudder, to writhe in his grip.

She would not enjoy this, she screamed to herself as he continued to redden her rear, making it blush, making her entire body heat with the forbidden pleasure. And each second of it reminded her of his words, the image of him behind her, parting the cheeks of her ass and forcing his cock into the dark hole there.

She screamed as another blow landed, the sensations spearing deep inside her pussy, rioting through her clit until it became engorged with the need for release. Each heated strike to her rear had her twisting on his lap, common sense and sanity retreating further into the ether of lust as she began to moan in compliance, in desperate pleasure.

"Fuck!" She could hear the rough tone, almost awed, definitely surprised as he halted the erotic spanking, causing her to arch her back to lift her ass to him for more. She was so close—didn't he understand how close she was to attaining that final pleasure?

"Angel?" His voice was almost guttural as his fingers slid between her thighs, rasping against the black silk of her panties as she shuddered in ecstasy at the touch. "Oh, baby, you're so wet. So fucking hot and wet."

He moved then, lifting her from his lap, tearing the gag from her lips as he stood her before him.

Her legs were unsteady she swayed, staring down at him, shocked by her own body, by the weakness assailing her. If it weren't for his hands steadying her, she wondered if she would have melted into a puddle at his feet.

Dazed, she stared down into his gaze, wondering at the near blackness of his once blue eyes as she felt the fingers of one hand move once again between her thighs.

"Jack," she whispered, unable hold back the shudder that racked her limbs as his fingers smoothed over the sodden crotch of her panties once again. "Jack, please."

She pressed her hips forward, tilting them, gasping at the fiery sensations as his hand cupped her mound, his upper palm rasping against her clit and sending it rioting in extreme ecstasy.

"Such a naughty, wet little Angel," he whispered again, causing her pussy to spasm in greedy hunger as she felt his fingers move beneath the elastic leg band. "So wet . . ."

Like an erotic whisper, the pads of his fingers smoothed over the drenched curls as Angel felt the breath rush from her body. It wasn't hard enough; the touch was too soft, barely there. She needed more. Needed something harder, something hotter.

A second later her hands flew to his shoulders, gripping them in desperation as he began to part the tender, sensitive folds, his fingertips rubbing against nerve-laden flesh as she trembled violently. Waiting. Oh God, the waiting was killing her. She wanted him to rip the silk away from her body, feel his fingers plunging inside her, hard, fast, ripping away her sanity and throwing her into the endless abyss of pleasure that she could feel waiting just out of reach.

It was this that had drawn her to him during the weeks he had spent in Ireland. The naughty, wicked sexuality. The knowing glint in his eyes assuring her that she would find delights in his arms she had never known in another's. He was like a flame, and she was the moth, desperate to be burned.

Her lips parted, her mouth opening as she fought for breath, fought to keep her eyes open, her gaze locked with his as she felt his fingers, broad and callused, nearing the spasming entrance to her burning pussy. So close. She wanted them inside her, filling her . . .

"Jack . . ." The low keening cry echoed around them as her hips jerked, pressed closer, the honeyed, slick juices spilling from her cunt as his fingers paused, holding rapture just out of reach while she gasped in lust-crazed desperation.

"Fuck, this is insane!" His sudden curse was followed by the removal of his fingers from her burning flesh as he bent, grabbed the waist of her pants, and jerked them quickly back to her hips.

"No. Damn you! What are you doing?" She pushed at his hands, only to have him grip her hips as he rose, turning and pushing her to the bed.

"Not like this," he growled, breathing roughly as she steadied herself, staring up at him in shock. "Shit." He raked his fingers through his hair, watching her with a shocked expression she felt must mirror her own.

Angel blinked back, fighting to breathe, to make sense of the sudden shift from hungry passion, greedy lust, to being bereft of his touch.

"Stay put, damn you!" he ordered, his tone guttural as she moved to rise.

She shook her head, her eyes lowering, only to widen again as she realized how very close she was to the instrument of pleasure she needed so desperately. The bulge of his cock was only inches in front of her face, pressing against his jeans, the thick length clearly discernible beneath the material.

Dazed. Uncertain where her daring originated from, she reached out, her hand running over the hard ridge as his body tensed violently. A sizzling curse escaped his lips as his hand caught her wrist, the other gripping her chin to raise her head.

"Think about it," he snarled heatedly. "I'll fuck your mouth until you can't scream, can't whimper because you're so full of my dick. And when you think it will never stop I'll bury myself between those sweet lips and shoot every drop of my come down your throat. And it won't stop there, girl. I'll strip you down and fuck you so hard and deep you'll never forget the feel of me. Ever. Think about it, damn you, because once I have you—once I taste that sweet pussy or bury my dick inside you—I won't let you go until I own you. Body and soul, little witch. I'll own you. Make certain, very damned certain you can accept that before you try to accept me."

He had lost his mind. Jack raked his fingers roughly through his hair as he stalked down the stairs, ignoring Angel's furious screams as she pounded on the locked bedroom door, her enraged threats almost amusing.

There was no room for amusement inside him at the moment. His guts were ripped in half, every bone and muscle in his body hurting with the need to fuck the tempting little witch, to hear her screams of pleasure rather than those of fury.

What the hell had happened? He had meant only to teach her a lesson, to spank that tempting little ass hard enough to teach her a measure of respect. Instead, what he had meant to be a disciplinary action had turned into an erotic lesson in his own self-control. Something so fucking hot, he felt blistered from head to toe.

What had she done to him? Jack paused at the foot of the stairs, raking his fingers through his hair as he realized his hands were trembling. He could still smell the sweet, hot scent of her body. She smelled like honey, warm and slick, tempting the senses and reminding him of why he hadn't pushed the sexual boundary she had placed between them after that first kiss in Ireland: because he knew, one more taste—taste, nothing—one more touch and he was addicted.

He could feel it, that compulsion for more. The driving need to lay her on that bed and taste every creamy inch of her.

"Damn." He paced into the living room, twisting his head and shoulders as the furious screams above began to abate.

Walking away from her had been next to impossible. Turning away from the fiery, hot feel of her body had torn something apart deep inside him. He wanted to go back. He wanted to stalk into that bedroom, throw her to the bed, and drive his dick so hard and deep inside her that he couldn't tell where he ended and she began.

He grimaced painfully, one hand dropping to the heavy bulge beneath his jeans as the material bit at the sensitive flesh of his cock. A groan tore from his throat as pleasure whipped through his body.

"Son of a bitch," he cursed, throwing himself into the wide, heavily cushioned chair that sat beside the picture window.

He leaned his head against the back of the chair, breathing out roughly as he fought the nearly over-whelming impulse to go back upstairs. To finish what he had started. To take her, to hear her cries, her pleas, to feel her tight and hot around him. To let loose the con-trol he fought so hard to maintain, and for the first time in his life, to immerse himself in the woman he would have beneath him.

It was that damned torque's fault. Had he not bought it, had he ignored the stubborn challenge in Angel's eyes and let the piece be, then he wouldn't be in this situa-tion, he reminded himself. Hell, he didn't even like the damned thing. But he had known she did, and he had known that if he didn't buy it someone else would. Someone who wouldn't have made certain, in time, that it was hers again.

But he was also honest enough to admit that there wasn't a chance in hell he was going to walk away from it now. He had probed at Angel's guard the full two weeks he had stayed at her father's estate. Teasing her, tempting her, growing unreasonably aggravated by her cool demeanor of unresponsiveness. No other woman had ever tempted him as she had. He had known that even then and he had fought it. Angel was different, and he didn't want her to be. He wanted her to be like every other woman he had known in his life. Easy to walk away from. Easy to maintain his control with. There was going to be nothing easy about the confrontation rising between them now.

He should stalk upstairs, pull the bit of jewelry from his luggage, and just give the damned thing to her. It would belong to her then. She would have sole ownership of it, and he could have some peace.

And he would have, if she hadn't tried to steal from him. No, it wasn't even that. He stared at the ceiling in furious realization that he wouldn't return it to her simply because he knew if he did, she would walk away. There would be no further reason for her to stay. And he had no desire to have her leave.

"Jack Riley, you dirty, blackhearted bastard." Something crashed against the bedroom door as his lips kicked up in a grin.

Damn, she was a hellcat. And hotter than anything he had touched in his life.

He breathed out roughly, wearily.

Something inside him warned that if he took her, if he let himself touch her again, then it would be the greatest mistake of his life. But Jack knew himself well enough to know that he wouldn't leave her alone long.

SEVEN

Dawn was nearing when Jack finally made his way from the guest room he had slept in through the early hours of the morning. He unlocked the door quietly, opening it slowly as he stepped into the room.

He throttled the groan that threatened to escape his chest at the sight that met his eyes. This was not a sight designed to aid a man in keeping his control. To the contrary, it was like adding fuel to the flames.

She was stretched out in his bed, wearing nothing but the little black thong and a silk-and-lace bra that cupped the full, creamy mounds of her breasts in a wicked, erotic frame. Long, slender legs were slightly parted; a graceful hand lay on her slightly rounded abdomen. Long, black curls framed her sleeping face, and her soft pink lips parted as she breathed in and out in relaxed slumber.

His cock hadn't abated through the night, despite the hour he had spent jacking off before he got out of his bed. A frown creased his brow as he felt a spurt of anger rising inside him. In Ireland she had taunted him with a cool facade, teased him with her haughtiness, and then attempted to steal from him. She had kept him erect, hot, and out of sorts for weeks, and he was trying to be a gentleman?

His fears from the night before, his knowledge that taking her would somehow change him, receded beneath the arousal twisting his guts in knots. God, he wanted her. He could see clearly, imagine with a realism that shocked him, the sight of her on her knees, dressed in nothing but silk and lace, her lips surrounding his cock, sucking him to her throat, creating a fire inside him that would burn out of control.

He shook his head, fighting it, fighting his own arousal.

"Rise and shine, Angel-mine." He moved to the bed, gripping her slender ankle and pulling at it firmly as she jackknifed in the bed.

A frown pulled immediately at her brows as fire shot through her gaze.

"Take your hands off me, toad," she snapped, jerking her ankle from his grip as she pushed the thick strands of black hair away from her face.

"Such a sweet disposition," he chastised her mockingly as he stood by the bed, staring down at her. "Get out of bed." He bent, picking up her clothing and tucking it beneath his arm as he grinned down at her. "You can wear one of my T-shirts while I wash your clothes. I'll see about having you a few things delivered today to wear. Be a good girl now and get cleaned up for breakfast."

"Excuse me?" she snapped, scrambling across the bed as she attempted to jerk her clothing from him. "Give those to me. I won't be staying here so I'll no need you to get me anything."

"Tsk-tsk, Angel-mine." He shook his head in reprimand as he held her clothing out of reach. "Remember the sheriff? The pesky tabloids? We'll discuss this over coffee and food. But I think you might want to reconsider your position here. Jail can be a very bad place."

She pulled back, wondering how serious he was. The one thing she had learned about him while he was in Ireland was that he could be counted on to keep his word. If he set his mind on having her arrested, she had no doubt he would.

The fury of the night before had receded beneath not just her normal common sense, but also the arousal he had fired inside her. But that didn't mean she would immediately bow to whatever his arbitrary rules would be. There were other ways of fighting this battle. Jack Riley did not hold all the cards as he believed he did. She wasn't the only one who had been caught in the web of lust and pleasure the night before. He, too, had burned, and she knew it.

Narrowing her eyes, she allowed her gaze to rake over him. From his darkened blue eyes, lower to the heavy bulge beneath his jeans. She could feel her pussy throbbing, her breasts swelling as the memory of the night before whipped through her head. His touch, his fingers parting the folds of her cunt, rubbing against the entrance to her weeping vagina. There had been a lesson to be learned in those all-too-brief moments when he had touched her. Some pleasure was so extreme that it wasn't worth losing. Never had she known such intensity. Such promise of more to come. She wanted, needed more. As though his kiss, his touch was a drug that was rapidly becoming addictive.

She leaned back, propping her weight on her elbows as she watched his gaze flare at the way this pushed her breasts forward prominently. She loved that look in his eyes, and even though she highly distrusted him emotionally, she had been unable to stem the arousal he could spark inside her.

"Very well." She shrugged. "Rather than buying me clothing, ye could just have my things collected from the motel in town. I'm sure that would much easier on ye."

His eyelids lowered, his gaze raking over her body, centering on her thighs. The rapidly moistening folds beneath the silk began to pulse in excitement. Her clit was like a living flame, burning out of control with her hunger to feel his mouth suckling at it, his tongue moving around it. She had a feeling she had never truly known lustful pleasure, but that this man could teach her much about it.

"You're playing with fire, Angel," he told her then, his voice deepening, roughening. "You may find that what you're asking for is much more than you can handle."

She rolled her eyes. "Americans are so dramatic," she sighed. "Do you delight in the warnings? Do they bring you some measure of heightened pleasure? Or do you just enjoy the theatrics?"

His blue eyes flared at the challenge. Sensuality covered his face, giving him a darker, more wicked demeanor than ever before. She had never known an

American lover, she admitted. The few men she had allowed in her bed were cool, well-bred Englishmen who performed between the sheets in the same manner that they performed in public. Coolly. With dignity. With very little excitement. Were all American men like her captor?

"You're asking for trouble," he growled.

Her fingers played, with apparent nonchalance, against the flesh of her abdomen, mere inches from the elastic band of the thong as she sighed with mocking patience.

"Very well, Jack. I will don your pitiful excuse for clothing and come down for breakfast." She rose on the bed, moving slowly as she swung her legs over the side and stood up, watching him, her gaze locked with his as he stood silent, merely staring back at her.

The move placed her much closer to him, mere inches from the heat of his body as his eyes darkened, heated sensually. The look had her breathing accelerating, her mouth drying out in anticipation. There was a message in that look, one that backed up his previous warning that she was playing with fire.

"Any particular shirt I should wear?" She tilted her head, keeping her voice soft and suggestive as she moved away from him, deliberately turning to give him a view of her naked buttocks while she walked to the chest across the room.

She made it perhaps a few feet before his hand wrapped around her upper arm, bringing her to a stop.

She turned, staring at him over her shoulder, her brow lifting in a haughty demand despite the dark sexuality that covered him like an aura.

"Tell me, Angel-mine," he whispered then. "Do you have any idea of the dirty little games men can play with soft flesh like yours?"

She licked her dry lips. No, she had no idea, but she was curious about the games he could play.

"You wouldn't hurt me," she finally whispered. "Others might, but you wouldn't."

His expression was almost savage now. His cheekbones seemed higher, sharper, his lips fuller, more sensual than before as he watched her broodingly.

"And you know this how?" His fingers tightened on her arm as his expression darkened with some undefined emotion. It was gone so quickly that she couldn't analyze or decipher it, but the shadow of it ran deep.

"If you were going to hurt me, you would have finished what you started last night, Jack," she whispered then. "I trust ye with my body. I would trust ye in what ye call yer dirty little games." She gave a sad smile. "But I would know better than to ever trust ye with my heart."

It was there again, that shadow of emotion. For a moment, bleak, almost overwhelming pain flashed in his eyes before it disappeared once again.

Angel felt her heart trip in dread, felt her chest expand and ache with the need to soothe something she was certain he would never let her see. Why would her declaration that she could never trust him with her heart hurt him? It was apparent it had.

"And you think your heart is so safe, little Angel?" he asked her, the curve of his lips mocking, almost a sneer as he stared down at her. "What makes you think I couldn't make you love me?"

She turned to him, moving her hands until they were

braced against the warmth of his cloth-covered chest, feeling the hard thump of his heart as it battered against the flesh there.

"Would ye want me to love ye, Jack Riley?" she asked him, a wry smile tilting her lips. "If I would risk your ire, and your justice system, to steal back a mere torque I feel is mine, what more would I do to punish one who stole my heart and broke it heedlessly?" Her hands caressed him subtly, moving against him with slow, sensual strokes. "Were you not the one who called me a blackhearted witch with no more sense than to cut my nose off to spite my face? Trust me, Jack, I would cut off the cock of any man stupid enough to steal my emotions and toss them away as though they were no more than trash from the day before. Believe that one well before you make the mistake of taking up a challenge I have not yet offered."

One hand retained its grip on her other arm, and it was joined then by his hand at her opposite hip, his fingers cupping it, drawing her closer as his head began to lower.

Angel felt her heart slam in her chest, her mouthwatering with the sudden need, the anticipation of the kiss she was so longing to taste. Her tongue flicked out to dampen her lips, her eyes widening as a throttled growl of hunger left his chest.

"You just have me shaking in my boots," he whispered, no more than a breath from her lips as she fought to hold her eyes open, to catch the flash of emotions that flared in the dark centers of his gaze. "Trust me, baby, it's not your heart I want. So if you lose it, you do so at your own risk. Now, that sweet, hot little pussy is another matter . . . After breakfast."

Angel was beginning to believe that American men were all tease and no true intent. Twice. Twice Jack had pulled away from her. Was it her willingness to have him that made him draw back? Her mother had always said that men wanted a challenge, not a willing sacrifice.

She brooded over that thought through breakfast in the large kitchen, sitting at the table and staring outside the window to the bleak Texas landscape beyond and sipping the after-breakfast coffee Jack had provided.

She had no time for games. She was never a game player, especially not in any relationship she had ever conducted. She pouted silently. She was now ready to merely go home. It was evident Jack was not going to give up the torque, no matter how she pleaded. And what proof would he have that she had broken into his home with the intent to steal it? There was little he could truly do unless she was honest with the law enforcement officials. Who said she had to be honest?

She sighed in disgust. She hated liars. Of course, as insane as she was, she would have to be honest. Besides, she was a lousy liar. Her father had always known when she was attempting to cover the truth with him.

"My coffee doesn't taste that bad." His rumbling voice drew her from her thoughts as she turned her head and watched him sit once again in the chair across from her.

"It could stand to be a bit stronger, but it's fair." She shrugged her shoulders. The coffee really didn't matter.

He leaned back in his chair, his expression thoughtful.

"You're too quiet," he said. "What are you up to?"

She rolled her eyes. Why did men always think that silence from a woman was a direct insult or possible threat to them?

"Nothing." She lifted her cup to her lips, sipping the dark liquid before returning it to the table. "I was merely wondering how long you intend to force my presence here in your home."

He lifted a dark-blond brow mockingly.

"I didn't invite you here, or force you here, darlin'," he drawled. "You arrived of your own free will."

"And I am now ready to leave," she informed him coolly. "I came, I failed. The torque, as you say, is fairly yours. I should have heeded my better sense rather than my emotions in coming here."

It was a bitter disappointment, losing that torque. Legend held that as long as it stayed within the bloodlines it was created for, then happiness and true love would come to that family. Her mother had known such a marriage. Her parents had loved each other deeply, so deeply there was little left for the children who lived in their shadow.

"Maybe I'm not ready to let you go." His expression was once again shuttered, brooding.

Mockery twisted her smile. "You can't keep me here forever, Jack. I have a life and a job to return to soon. I'm certain that matters little to you, but other than the torque you purchased from my father, it's all that matters to me."

A smile quirked his lips. "You need to widen your

horizons, darlin'. A woman needs more than just a career to keep her warm at night."

"I have an electric blanket. It works quite well and bitches much less," she responded drolly. "What more could a woman want?"

"An orgasm?" he questioned in amusement.

"My vibrator does the job." She lifted her shoulders in a shrug. Men were so insane.

"Hmm," he murmured. "Well, we'll let you get back to your vibrator and your blanket eventually. Until then, I think it's my duty to punish you for your criminal activities. I mean, hell, I let you get away with this, only God knows what you'll attempt next. Bank robberies, assault—the list goes on and on. I think someone needs to teach you the error of your ways."

She would have laughed if his high-handed mocking attitude didn't spark a flame to a temper already out of sorts. The fact that her mother had always said Angel only raged at those she loved was just a distant memory. She'd been a girl then, not a woman.

"Excuse me?" She drew herself rigidly erect as offended fury began to fill her. "And what makes you think I'll allow you to be my judge and jury in this matter? You know what that torque means to me, Jack."

He grimaced with mocking sobriety. "Sorry, sweetheart. It's me or jail."

"It's your word against mine," she reminded him furiously.

"Yeah, but the sheriff is a real good friend of mine," he pointed out. "Hell, we're almost family. I think he'll believe me over you."

This was a nightmare.

He looked entirely too confident, too superior for her to doubt his word. Of course the sheriff would believe him over her. Small towns in America would be no different than in Ireland. It would make no sense if they were.

"So much for American justice," she harrumphed. "So how much longer do you intend to hold me prisoner here?"

He tilted his head, watching her with a thoughtful, considering expression. "Oh, I don't know. How long do you think it will take you to learn your lesson?"

Angel snorted. As though she would attempt to deal with an American again. "Five minutes after I realized you were aware of my presence?"

The expression on his face assured her he wasn't falling for that one.

"Fine, Jack, you're going to punish me." She waved her hands dramatically. "So what exactly do you have in mind? Scrubbing floors? I can do it well enough. Where should I start, me lord?"

She allowed her accent to thicken, her expression to become disdainful. Damn man. "You'll definitely be on your knees," he growled then, his gaze filling with infuriating male arrogance. "But it's not the floors you'll have your attention on, woman. Rather, my dick. So open wide and get ready to suck."

Before Jack was even aware of his own intentions he was out of his chair and pulling Angel into his arms. That smart mouth and haughty air made him crazy. It made his cock so damned hard he wondered how he managed to contain it beneath his jeans. It should have been bursting through the material and aiming directly at that hot little pussy between her thighs.

"Jack, you wouldn't dare . . ."

He broke the exclamation by the simple means of covering her lips with his own. His head tilted, slanting over those pouty curves as he pressed home his advantage and speared his tongue between her lips.

She was one of the most infuriating, aggravatingly smart-assed women he knew. She was also the softest, sweetest bit of female he had ever taken in his arms. Her gasp against his lips inflamed his lust, the way her body tensed and shuddered, the obvious fight to hold back the response he could feel trembling through her.

Her hips jerked against his, the soft pad of her pussy tilting to accept the pressure of his cock as he bent his knees to drive it against her.

There was that little gasp again. Shock and pleasure as her tongue tangled tentatively with his, as though she were wary of her response to him. But he could feel the flames burning inside her, reaching out to him, heating his own hunger.

What was it about this woman? His little thief. If he wasn't careful, she would attempt to steal more than just the torque she came looking for; she would steal a part of him he had sworn no other person would ever hold.

His arms wrapped around her, one going around her shoulders as his fingers tangled in the soft weight of her witchy black hair. A fine payment for the slender fingers clenched in his own now, holding him still against her as she allowed him to eat at her lips.

She was as sweet as sugar, as hot and spicy as a ripe

cayenne. He had always been partial to the little fire-hot peppers, and even more so now. She was a temptation, a challenge; everything about her dared a man to tame her, to take her, to find the nasty, sexual creature lurking behind that innocent, too-cool gaze.

He would find that woman.

He lifted his head, staring down at her, feeling some emotion clench his chest as she stared up at him in equal parts dismay and arousal.

"On your knees," he whispered then, dying inside, craving the feel of her lips around his tortured cock in a way he couldn't explain, even to himself.

She stared back at him, her expression such a challenge that it had every bone and muscle in his body clenching.

"And if I don't?" she whispered, obviously, deliberately pushing him.

"Then I tie you down and see just how long I can tease and tempt that pretty little body. And how long it takes you to beg me to let you on your knees before I put out the fires both of us know I can stoke inside you, baby."

She seemed to think about that one for a moment before a mocking little smile of submission crossed her lips.

He got more than he bargained for.

Standing in the middle of the Mexican-tiled kitchen, the rays of the sun sending shafts of fire washing over his body, he watched as slender, graceful fingers began to loosen the buttons of his shirt.

"Straight to my knees?" she asked him as her violet eyes darkened in response to his warning growl. "Or may I play in between?"

What was that little warning at the back of his brain? The one screaming at him to get her the hell away from him, out of his home, out of his life?

Whatever it was, he didn't want to hear it.

He didn't want to hear anything but that pleased little murmur that escaped her lips as she spread his opened shirt back from his chest. Her face flushed, her eyes nearly black as she lowered her head to lick at the skin teasingly.

Jack had to grit his teeth to keep back the groan that would have escaped. He allowed his hands to hang loosely at his sides, wondering how far she would go. How brave she would get.

She licked her way across the expanse of suntanned flesh to a hard, flat male nipple. He expected no more than a perfunctory little lick. What he got instead had his fingers clenching into fists as he fought for control.

Those sharp little teeth of hers raked against his nipple slowly as her hot, wicked tongue licked over it. Flickering flames danced across his skin, scouring his nerve endings and causing his cock to jerk in painful need.

He stared down at her, entranced by the apparent enjoyment she was receiving from touching him. One hand moved lower along his side to the tense flesh of his abdomen as the other tweaked and caressed the mate to the nipple she was tormenting with slow strokes of her tongue and gentle nips of her teeth.

He had never known how sensitive his own nipples could be. It was a vaguely disconcerting feeling, that tingle of awareness that shot straight to his balls and tightened them painfully.

Then those wicked, mischievous lips moved across his chest to the small nipple her fingers had tormented with such insidious heat. He was going to explode, he thought in surprise. Surprise, because he had never known a time when a woman hadn't gone straight for his dick, or hadn't demanded a romantic, deeply involved kiss before going down.

Women were strange creatures, but he could always count on those two rules to remain steadfast and true. Until now. Now one small bit of Irish fluff was blowing all he had known straight to hell and burning him alive in the bargain.

She licked, kissed, and stroked his chest. Her tongue painted circles around his nipples as her teeth scraped erotically against the hair-spattered flesh. Sweet heaven, her mouth was hot. If she managed to make it to his cock, he would burn in the inferno.

"You're so hard, so warm," she whispered as her lips began to ghost along his tense stomach. "I can feel your muscles just under the skin. They feel so powerful. So strong."

She bit into the hard flesh of his upper stomach, and his head fell back with a groan. Son of a bitch, his knees were even growing weak.

He reached out, his fingers burying in her hair, intending to halt her play, until he felt her fingers at the buckle of his belt. He had to fight to keep from trembling like a weak-kneed greenhorn. Dammit to hell, she was destroying him, her fingers moving at a snail's pace as she tracked each corded muscle of his abdomen with her destructive mouth and heated tongue.

And for all the protests against allowing her to continue his mind was throwing out, she was delaying his pleasure—hell, no, she was accelerating it to a depth he could have never imagined. He had demanded a blow job, not a damned map made with her tongue across his flesh, but what pleasure that seemingly aimless journey was creating.

He stared down at her, seeing her on her knees now, just as he demanded, her hands parting his jeans, pulling them lower, revealing, inch by thick hard inch, the erection straining beneath it.

He expected her to devour it. To take it in her mouth and begin the hard, fast suckling that would have the event quickly finished. Hell, this was one time he wanted nothing more than to release the pressure building in his balls.

But did she know that?

Was she kind enough to do as any other of her sex would have done?

No.

"Fuck!" Thighs were not supposed to be fucking sensitive. Son of a bitch.

Her teeth raked over the inner flesh before her lips opened, pulling a bit of the skin into her mouth for a heated caress.

Once again, her mouth was an aimless destroyer, moving from one thigh to the other, licking and stroking, destroying him as he felt his legs shake. Yes, his fucking legs were shaking. So what? What man's legs wouldn't shake with such beauty worshipping something so seemingly undeserving as the sensitive flesh of his thighs?

"Witch!" His strangled groan surprised him, but the liquid heat washing over his balls shocked him more.

Almost timid now, searching, learning, her tongue moved over the tight sac, probing at it, circling the hard spheres beneath the flesh before she gently, tenderly sucked one into her mouth, tonguing it like a favorite treat.

Pre-cum spurted from the tip of his cock, running in a silken trail down the throbbing shaft as she tortured him with her mouth. And it was fucking torture.

Lightning bolts, whipping fingers of white-hot heat shot through his body, searing nerve endings and curling his toes inside his boots as she began to lick at the creamy trail of liquid that had escaped the pulsing crest of his erection.

She moaned in pleasure, as though his taste pleased her.

The woman was fucking crazy.

His hands tightened in her hair as he watched her unman him. Bit by bit she was ripping away his preconceived notions of a head job and replacing them with pure, undiluted ecstasy.

"So hard and hot." The thick Irish accent had to be the sexiest sound he had ever heard in his life. "Throbbin' as though it has a heartbeat all its own."

He would have replied. He was certain he could have found some kind of smart-assed mocking comment drifting around in his mush-head if she hadn't chosen that moment to envelop him in the dark, lava-hot depths of her silken mouth.

His abdomen convulsed. He could feel his balls tightening further, drawing close to the base of his cock as warning fingers of impending release scraped up his spine. Her mouth . . . God help him if he thought another man had known such pleasure from that mouth . . . it was making him crazy. He felt like howling with the sensations.

Instead, a broken groan tore from his chest as he thrust in deeper, feeling her tongue caress the sensitive underside, her lips tightening on him, her mouth drawing on him.

Hell, yes! A rebel cry was building in his head. "Fuck, yeah. Suck me, baby. Suck my cock . . ."

His hands held her head in place as he stared down her, meeting the pitch black of her eyes as he watched his cock shuttle between her stretched, reddened lips. Her cheeks were flushed bright, her eyes glowing, his dick glistening with the moisture from her mouth.

She sucked him, all right. Her tongue twisted around the head, probed at the underside, flattened and stroked while she moaned. The sounds of her pleasure vibrated against the crest as he pushed it nearly to her throat, feeling her fingers caress the rest of the shaft as her honeyed mouth sucked him to his destruction.

Then the fingers of her hand became a devilish instrument of erotic devastation. They began to play with the tight sac below, cupping and caressing, nails raking as he fucked against her lips with a hunger he knew he would never forget, no matter how long or how hard he might try. Her mouth, lips, tongue played in harmony, drawing on the tortured flesh of his cock as her fingers tortured other areas. He could feel the warning tingles of impending release. Knew there were only seconds, no more, before he erupted.

"Angel . . ." He groaned her name. He couldn't, wouldn't spill his seed into her mouth without her permission, without her knowledge. "I'm going to come, dammit. Stop now, or you're going to get something you might not want."

"Mmm . . ." Her mouth tightened and her stroking fingers moved faster as she sucked at him harder.

Destruction.

He gritted his teeth as his head fell back and he felt his release explode through his system. The white-hot flares of pleasure exploded through his body, tightening his muscles, his bones, sending a cry of near pain past his lips as he felt the semen shoot from the tip of his cock to the depths of her mouth. The stroking, swallowing, taking-every-damned-drop-of-his-cum mouth.

He could feel her cries, echoing from her throat to his erection. Aroused, hot little sounds that sent his blood pressure soaring back to the boiling point.

Not yet, he cursed viciously, his head lowering, his eyes opening to stare down at her as he eased his still hard flesh from her lips.

"Jack?" She whispered his name, the sound echoing with her own arousal, her own needs.

Hell. What had he done? What had she released inside him? He could feel an unnamed, unknown emotion riding on the back of the pleasure still pulsing through him, one that intensified not just his lust, but his pleasure as well.

"Witch," he whispered again. "Hot, seductive little witch. I'm going to fuck you until you scream for mercy . . ."

EIGHT

Angel gasped breathlessly, anticipation rising hot and hard inside her as Jack pulled her ruthlessly to her feet. Staggering, she cursed her weak knees and the arousal blistering through her body. She wanted to climb him, to wrap her arms around his neck, her legs around his hips and ride. What was that saying? Save a horse, ride a cowboy? Oh yeah, she could definitely adopt that sentiment as her own.

Never had she done anything so erotic in her life. The sheer sensual sexuality of the act she had just performed left her dazed, her body throbbing in agonized arousal. Every nerve ending, every cell was screaming out for relief, for release.

"Come on." He took only the briefest moment to secure the snap of his jeans before he impossibly, surprisingly, lifted her into his arms and headed for the stairs. The world tilted on its axis as her arms wrapped around his neck, her lips moving for the strong, tanned column of his neck. She needed the taste of him, any part of him. Strong, heated, all male, it was an aphrodisiac she wondered if she was now addicted to.

"Little witch," he growled as he started up the stairs. "Keep that up and we'll never make it to the bedroom."

Who the hell cared? The stairs suited her fine.

Her teeth scraped his neck, her tongue stroking the tough skin as her hands buried in his hair to hold his head in place. She wanted more of him, now. She gripped the flesh between shoulder and neck, gripping the tough muscle there with her teeth as she began to draw on it erotically. God, he just tasted too damned good.

"Son of a bitch!" He stumbled against the wall, breathing in harshly as a hard shudder racked his body. "Woman, I'm going to fuck you on the stairs if you don't stop that."

Good. She wasn't alone. She was horny and ready now. Readier than she had been for the tough American who had invaded her life, possessed her torque, and now possessed the very essence of her pleasure.

"I'm game if you are," she whispered against his ear as her lips lifted from his neck, her tongue curling over the lobe of his ear.

"I'm going to paddle your ass," he grunted as he continued to the bedroom. "And not in a good way, Angelmine."

Her womb clenched at the very thought of another of those erotic spankings. As though he could do anything more sinister. The sound of his voice did not lend itself to a painful beating, but rather to a sensual firestorm of pleasure.

"Any paddlin' you gave, cowboy, would be no less than pleasure." She smiled up at him as he placed her on the bed, staring down at her intently.

Her breasts were swollen, pressing against the T-shirt demandingly as her nipples rasped against the material. Below, her pussy was a rioting, gluttonous heat that pulsed and wept in hunger.

She licked at her suddenly dry lips as he began to strip. First the white shirt, revealing the powerful muscles of his chest and shoulders. Sitting on the bed, he pulled his boots from his feet, tossing them carelessly to the floor with his socks before rising again and jerking his jeans loose. Seconds later he stood before her, completely naked, a sun-bronzed warrior, a sensual conqueror.

His rampant erection stood straight out from his body, a heavy, sensual weapon intent on impalement.

"Take off the shirt."

His voice was a rough growl, sending tingles of sensation rioting over her flesh.

She sat up on the bed, removing her shirt slowly, watching him from beneath lowered lids as one broad hand circled the shaft of his cock and began stroking it lazily.

It was a mouthwatering sight. That lovely, pleasure-giving cock, the dark stalk, the purplish crested head, the pre-cum glistening at the tip. She licked her lips slowly.

"Now the bra."

She unclipped the bra, discarding it slowly, panting for breath.

"Lie back." He moved closer to the bed, his eyes

heavy-lidded, his lips heavy with lust. He looked like a dark, lustful warrior. A man determined and willing to take what he wanted. To give what he knew she craved.

How could he know what she craved? How had he tapped into a hunger, a need that even she had been un-aware of until now?

Angel lay back on the bed, her breath rough, ragged as he stopped at the mattress. "Take off the panties," he whispered. "Slowly."

Slowly. She smoothed her hands over her abdomen, allowing them to meet at the silken band just above the rise of her aching pussy. Her thumbs hooked in the elas-tic as she peeled the material over her hips with excru-ciating hesitancy.

Tension thickened the air, burning her lungs with the incredible, sexual heat.

Jack watched every move, his gaze intent as the pan-ties passed over the swollen folds of her aching pussy, down her thighs, until she was able to move her legs to aid in discarding the last shield between her and his eyes.

She lay still beneath his regard then, fighting back the whimpers of anticipation as he watched her.

"How pretty." His voice was a hard rumble. "Spread your legs for me, Angel. Let me see paradise."

Angel shuddered, the sensual blow to her womb nearly kicking her into climax. A man should not have such power over a woman that his voice and gaze alone could cause such a response.

She opened her thighs slowly, her hands smoothing up them, framing the mound of her pussy as he placed one knee on the bed, his cheeks flushed a brick red as he watched her hands.

She watched, entranced, as his head lowered.

"Open yourself for me," he demanded roughly. "Part that pretty pussy for me, Angel-mine."

She whimpered, shocked that the hungry mewl had actually come from her throat. Her fingers moved, parting the swollen, sensitive folds as he hovered over her.

"Oh God, Jack . . ." She breathed the small prayer for mercy as he blew a waft of breath over her throbbing clit, sending the hot juices flowing freely from her vagina.

He bent over her as she watched, her eyes widening, the breath halting in her throat until she felt the rapid, fierce strike against her aching clit. The sweep of his tongue was like wildfire, sending her hips arching closer to his mouth as a strangled scream erupted from her throat. Another hot lash and she was twisting beneath him, her knees bending, feet pressing into the mattress as she lifted closer.

"Stay still." His hand landed on the open flesh of her cunt.

Shock resounded through her. She felt the explosion trigger in her clit, setting off fireworks in her pussy then in her womb as her orgasm took her by surprise. A strangled scream of rapture tore past her throat as she pressed her head into the pillow, her eyes closing as she shuddered through the extraordinary pleasure.

"Jack . . ." She still ached. She was empty, burning.

"Oh, baby, how greedy that little pussy is."

She realized then that she was still holding herself

open for him, giving him a clear view into the spasming opening to her vagina.

He moved slowly between her thighs.

"We can play later." He lifted her hands, holding her by the wrists as he lay them by her head. "Stay there. Stay real still, baby, and I'll see about feeding that hungry little cunt."

God, he looked so wicked. With his long hair hanging around his face, those dark-blue eyes glittering beneath the lowered eyelids, his lips fuller, more sensual than before. He resembled the wicked, sexual dream vision she had lusted after for so many years. The one that came to her only in the dead of night, his features hidden, only the gold torque encircling his neck a familiar sight to her.

And how she longed to see that torque there now. Gleaming dully against his sun-rich flesh as he made a place for himself between her legs.

Her gaze went lower, her mouth drying at the thick length of his cock as he paused, kneeling between her thighs, watching her, driving her insane with the wait.

"Lift to me," he growled. "Raise your hips for me."

She did as he commanded, bracing her feet against the blankets and lifting her drenched pussy for the stretching she knew was coming. Her previous lovers hadn't been exactly endowed, but Jack had taken more than his fair portion in that department.

He gripped the steel-hard flesh, running the thickly crested head through the honey-rich slit before it.

"Fuck, you're hot," he groaned as he tucked it at her opening. "Hot and wet and so very, very greedy."

"Oh God, Jack, have mercy." Her hands fisted in the blankets beneath her as the head began to press into her. Her head thrashed, stars glittering behind her closed eyelids as she felt him separating her, slowly, so very slowly she thought she would die from it.

"You're so tight, Angel-mine," he whispered as he gripped her behind the thighs, holding her in place as the smooth flesh of his cock began to pierce her. "So tight and sweet, it's enough to make a grown man cry in pleasure."

Her head tossed, her eyes fluttering as she fought to keep them open, fought to watch the slow impalement of her cunt.

She couldn't watch. She could only feel. Her eyes dazed and lifted to his, her body bowed, tension tightening it to a near breaking point as she felt him slowly, oh so very slowly, working his cock past the tight, tender tissue of her pussy.

"Ye'll kill me . . ." She was aware of the thickening of her accent, but could do nothing for it.

"Fuck. Stay still, woman," he growled as she twisted against him. "You're so fucking tight I'm going to lose control any minute."

Yes, she wanted that. Needed it.

"I'll never survive this pace," she cried out, frustration eating her alive. "For pity's sake, Jack. Fuck me. Fuck me or kill me, whichever ye've decided to do. But do it right quick. No' this slow."

"But I like slow, baby." His hands tightened beneath her legs. "Slow and tight, feeling every sweet muscle in that tight little pussy gripping my cock."

His expression was a grimace of pleasure and arousal.

A frustrated, agonized moan slipped past her throat as he filled her more. Mere inches, stretching her so deliciously, heating her, sending her blood pressure to the boiling point as she endured a pleasure never before imagined.

She couldn't take it. She needed more. Needed him deep and hard inside her.

She clenched around the portion of his cock that was there. Stroking it with her inner muscles as she fought for an anchor in the tumultuous storm overtaking her. There had to be something, some way to at least hold on to her sanity. What minute portion of it he had left her with at this point.

She knew the slow, fierce digs into her cunt were driving her past sanity. She needed to be filled, not teased to death.

"You're a demon, Jack Riley," she accused him harshly as he kept his hesitant, teasing pace. "A torturous, arrogant demon."

"And you're a witch. A black-haired, violet-eyed, hottest-fucking-pussy-I've-been-in witch," he groaned, sinking in deeper as she gritted her teeth and fought to hold back the cry that escaped against her will.

"Son of a bitch, Angel . . ." The desperate curse heralded a sudden hard push that gave her more. Then more.

"Yes. Oh yes, Jack. All of it. I need it all." She was gasping, fighting to press closer, to feel every inch stretching her wide.

Until he pulled back.

Baring her teeth in a snarl, Angel arched then forced herself forward, her hands gripping his shoulders as she came astraddle his hard thighs, then forced herself onto the hard wedge of male muscle tormenting her.

Her keening cry echoed in the air around her as she felt him fill her, the head butting into her very cervix as her teeth gripped his shoulder like an animal in heat. His hard hands now gripped her buttocks, clenching in the soft flesh there as she felt his cock throbbing hard and heavy inside her.

Her knees clasped his thighs, her feet pressing into the mattress as she began to ride her cowboy. Moving up until only the crest remained inside her hungry pussy before sliding back down in an erotic dance that had the breath slamming from her throat and pleasure overwhelming her.

"Save a horse, ride a cowboy," she whispered before nipping his ear and clenching on the invader with a tight, caressing grip.

She wasn't anticipating his reaction.

Before she could do more than gasp he was moving. He slammed her back on the bed at the same time his cock slammed into her pussy and he gave her what she had been pleading for. Hard, driving, fierce strokes that drove her headlong into the storm swirling within her body.

He fucked her like the demon she had sworn he was. Holding on to her, his cock shuttling in and out in a rapid, destructive pace that had her tightening, clenching, rapidly ascending a peak that alternately terrified and exhilarated her.

She stared up at him, dazed, feeling the fires swirling in her veins as her legs lifted, clasping his hips, opening herself further for the tumultuous invasion.

"Harder," she panted, feeling it, the orgasm she knew would change her forever. "Harder, Jack. Fuck me harder . . . harder . . ."

He gave her harder. He gave her deeper. Shafting her with a ferocity that had her screaming, exploding, dying in his arms as the flames consumed her.

Angel was only distantly aware of his release, the feel of his semen shooting inside her, prolonging the orgasm tearing her apart as she shuddered beneath him. Her arms and legs surrounded him, refusing to let him go as he finally stilled against her. Glowing aftershocks repeatedly shook her frame, leaving her breathless, astounded.

Such pleasure should not exist. It was destructive to the mind. It was destructive to the heart. The one part of herself she swore she wouldn't lose, she feared was the first part to go.

"Ah, Jack, if only . . ." She whispered the words at his ear as he moved from her grip, falling to his side and pulling her against him. "If only . . ."

If only ye were mine . . .

Jack came awake in a rush, certain Angel was gone, that the pleasure he'd had was only in his dreams. Sitting up in the bed, he met those violet eyes as she walked slowly from the bathroom, a towel held tight around her body.

"Damn, I hope you don't wake up like that on a regular basis," she snorted, irritation flashing in her eyes. "You nearly scared me to death, jumping like that."

He blinked, feeling his chest clench as he watched her.

Ignoring the feeling, he snorted at her comment,

moving from the bed as he checked the time on the clock.

Nearly four. How long had he slept anyway?

"I'm surprised you're still here." He moved from the bed, scratching his chest before stretching the sleep from his limbs.

She tilted her head and shrugged. "Beats jail."

Jack shot her a sharp look. Did she mean it? Hell, no, she didn't. He wasn't falling for that shit. She had met the heat, the wildness that reared inside him perfectly. That was not an unwilling lover, giving in to a fate little better than another that could await her.

She smiled. An all-too-innocent smile that didn't cover the feminine knowledge in her eyes. Damn her. She had been making him crazy for too long. The time he had spent between her thighs earlier wasn't near enough to make up for the many weeks she had been making him crazy at her father's estate.

"Tell me about the torque." He moved to the dresser, pulling out clean clothes as he glanced over his shoulder.

She shrugged her bare shoulders. "It was gift from an ancient Celtic priest to an English warrior who was set to wed the priest's favorite daughter. Even though the warrior was given orders to kill all the priests, still, he stayed his hand to bring peace with the bride he'd wed and the people he would rule. As long as the torque remains within my line, it's promised that we'll always know happiness and love in the marriage bed and the lands . . ." She swallowed tightly. "The family would always remain prosperous. Should it ever be taken away, then the blessing placed upon us goes away as well."

He shifted uncomfortably. Marriage he could do

without. He didn't want marriage. Then he looked at her again, remembered her in his bed, and frowned at the unfamiliar surge of longing that struck his chest.

What had she once said about a woman who would love him? One who would greet him, knowing his needs, his hungers? The pleasure of loving and being loved?

Hell, no. No marriage.

Besides, he doubted she would give up her nice cushy life in Ireland to be a rancher's wife. He had decided while on the Manning estate that his days of traveling, buying, and selling were coming to an end. He was tired of traveling, of never sleeping in a bed he called his own.

"A piece of jewelry doesn't make a good marriage," he finally grumbled. "It's the people."

"I agree." She shrugged, her voice quiet. "But the blessing could make certain that those two meant to be together, come together. Whichever. Fact or legend. It's the one piece of our family that we have left from centuries of history. A piece that has passed from mother to daughter since it was given to the first warrior."

"Then why mother to daughter?" His tone was a shade mocking, and he knew it.

"Because it was given to the husband of the female of that land. Not the son. But as I said, that is beside the fact. Father had no rights to sell it. Mother's early death prevented her from making the will she had planned, leaving the torque to me upon her death. Though their joint will left it to me upon Father's death. And the estate in my care. Should I decide to sell or no longer remain in Ireland, then my brothers would be given stewardship of it."

"The estate is worth plenty," he pointed out.

"The torque is worth just as much to me, if not more." She stared back at him, her violet eyes filled with emotion. "I'll let it go eventually, Jack. There's no sense in rubbing salt into the wound now."

He grunted, moving for the shower rather than replying to her comment.

"Don't bother dressing," he warned her as he passed. "I won't be long."

NINE

Arrogant ass. As though she had any of her clothing to dress in. Though if she did have anything clean, she would have definitely put it on just to spite him, she thought nearly twenty minutes later as she stood in the kitchen, dressed only in another of his T-shirts.

She was hungry. And she refused to cook naked. It just wasn't going to happen.

As she pulled eggs and omelet ingredients from the refrigerator, she frowned, wondering at his strange behavior before he disappeared into the shower. What would it matter to him where the torque came from, or the legends behind it?

It mattered to her. She might have hoped the legends were true, that the torque could lead such a man to her, but it wasn't just that. She loved the thought of all the centuries of happiness it had seen, had been part of. To have come from a man believed to be one of the most powerful Druids to have lived, created and empowered to protect the child he loved and the daughters of her line. It was the very heart of love.

For a very short time she'd wondered if the torque had brought Jack to her life with its power. She'd hoped, because her reaction to him was so odd, that he would be hers. That he could love.

Still, he had grown on her. She had enjoyed sparring with him, rebuffing him only to see what new game he would come back with. It was exciting, titillating; it had kept her arousal and her intellect challenged as no other man ever could.

But he had taken the torque. Despite her furious pleas, he had bought something that was priceless to her and taken it from her. He had taken the one thing left of the glorious past her ancestors had lived and loved through.

"You dressed." His voice was dark, forbidding as he stepped into the kitchen.

Angel placed the first omelet on its plate and poured the second into the pan.

"So I did." She glanced at him over her shoulder, once again seeing his features in the fuzzy image of her dream lover.

He was going to break her heart and she knew it. She could feel it in the vague, hollow ache in her chest, and she hated it. Despite her determination to hold her heart from him, he had taken it as easily as he had the torque.

How was that? she wondered. He had stolen the torque. Had purchased it. It had been no gift, it had not come to him through their marriage . . .

Yet neither had it come to its first wearer in such a way. She remembered the legend of the first bearer of the torque. The English warrior who had been gifted the emblem by the father of a conquered maid. A peace of-fering. A promise . . .

She shook the thought away. This wasn't centuries past, this was here and now, and Jack wasn't an English lord, nor was he a conqueror or a warrior. He was a cow-boy, one with a gift for acquiring things that should have never been his. Things such as her torque . . . and her heart.

She slid the second omelet to a plate and then placed both on the small round kitchen table along with silver-ware. Turning back to the counter, she poured two large mugs of coffee and set them by the plates before taking her seat.

The feel of the cool wood against her bare rear was a shock. She drew in a deep breath, sighed at the distrac-tion, then picked up her fork.

"You can eat or you can fume because I'm not flashing body parts for your pleasure. Doesn't make a difference to me, I'm going to eat," she informed him coolly, refus-ing to turn to look at him.

"You're a stubborn woman." He made it sound like a curse.

"I consider it one of my better qualities." She lifted a bite to her lips, inhaled the aroma, then devoured it. Sex with Jack made her hungry.

Another of those male snorts sounded behind her be-fore he moved around her to the opposite seat and the plate awaiting him.

He looked more amused than displeased with her.

Silence reigned as they both ate, though Angel could feel the tension growing between them.

"I have to return tomorrow," she finally announced as she stood and collected the empty plates.

"You mean if the sheriff lets you?" He lifted a brow mockingly.

"Sheriff or no, I have no choice." She shrugged indifferently. "I haven't moved to America, Jack, I was only visitin'."

She turned back, her gaze moving to the window and the land outside it. It appeared barren, scruffy, but there was a beauty within it that she hadn't expected to see, a beauty she feared she would miss when she returned to Ireland.

He leaned back in his chair, a frown crossing his face. "Forget it. I'm not ready for you to leave yet."

She smiled at his stubbornness, shaking her head as his arrogance reared its head. He was really quite charming, even when he frowned like that.

"Then in the morning, I suggest you notify the sheriff of my attempted theft of your property. Because by afternoon, I will be gone. This isn't my home."

So why was regret eating at her soul?

"And you think two nights is enough to make up for the near month of hell you put me through while I was trapped on that estate of yours?" he growled, rising to his feet. "I don't think so, little witch."

"Angel," she corrected him, her smile mockingly innocent. "Remember?"

He crossed his arms over his bare chest. "I want a month."

"You're a big boy, Jack. Your wants won't hurt you." But some of hers did. Because she didn't want to leave.

She wanted to stay with a strength that actually made her chest ache.

He made her ache. Just staring at him, seeing not only the incredibly sexy male body, but the man as well. The one who made her laugh, made her scream in frustration, and made her hotter, wetter than any man ever had, than she knew any other man ever would.

"You're not leaving."

His declaration was a surprise. The frustrated look on his face was even more so, as though he had surprised himself with the words as much as he had surprised her.

She adopted his stance, crossing her arms beneath her breasts and watching him with curious amusement. He rather looked like a little boy not getting his way. It was oddly cute. Exasperating, but cute nonetheless.

"Tomorrow I leave, Jack," she reiterated. "Unless you are proposing more than a fly-by-night affair?" She lifted a brow suggestively.

His frown, if possible, became darker.

"I didn't say that." His response was immediate. A second later a thoughtful glimmer entered his blue gaze as he shifted uncomfortably. "Why, do you want more?"

She arched her brow. That bit of confusion, of ill ease, would have been endearing if it weren't her heart he was playing with.

"I'm merely pointing out we both have lives," she finally answered coolly. "The sex is incredible, Jack, but I have a life. Sex, no matter how incredible, is not the be-all and end-all. I have to return to my home."

"So take a vacation," he snapped impatiently.

"Ireland isn't America." She rolled her eyes at the demand. "I can't just vacation whenever the mood hits me. The matter isn't up for argument. Tomorrow . . ."

"I won't let you leave."

Arrogance, pure and simple. There was nothing uncomfortable about that statement.

"Kidnapping is illegal in America as well," she pointed out.

"I didn't kidnap you. I'm just keeping you." It was obvious he wasn't seeing the complications here.

"You, and whose army?" she mocked.

"Who needs an army, sweetheart?" He smiled, a sensual wicked curve of his lips that made her want to groan. "I have handcuffs. Velvet-lined and soft as sin. They'll keep you in place. I promise."

Why couldn't he let her leave? Jack moved slowly across the kitchen, his cock aching like a wound as he stared into her confused, amused expression. She had no idea how very serious he was. Hell, even he was unaware of how serious he was until she mentioned leaving.

Everything inside him screamed at him to keep her there, in his bed, in his life. He couldn't imagine not having her there, the sweet heat of her pussy gripping his cock, her kiss making him hot and hard. Her laughter filling the house.

For so many years this place had been a silent tomb, a place to sleep, but nothing more. In the last two days, it had become that something more. It seemed lighter, brighter; it echoed with life. Just as she had lit something within him during his stay in Ireland. Something he had been unaware of until now.

But she was entirely too serious about leaving him.

He backed her into the counter, his arms braced on each side of her as he stared down at her, his eyes narrowed, everything inside him rejecting her announcement.

Her hands flattened on his chest, delicate fingers trembling against his bare flesh as her gaze lowered.

"Don't." She said that hated word. Dammit, he hated it when she did that.

"Don't what?" He lowered his head, nudging her chin up before allowing his lips to whisper across hers. "Don't tempt you into spending more time with me? What would it hurt, Angel? A week, maybe two?"

Something flashed in her gaze, a glimmer of pain, a shadow of fear as her lips parted before the soft stroke of his tongue.

She was soft and heated, her tongue flickering against his as it licked over her lips. Damn. His muscles clenched at the deliberate temptation of the caress. She made him so damned horny, he forgot what patience was. He wanted nothing more than to lift her to the counter and fuck her like an animal in heat. The nearly overwhelming urge to do just that sent a shudder up his spine.

"Jack." Her hand lifted, her fingers smoothing over the stubble roughness of his cheek. "If I stay, you'll break my heart. Is this what you truly want? Let me go now, while I can still retain the memory of what we had, without the pain of losing it forever. Leave me something for the future."

Her eyes were like large, bruised violets, dark with emotion, with a feminine plea for mercy.

A frown pulled at his brows as once again the dream

from that morning swept through him, the emotions that had pulled at him then pulling at him now.

"No." He shook his head, not clearly understanding why the word came so naturally to his lips.

"No?" she questioned him roughly. "Jack, you can't make me stay. Handcuffs and sheriff aside, you can't force it on me."

Her accent thickened with her anger. The smooth, soft lilt of her voice became a thick brogue that had his cock hardening further, every instinct in his body screaming out that he take her, bind her to him, never let her go.

"Son of a bitch." He pushed his fingers roughly through his hair as he let her go, turning away from her and the erratic, erotic temptation of her slender body. "Fine. Tomorrow you can leave. But that still leaves tonight, in my fucking bed." He turned on her swiftly, catching her swift intake of air, the pain that flashed across her face. "And my bed is not in this kitchen, Angel. Get up there."

She wasn't going to cry, Angel promised herself. He was giving her what she asked for, no more, no less. He would let her go and leave her something for the future. But what?

She moved up the stairs, aware of him stalking slowly behind her, his gaze never leaving her back, heating the air around them. She had never seen him like this, determined, almost savage, the playboy exterior eroded away to show the steel core of the man beneath. A man who aroused her, fascinated her, and threatened every part of her woman's soul. This was a man who could destroy every dream she had for her life.

And still she was moving up the stairs, heading for his bedroom, every cell in her body screaming out for him, her pussy drenching with the hunger rising in her body. She entered the doorway, stepping slowly into the room before turning to face him.

He was stepping out of the sweatpants he had worn downstairs, his cock a rampant impaler standing out from his body, engorged with lust. His expression was one of fierce determination.

Before Angel could do more than breathe in sharply, he was pulling her to him, his mouth coming down on hers, slanting across it as he sent his tongue pressing firmly between her lips.

Her head fell back on her shoulders as a weak moan of submission left her lips. She couldn't fight him. She didn't want to fight him. She wanted nothing more than to be held in his hard, muscular arms, to feel him, dominant and powerful, overtaking her.

She heard the material of his shirt ripping from her body. The sound sent a surge of excitement powering through her veins as a rush of heated juices ran from her pussy. God, he made her wild. Too wild. He took too much of her, made her feel too much. It wouldn't matter when she left; she knew she was leaving her heart behind.

Her hands moved, unable to keep still, to keep from touching him, holding him. She needed to feel his flesh, to memorize the texture of it, the warmth and power of the muscles beneath the hair-sprinkled, suntanned skin.

They roamed over his chest, his shoulders, finally sinking into the silken texture of the overly long blond hair. Who would believe that she had fallen in love with a cowboy? A devil-may-care charmer who cared nothing for her heart, only the relief he found in her sexually. It made no sense to her, but she knew that forever her heart would linger in this dry, rough land, always longing for him.

"God, you feel good." His voice was as rough as his breathing, as intent as the cry that slipped past her lips.

His hands smoothed over her breasts, cupping, his fingers rasping her nipples as his mouth followed suit. His tongue licked over one as his hands moved lower. His lips covered the hard tip, his tongue licking with all apparent enjoyment as the fingers of one hand slid between her thighs.

Heated fingers of lightning crashed inside her as sparks dazzled her vision. The pleasure was so intense she wondered if she would survive it this time.

"You're wet, Angel-mine," he growled, his fingers caressing, sliding through the cream flowing from her vagina as she arched against him.

"So fix it," she panted, feeling his lips stroking her nipple as he spoke, causing tiny shards of sensation to travel from the hard tip to her womb, convulsing it with pleasure.

"Is it fixable?" he drawled, his voice sexy and dark as his lips moved to her neck.

Hell no, it wasn't.

"I'm sure you can find a way if you think about it a second." She arched closer, feeling his cock against her stomach, a hard, hot, living stalk of pleasure.

A rough laugh vibrated from his throat as he smiled against her neck.

"There's no cure," he warned her. Something she was well aware of. "Only intense therapy. Lots and lots of this . . ."

His hands cupped her buttocks as he lifted her against him, his cock sliding between her thighs to notch at the tender opening of her pussy.

Angel's eyes opened wide as she gasped, her legs automatically lifting, her knees clasping his hips.

"There you go, baby." He nipped at her neck erotically. "Ride your cowboy now."

She felt him brace himself, holding her close as he began to work his erection inside her. Sliding in, pulling back, shafting the sensitive channel with burning thrusts, sending him deeper with each stroke, stretching her further as she began to keen in pleasure.

God, she had never imagined being taken like this. He held her weight confidently, his legs braced apart, his cock spearing inside her, stretching her when she was certain she could take no more, stroking nerve endings still sensitized from the morning's play.

She was shuddering, needing him, aching.

"God no. Don't you stop . . ." she demanded fiercely as he slid from her, his soft laugh one of strained control as he moved to the bed, dropping her to it as he followed her down.

But he wasn't moving to reclaim the territory he had possessed moments before; instead he spread her thighs wide, lowered his head, and used his tongue to still any protest she would have voiced.

Shock held her rigid for long moments, but the pleasure was more than she could have imagined denying. Her hands clenched in his hair as a long, low moan passed her lips and she gave in to the pleasure building inside her.

His tongue was like a whip of burning pleasure. Licking . . . licking as though he were devouring a favored treat as his tongue slid through the thick, heavy juices of her pussy.

The sounds of his enjoyment vibrated from his lips to the folds of her cunt, and the cries of her pleasure pierced the air as his lips wrapped around her clit and his tongue probed at the nerve-laden knot.

He was making her insane. She was going to die of the pleasure.

Angel writhed beneath him, lost in the dark storm of excessive sensation, reaching, climbing higher with each diabolical stroke of his tongue. She was close. So very close to an orgasm that she knew would steal her soul, and she fought it with every breath.

Until two hard, broad fingers slid inside her clenching pussy, opening her, fucking her with smooth strokes as his mouth and tongue licked and sucked and threw her headlong over the precipice she had fought so desperately.

Her hips bucked, arched. The orgasm tore through her, taking her breath, tightening her muscles to near breaking point as it exploded through each nerve ending.

Wicked, lustful demon that he was, Jack chose that moment to move to his knees, position the thick head of his cock, and push inside the contracting, gripping tissue of her cunt.

She screamed with her last breath. She bucked against him, seeing stars in front of her vision as his cock surged inside her, beginning a hard, fast rhythm she couldn't fight, couldn't deny. There was no time to save herself. No time to pull her defenses around her before he stripped the last of her fragile control.

She was a creature of pleasure. One long, rapidly exploding, melting orgasm that refused to stop. She dissolved around him, shuddering helplessly, going from one pinnacle to another, only to be driven higher, higher, until the gripping, destructive, final release sent her juices pouring around his cock as it spurted inside her, filling her with the heat and strength of his seed.

She collapsed. There was barely the energy left to breathe, to remain conscious as she drifted in a sea of bliss unlike anything she had heard or read about. She was only distantly aware of the fact that he had covered her, that her hands were locked around his neck, her fingers buried in his hair. She couldn't release him. She had a death grip on him—or was it a soul grip, for surely she still lived?

When he moved to take his weight from her, his arms wrapped around her, pulling her with him as her head fell naturally against his shoulder. "What do you do to me?" he whispered into the darkness as her hand lay on his chest, just stroking him, easing him.

His hand was buried in her hair, holding tight to the strands as though it would hold her there, hold her to him. As though it would keep her from walking away from him.

"When ye came to the castle to visit with Joe, you were, are, so cocky." Her laughter whispered over him, her voice low, pure pleasure riding her voice. "It was all I could do not to be snappish with ye, ya know?"

He snorted at that. "You were an icicle."

"So one might have thought." Satisfaction filled her voice. "When I was a girl, my temper was terrible. I fought everyone, anyone, I didn't care. I would scream at the smallest slight, and was always looking for reasons to set my temper free." She stroked his collar bone to his shoulder. "Da and Mother sent me away," her voice lowered and he heard the aching loss in her voice. "To boarding school, thinkin' a stricter atmosphere would quell my temper." She didn't say anything for long moments as Jack stared up at the darkened ceiling waiting, aching for the child she had been. "I wasn't to come home until I could be a good child. Until I could control myself and my temper." She shrugged. "I wanted to come home. Even though I knew returning meant once again knowin' all that anger because no matter my antics, my parents' world was for each other, not for the children they brought to this world."

He frowned at the admission. "And you didn't want to be sent away again," he said, seeing now why she restrained herself, why she kept so much inside.

"The time at the school was a good thing. No one was cruel to me, though the counselor I had was a bit stuffy." She shrugged. "I wanted to be home. I felt like a plant missin' its roots, because I knew nothing, had no ties to anyone at that school. So I became a good child. And after a year, Da let me return. I haven't had to leave since." She paused and he felt her smile against his arm. "Until ye showed me, Jack, that by holding back all my emotions, I was giving myself very little to draw anyone to me. Perhaps . . . Ah well, perhaps I need to consider how much I allow others to see."

So she could draw a husband to her?

He frowned at the thought but didn't speak it.

"I laughed at ye often after ye'd leave a room," she admitted, humor filling her voice. "And I hadn't really laughed in a long time, Jack. I thank ye for that."

He released her hair to play with it instead, still staring at the ceiling, frowning, trying damned hard not to think.

"Yer worthy of my torque, Jack Riley," she whispered then. "It was I who was unworthy of it. Perhaps one day ye'll give it to the man who would steal the heart of a daughter ye have, and give him the story of its fine history. The power could be in the knowledge of what the torque represents, and not the torque itself. Do ye think?"

She asked a question.

She asked him a question. He felt like a weight was pressing against his chest, making it difficult to breathe, to understand what he was feeling and why those words hurt him.

"I'll miss ye, Jack Riley," she told him softly, settling against him. "I'll miss ye verra much."

Silence filled the bedroom and Jack was damned if he could find anything to say, if he could explain even to himself what he was feeling.

TEN

There were tears in her eyes. He saw them, even though she was careful to keep from looking him in the eye as she finished dressing in the black jeans and black shirt. She looked like the dark angel she was, flitting about the room to hide the trembling of her lips, her hands.

Jack sat on the edge of the bed watching her, the torque clenched in his hand, hidden by the blanket at his side.

"The cab will be here soon." She lowered her head again as she faced him. "I'll miss ye, Jack."

The words tore through his chest.

Fuck. Fuck. What had she done to him? Letting a woman go, no matter how hot and sweet her pussy was, had never hurt.

He rose to his feet, stepping before her and caught her hands. Slowly he placed her precious torque across them, watching the dull gleam of the gold as she held it.

Her gaze flew to his.

"I would have brought it back to you," he told her then. He had denied it at the time, but he had known he was only buying the damned thing because of her.

He wanted to please her. To bring a smile, some glimmer of joy to her face. Instead a tear slipped down her cheek as a sad smile crossed her lips.

She lifted her hands, spreading open the neckband until she clasped it around his neck, allowing the ring to encircle the wolf's head as it rested at the center of his collarbone.

The weight of it was odd, the heat from it warming his flesh.

"It's yours," she whispered. "Not only fairly bought, but freely given to ye. Remember me, Jack," she said, repeating his words from the night before. "Just as I'll always remember you."

He stood still, frowning down at her as she placed a quick, tearful kiss on his lips before rushing from the room.

He could feel himself fighting for breath, feel the urge to go after her, sling her over his shoulder, and force her to stay. But he knew it wouldn't be enough. Force would never work with his proud Irish lass. What would?

Love?

Love did not exist. Not for him. Not in this world. He had admitted it to himself years before. No matter how much he had longed to find that perfect woman and make a home somewhere, anywhere, he had been unable to. He couldn't feel those emotions. Not that intense overriding storm of feelings he heard love was.

He had given up.

He had traveled the world more than once, searching

for priceless treasure, for that one great adventure, but the search had begun with the search for love, hadn't it?

He sat back down on the bed, feeling the torque like a weight of incrimination.

At twenty-two he had realized what he searched for didn't exist in Madison, or the small towns that surrounded it. It wasn't in Dallas, or in Fort Worth. It hadn't been found in New Orleans, Fort Smith, or any of the other cities he had traveled and worked his way through.

Eventually, he had stopped looking for elusive emotion and concentrated instead on profit. On prosperity. On making the land he owned something he could find pride in, something worth fighting for.

The emptiness of the house mocked him now.

Outside he heard the cab pull into the drive. Less than a minute later it left. And he was alone.

Alone in the house he had built from the money he had made as he traveled the world conquering adventure.

And losing himself.

"Fuck!" He rose to his feet, pacing to the window to stare into the dry heat of another Texas morning.

Damn, he thought he loved it here until he'd driven onto the land Joe Manning owned and felt the beauty of it clench his heart. Then the beauty of his Angel stole his breath. He thought this was home, but honest to God, the only hours he had found peace here, felt fulfilled, were those Angel had filled with her presence. Just as she had her father's estate.

Her laughter. Her irate voice. Her soft sighs.

She haunted him, and she was no more than a few miles from the driveway, he was certain.

He lifted his hand, releasing the torque from his neck before staring at it, holding it in the sunlight, staring down at it with a frown.

He hadn't even wanted the damned thing, so why had he really bought it?

Because she claimed it.

It was the one thing he could possess that would anchor her to him. It was the only thing she truly loved at one time, her father had claimed.

In that moment, he realized that he had wanted it. From the moment he saw it, held it, it had been familiar, felt comfortable in his grip. Just as it felt comfortable around his neck.

He clasped it around his neck once again, his eyes narrowing as he stared into the vivid blue of the sky.

He told her she wasn't leaving him, and by God he meant it.

He showered, dressed quickly, then walked to the dresser, opening the middle drawer. Staring at the assortment of adult articles there, he decided quickly which ones to take along.

Handcuffs were a must. The black silk kerchief. Couldn't have her screaming too hard at a hotel; someone might call the sheriff. A few toys. Definitely the small tube of lubrication, just in case he decided to get adventurous.

He threw them all into a small bag, pulled his boots on, grabbed his keys, and headed for the front door. It was time to bring his woman home.

Angel held back her tears as she rode into town. She kept her head turned away from the rearview mirror.

She didn't want the cabbie to see the tears swimming in her eyes, or the pain that raged through her.

Walking away from Jack was the hardest thing she had ever done. Watching the Texas landscape pass by, the flat valley filled with grass, the rolling hills beyond thick with trees and a hardy wildness that called to something in the very depths of her soul.

She didn't want to leave. She wanted to stay, if only for the few weeks he had suggested. But if it hurt this horribly now, how much more would it hurt weeks, or even days from now? It would destroy her.

She closed her eyes and let the image of him form in her mind. His crooked smile. His brilliant-blue eyes. His broad, callused hands. Every inch of his body was adored by her inner vision as she silently forced herself to say good-bye.

The old writings that had passed through the ages with the torque told of its first owner. A proud English warrior who had wed the daughter of the Celtic Druid so many centuries before. The MacTaidhg family lands had fallen beneath the sword of the one called the Hewn Wolf. A blond-haired warrior who had found favor with the English king and been given the Irish lands and the order to conquer the wild hearts that fought against the Crown so fiercely.

He had moved to the very heart of the land, wedding the daughter of its hidden priest, and protecting the secret that would have seen her beheaded. It was said he was a scourge of the people, until she tamed him. That she had bewitched the wolf and brought him to her feet. Though the tales Angel's mother had told hinted that both warrior and proud Irish lass bowed to each other.

The torque will bring the warrior destined to tame your wild heart, Angel, her mother had told her countless times. Before Megan Manning had died, she had spoken often to her daughter about the legends. Those that assured love and happiness for the female descendants of that first blessed marriage. As long as the ancient neckband stayed within the family it had been given to, then its power would remain true.

And now it was gone. Sold by her father to the man who had stolen Angel's heart and would be lost to her forever.

She would begin the legacy of discontent now, rather than one of happiness.

She blinked back her tears, raised her chin, and stared into the hazy reflection the window provided. She looked as broken as she felt. And that just wouldn't do. She wouldn't give others the knowledge of her pain, for surely if she did, news of it would reach Jack. It wasn't his fault he couldn't love her, and she wanted no guilt to be heaped on him.

Loving him had been her choice.

"Here we are." The cabbie stopped in front of the small hotel in the center of town. The three-story building had all the quaint charm of the West on the outside, though the inside was fully modern.

"Thank you." She pulled several bills from the pocket of her jeans as she stepped from the cab.

"Thank you, ma'am. I hope your stay at the J. R. Ranch was a good one. Ol' Jack's not home often, so not many get to stay in that nice new house he built a few years ago."

"It's a beautiful house." She fought the burning tears behind her eyes. "Thank you again. Good day, sir."

She moved away from him quickly, heading inside the hotel and to her room. The dark wood lobby was decorated in the style of the Old West. Heavy brocades and large pieces of furniture.

She passed through it, for once taking no time to admire the unique decorations. Her room was on the third floor, and if she hurried, she would have time to shower and pack before heading to the airport and the late flight she had booked back to Ireland.

Entering the elevator, she moved to the back corner, wrapping her arms around her as she lowered her head to stare at the rust-brown carpeting beneath her feet.

She missed him. She ached for him.

Leaving him was ripping her soul apart . . .

Hotel security in Madison, Texas, could really suck. Jack slid the stolen key card through its computerized pad, waited for the green light, then eased it slowly open. Few people thought to use the metal latch on the other side to prevent access. He wondered if Angel had been diligent enough to use hers.

Nope. The door eased fully open, not even a squeak of the hinges to give away his presence.

The bathroom door at the side of the entrance was closed, the sound of the shower running assuring him that Angel was suitably busy. A slow, wicked grin crossed his lips as he closed the door behind him, sliding the latch over onto its metal peg to assure privacy. He didn't

want one of the housekeepers coming in at the wrong
time in the morning.

Moving farther into the room, he set the duffel bag
on the bed, quickly opened it, and began preparations
for Angel's final fall. She might think she was leaving
him, but he was going to show her differently.

Soft, padded cuffs attached to long chains came first.
Looping the ends of the small chains to the bed legs, he
clipped them in place before laying the padded cuffs on
the pillows. Next were the ankle cuffs, which he arranged at the lower corners after securing them.

The tube of lubrication was laid on the table along with
nipple clips, a dildo, and a butt plug. Finally, he undressed,
folding his clothing neatly before sliding them into one
of the empty drawers of the dresser by the bed. He was
going to play, and Angel was going to be his personal
little toy in the games he had planned.

The shower shut off.

Smiling in anticipation, Jack moved to hide along the
wall, waiting until she walked through the short hallway.

It didn't take long. A few short minutes later, he heard
the bathroom door open and watched as her shadow
neared. Emotions swamped him in those fragile seconds. Possessiveness, love, love unlike anything he could
have imagined, and tenderness.

She stepped past him.

Moving quickly he came behind her, his arms sweeping around her, pulling her around, giving her only a
second to glimpse his face before his lips lowered to
hers. But he had glimpsed hers as well. Her eyes reddened, tear-drenched, her cheeks pale, her expression
miserable.

"Shh," he whispered against her lips as her lips opened to cry out. "It's okay, baby. It's all okay now . . ."

One hand cupped her cheek as his chest clenched at the dampness he felt there. He had made her cry. Pain streaked through him at the thought of that.

"Don't cry, Angel-mine," he whispered, sipping at her lips, his tongue stroking over the swollen curves as her breath hitched, a small, strangled sob coming from her as her hands gripped his arms, her nails biting into the flesh. "No more tears, baby. Only this. Only this."

His lips swallowed the words, parting her lips, his tongue driving deep as he maneuvered her slowly to the bed, holding her to him as he lifted her to the center before laying her back.

He ignored the gasping little moans that left her throat. Rather than allowing her voice to her questions, he snapped the cuffs on one wrist. She jerked beneath him as he did the same to the other.

Then he released her lips, staring at the kiss-reddened flesh with a sense of satisfaction.

"What are you doing?" Her voice was hoarse as she tested the strength of the chains.

Jack moved back, going to her ankles, chuckling as she kicked out at him.

"Jack, have you lost your mind?" Another question. She struggled furiously as he restrained her ankles, testing the length of the chain for enough freedom of movement to allow him his play. She could bend her knees, but she wasn't going anyplace. She couldn't turn from him, nor would she be able to writhe from his grip.

"Let me go!" she snarled up at him, her violet eyes still damp with tears as she fought against the restraints.

"Do you think this will solve anything? That it will make it better?" Her voice trembled. "For God's sake. Don't hurt me like this, Jack."

He sighed, shaking his head in chastisement as he watched her.

"Shame on you, Angel, thinking I would just let you walk away," he said gently, amazed at how free he suddenly felt, at the joy that rose inside him.

He had no idea how much he did love her, how much he had loved her before he ever left Ireland. Until now, staring into her pain-ridden gaze and seeing a reflection of the pain he couldn't explain within himself, he hadn't a clue how much she meant to him.

She opened her lips to berate him further when her gaze fell on the torque circling his neck. Her eyes widened then, a gasp leaving her lips as shock filled her eyes.

"I won't let you go," he whispered then. "Not ever, Angel-mine."

Then he lowered his head, taking her lips in a kiss that swamped him with pleasure, with emotion, with a sense of coming home.

Angel moaned beneath his kiss, her lips parting for him, her tongue tangling with him as he began to sip at her lips, to nibble and stroke as he inflamed every cell in her body with the pleasure.

He was the dream. The one who had tormented her for so many years. And now she knew why she had never been able to look beyond the torque to see his face. Why she had been filled with such a sense of wonder and overpowering emotions. Because she had given up on the dream, just as she had given up on the torque.

Only to learn that the man and the neckband went hand in hand.

"Jack." She moaned his name as his head lifted, his eyes, brilliant blue and filled with arrogant assurance, meeting hers.

"I love you." He whispered the words she had felt certain she would never hear from him. "I've waited a lifetime to say those words, Angel. Searched until my soul grew weary with disappointment. I'll not let you leave me."

She wanted to wrap her arms around him. Wanted to hold him to her and laugh aloud in overwhelming relief.

"Let me go." She jerked at the restraints. "I want to hold you, Jack."

He grinned. A devilish, wicked curve of his lips that had her lips parting in excitement.

"Not yet, baby," he growled. "We're going to play tonight. For hours and hours and hours. And when morning comes, you're going to be too damned tired to even consider leaving. You won't remember your name, let alone any desire to walk away from me."

She wasn't going anywhere now. She nearly whispered those words then held them back at the last second. What had he said about playing? Would her pleasure be better served in allowing him his way?

Well, duh, as the American students said. Of course it would be.

She relaxed back upon the pillows.

"Do your worst," she whispered, smiling herself as his eyes narrowed at her challenge. "But I bet I still remember my name well."

ELEVEN

"What's your name, baby?" Jack's voice was tight, hoarse, as she twisted beneath him, writhing beneath the steady penetration of the dildo filling her pussy as the plug in her rear stretched her unbearably.

She was on fire. She could feel the flames burning through her body more than an hour later as she begged, pleaded for release. He was killing her. He had been steadily killing her since the first kiss, making her beg for more when she swore she could take no more of the blistering torment.

She was panting; perspiration covered her, dampened her hair, her flesh, and the comforter beneath her body. Still, Jack lay between her thighs, fucking her slow and easy with the fake cock as she fought to get closer to him.

His tongue was a demon. It was evil. No pleasure such as this should be possible.

He licked his way around the straining nub of her clit,

flickering over it with devilish disregard for her hoarse cries as she arched closer to him, only to have him pull back.

"Please," she panted. "For mercy's sake, please . . . please . . ."

"What's your name?" he whispered again, pushing the dildo deeper inside her, forcing her to take it to the very depths of her pussy as her muscles spasmed around it, her juices flowing, her cunt weeping with the overwhelming need to orgasm.

She had held out as long as she could.

She tried to scream as one hand moved up, fingers tugging at the clips attached to her swollen nipples and sending pulsing fingers of sensation raking along her nerve endings to the overly sensitive depths of her cunt.

Her back arched, her head shaking as he sucked her clit into his mouth once again, never truly touching it, merely surrounding the swollen knot of nerves with moist heat.

It was almost enough. But in this game, almost counted for nothing.

"This is unfair," she wailed, a moan tearing from her throat as the dildo moved with slow precision until only the head rested inside her, stretching her opening, burning her before sliding back once again.

"Harder, damn you. Fuck me properly." She nearly screamed the words. She would have screamed them if she had the breath to do so.

"What's your name?" he whispered again, licking over her clit as every muscle in her body clenched at the nearness of release. "Tell me, baby. Do you remember your name?"

"Yes." She stared up at him then, her eyes dazed. "Jack's. I'm Jack's. Whatever he wishes to call me, whenever . . . For pity's sake, Jack . . . Please . . ."

He moved before the words were out of her mouth. The dildo pulled free of her body, causing her to arch, her feet bracing on the bed as she lifted, attempting to follow it.

Oh God, she was so empty. Too empty. She was dying . . .

"There, baby," he whispered as he came over, the head and steel-hard perfection of his swollen cock nudging against the opening of her pussy. "Feel how much better this is."

He pushed inside her.

Better? It was nirvana. It was ecstasy, rapture, it was fucking incredible.

She shook, trembling so hard her teeth nearly chattered as she stared up at him, feeling him push into the tightened channel of her pussy, passing the heavy weight of the plug still anchored in her rear, making her muscles grip him so snugly she wondered that there was room for him.

But he made room, working his cock inside her like a knife through melting butter as he penetrated the syrup-slick confines of her cunt.

Electricity whipped around her. It sizzled in the air, crackled along her flesh, preparing her for the explosion building with her. One she wasn't certain she would survive.

"Look at me, Angel," he whispered when her eyes began to drift closed. "Look at me, baby, let me see those pretty eyes when you come around my cock. Watch me, sweetheart . . ."

And he began to move.

Each powerful, straining thrust had his pelvis raking against her clit as his erection burrowed hard and deep inside her. The thick length stretched her, burned her, sent her senses careening as her cry tore from her throat.

Her eyes widened as his strokes increased in speed, his hips slamming against hers as his face twisted into a mask of pleasure.

"God, I love you," he growled as his head lowered, his teeth tugging at one nipple clip as the fingers of his hand tugged at the other.

The additional flare of sensation, the destructive pleasure ripping through her, undid her.

Angel arched, her breath catching in her throat as she began to shudder, feeling the tension exploding within her as her pussy seemed to melt around him. Her clit pulsed, throbbed, then followed in the wake, sending brilliant arcs of fire to burn through her senses as she burned beneath him, only distantly aware of his release as well.

She was flying, soaring in a world of dark pleasure unlike anything she had ever known, feeling her body as though it were an alien creature, erupting again, then again, as her orgasm ripped through her soul and— rather than tearing her asunder—made her whole.

For the first time in her life, she was whole.

She didn't know how long she lay there, her body convulsing in the aftershocks of the pleasure, but she knew Jack was with her. His arms enfolded her, holding her tight, his face buried at her neck as his body shuddered atop hers.

Then his head turned, his lips ghosting over her ear.

"Angel-mine," he whispered. "I love you."

A smile tugged at her lips as she drifted sleepily within the waves of pleasure that still surged through her.

"I love you, Jack," she whispered in turn then. "Now remove these chains before I'm forced to kill you."

She tugged tiredly at the restraints. There wasn't a chance in hell she could sleep like this, and she wanted nothing more than to sleep.

A rough chuckle sounded, but he moved, hurriedly releasing her wrists and ankles before dragging his nude body back up the bed.

"Let me catch my breath and we'll try that again." He yawned as Angel brushed the nipple clips that had fallen beside them on the bed out of her way.

"Sure." She snuggled against him. "In the morning."

He sighed deeply.

"We're going home in the morning," he said, his arms tightening around her. "To my ranch. Then later, I think we might like to live in Ireland for a while. Later."

"Home." Her eyes closed, a smile tilting her lips.

Yes, she was going to go home.

EPILOGUE

Joseph Manning hung up the phone and stared at the portrait that hung over the fireplace of the family room his wife had so loved.

"I did it, my love," he whispered, smiling at the laughing violet eyes that showed the wit and charm that had been so much a part of her. "Just as you said I would. I found our daughter her American warrior."

At first, no one could have ever imagined Jack Riley was a warrior. A charmer. A playboy. Not a warrior. But the weeks he had spent at the estate had given Joseph another insight into the young man. A loner because he believed what he sought didn't exist. A man who feared love was an illusion.

And, ahhh, the sparks that had flown whenever his Angel was in the cowboy's company. She had lit up like a grand light, her eyes sparkling, her cheeks flushing as she fought against the attraction that was so very apparent.

In those weeks Jack had stayed with them, he had watched them seek each other's company, only to bicker like children fighting for supremacy.

He had known Jack for many years, but he had never seen him react so to a woman. And he knew his daughter better than she imagined. She had fallen in love so easily, yet had fought it so hard.

"Well, love, I was looking forward to returning to your loving arms," he sighed, though without regret. "But I think when we meet again you would like to know of the grandchildren that will soon be coming. Perhaps a fine granddaughter looking like yourself that the torque will bless as well."

He lifted the glass of wine that sat at his elbow and toasted the portrait.

"I miss ya, love," he whispered, his chest aching with the loss. "But I was blessed in you."

He sipped at the wine.

It had been many years since he had visited America. Perhaps it was time to return. To see the fine ranch Jack spoke of and to share in the happiness he could hear in his daughter's voice.

"Just a short visit, love," he whispered, glancing at the portrait once again. "Shall we go?"

She was gone these many years, but he knew she traveled with him, no matter where he went. She was his heart.

Just as Angel was now Jack's heart. As Jack was Angel's.

A generation for the torque to bless.

Coming soon . . .

FROM #1 *NEW YORK TIMES*
BESTSELLING AUTHOR
LORA LEIGH

COLLISION POINT

AVAILABLE IN MARCH 2018
FROM ST. MARTIN'S PAPERBACKS